FIENDISH DELIGHTS
THE THRILL OF THE HUNT
BOOK TWO

HELEN HARPER

RECAP OF BOOK ONE

Recap of *Tattered Huntress*, Book One of *The Thrill of the Hunt*

Daisy Carter is a low elf living in Edinburgh and eking out a living as a delivery driver. She is dispatched to Neidpath Castle to deliver a parcel to Hugo Pemberville, a celebrated high elf who is famous for treasure hunting. When she hands him his parcel and waits for his signature, he recognises the silver ring in her eyes that indicates she is a user of spider's silk, a dangerously addictive drug that Daisy takes to control the wild magic inside her. Hugo's demeanour changes instantly and, with considerable rudeness, he tells Daisy to leave. Before she does so, she spots some notes about the location of a special, long-lost locket necklace.

Upset at Hugo's attitude, Daisy suggests to a belligerent troll named Duchess that she leave her current habitat in favour of a more pleasant one under the bridge at Hugo's ancestral home. When Hugo discovers that Duchess has taken up residence there, he calls Daisy's boss and ensures she is fired because of her drug addiction. To retaliate, Daisy uses the information she spied on the notes to find the necklace before Hugo does.

Daisy takes it to a man called Sir Nigel. He is impressed that she found it and offers her a place in a treasure-hunting competition to find some chests of Jacobean gold. Daisy later realises that the locket on the necklace was enchanted; having opened it before she handed it over, she is now supposedly the boss of two very annoying brownies, Hester and Otis.

Daisy and the brownies joins Sir Nigel's treasure hunt to find three parts to a magical key which, when combined, will reveal the location of the treasure chests. There are numerous other competitors, including Humphrey and Eleanor, a friendly couple who are somewhat lackadaisical about the hunt.

The first key part is located in northern England. Daisy would have found it first, but she is delayed when another team is attacked by a giant snake. She saves them, but in the meantime Hugo and his team of Primes find the key part. Hugo initially thinks Daisy engineered the snake attack in a deliberate attempt to harm her competitors, but he soon realises the truth.

The second key part is located in the north of Scotland, in a concealed chamber behind an underground cavern called Smoo Cave. The entrance to the chamber is unlocked by another competitor – Gordon, a sorcerer who appears to have an uncomfortable history with Hugo.

Daisy discovers she is claustrophobic and panics when she is underground. Unable to continue searching for the key part, she falls through the ground in the cave and is knocked unconscious. When she awakes, she is challenged to a fight to the death by a one-eyed creature known as the Fachan. The Fachan eventually decides that she is not a worthy competitor, but he gifts her a sentient sword called Gladys and shows her the way out of the cave.

Suffering from spider's silk withdrawal symptoms, Daisy

starts hallucinating. Hugo finds her and helps her recover. His attitude towards her softens considerably. She re-joins the treasure hunt for the third key part located in one of many houses owned by a rich man known for his unpleasant behaviour. With the help of Hester and Otis, Daisy discovers that the man has been keeping magical creatures captive. She releases them, sneaks into the house and finds the key part. Before she can retrieve it, though, Humphrey appears and takes it.

With no key part, Daisy can no longer participate in the treasure hunt, and only Humphrey and Hugo remain in the competition. She is suspicious about Humphrey, so she secretly spies on the moment when all three key parts are put together and the location of the treasure chests is revealed. They are on the tidal island of Cramond, near Edinburgh, and Daisy quickly heads there to wait.

She witnesses Humphrey attacking Hugo with a terrible power known as blood magic and steps in to save him. Humphrey escapes while Hugo and Daisy are trapped on the island as the tide comes in. They are forced to shelter there for hours, during which time Hugo reveals that his best friend died as a result of a spider's silk addiction and Daisy confesses that she takes the drugs because otherwise her magic will overwhelm her.

Eventually they make it safely back to the mainland where they recover the treasure and ensure that Humphrey is arrested. Daisy is offered her old job back as a delivery driver – but she decides to become a full-time treasure hunter instead.

CHAPTER ONE

It's one thing declaring to the world that you're a treasure hunter but it's something else being one, especially when you possess few connections, little experience and limited resources.

Dogged determination and a LinkedIn profile were all well and good, but I was becoming the living embodiment of Catch-22. I couldn't get any decent treasure hunting commissions until I successfully found some treasure – and I couldn't successfully find any treasure until I had some commissions. That's not to say that I hadn't found work; it just wasn't the kind of work I'd envisaged when I'd started down this path a few months earlier.

'The tide will be coming in soon,' Otis informed me, buzzing in my left ear.

Hester flicked the lobe of my right ear. 'It's also starting to rain.' Her tone was disgruntled. 'And it's not the sort of refreshing rain that makes you glad to be alive. It's the sort of Scottish December rain that is grey and icy and seeps not only under your collar and into your bones, but also into your soul to make you wish you'd never been born.'

'It's only rain,' I muttered. I scuffed the sand at my feet, telling myself that I was having fun. I'd found a lot of broken shells, pretty sea glass and bits of rubbish, but I hadn't found Trish York's wedding ring.

'That's easy for you to say. Some of those raindrops are the size of my head,' she complained.

I crouched down and turned over a seaweed-covered rock to check underneath it. 'You can stay in my pocket. You'll be dry there.'

'Dry,' Hester argued, 'but musty and smelly. When was the last time you washed this coat?'

Otis sighed. 'Stop being rude, Hes.'

'I'm not being rude, I'm being truthful. Are you trying to tell me that you don't think Daisy's pocket smells like the rotting intestines of a rat's corpse?'

He didn't answer his sister, suggesting that her description was wholly accurate. Instead, he addressed me. 'I don't think you're going to find Mrs York's ring, Daisy. It's probably already been swallowed up by the sea. You've tried earth magic. You've tried a metal detector. You've walked up and down this beach eighty-four times. The ring is gone.'

'This isn't proper treasure hunting,' Hester added. 'It's lost and found. Where's the glory? Where's the fun? Where are the damned dragons?'

'Do you *want* to meet a dragon?' I asked.

'Anything would be better than this.'

The only dragons left in the British Isles were in Wales. While I thought it would be beyond cool to meet one, I doubted Hester actually wanted to come face to face with a curmudgeonly beast with fangs the size of a Mini Cooper. Dragons were dangerous. And they usually stayed well out of sight. Hester was right about one thing, though: this wasn't treasure hunting. Not really.

I pulled my bag off my shoulder, unzipped it and rummaged inside. I didn't need to look at either brownie to know that their expressions would display disapproval but they knew better than to say anything. I'd heard it all before and it wouldn't make a difference.

I located the small bag containing my supply of spider's silk and plucked out a pill. Without hesitating, I tossed it into my mouth. It fizzed on my tongue, the familiar bitter taste making my lips pucker before I swallowed it whole. Immediately my skin tingled and my muscles tightened. I raised my chin and, ignoring the rain, made a last-ditch effort to find the stupid ring by sending out a blast of air magic towards the damp sand.

My intention had been to blow away the top inch or so to reveal what lay underneath, but as I pushed the magic forth I stumbled, losing both my footing and my grip on the spell. The resulting burst of wind slammed into the beach with a deafening crash – and I was thrown backwards by at least several metres, landing with a painful thud on my back.

'Mmmmf!' That had really hurt.

I struggled up to a sitting position, blinking through the cold rain at the newly formed crater in front of me. Oops. That certainly wasn't what I'd intended.

'What the fuck was that about?' Hester screeched, her tiny cheeks bright red. 'Look at what you did to Otis!'

I glanced around and my eyes widened in alarm when I saw him. Shit. He was some distance away, having been turned upside down. The top half of his body was buried by sand and only his legs were visible, kicking uselessly in the air.

I scrambled towards him to pinch his feet and pull him free. He coughed and spluttered. His head, arms and torso were covered in soggy sand. I gently used the tip of my finger to brush it away while Hester continued to admonish me. 'You could have killed him!'

'I'm fine, Hes.' Otis coughed.

'He could have suffocated!'

'Honestly, it's not a problem.' He rubbed his eyes and blinked, trying to smile.

She didn't listen. 'How could you lose control like that, Daisy? He might have died!'

Guilt washed through me. She was right: it should never have happened. It had been years since I'd allowed my magic to get the better of me like that. 'I'm sorry, Otis,' I whispered. 'I'm so sorry.'

He blinked again and shook away the last of the sand. 'It's fine. Honestly. And look.' He pointed at the sand crater. 'Look at that.'

I followed his finger. In the very centre of the hole there was the glint of gold. I peered more closely. Yep, that was a ring. Triumph flooded me.

'Well done, Daisy,' Otis wheezed. 'You found it after all.'

Hester scowled. 'Big deal.'

I pumped the air with my fist, strode towards the ring and scooped it up. It was a minor success but I'd absolutely take it. 'Come on,' I said, grinning widely at the brownies. 'Let's get out of here.'

~

'We're not going to get rich from jobs like this.' Hester was still intent on complaining when we finally arrived home with a very small reward from Trish York safely in my back pocket.

'We've been through this, Hester. The financial reward wasn't why I took that job. Mrs York was ridiculously happy to get her ring back, and if she leaves a review it'll be more than worth the hours spent on Longniddry beach.'

It was true. The more reviews and testimonials I garnered, the more chance I had of being hired for a real treasure hunt by someone with a lot of money behind them. Frankly, reviews were worth their weight in gold – no pun intended.

One day I hoped to have enough resources and access to establish my own treasure hunts, but for now I was relying on the information and requests provided by other people. I couldn't afford to spend the better part of a year researching dusty archives for details of potential lost treasure. But in the future anything was possible and, bottom rung of the ladder or not, I wouldn't allow myself to be anything other than optimistic about what lay ahead.

'You should write to Sir Nigel again. He might give us some real work,' Hester instructed me.

'He's out of the country.' I started to peel off my damp – and, yes, smelly – coat. I'd be finding grains of sand in my clothes for weeks if not months, no matter how many times I washed them. Sand was sneaky like that.

'You could approach Hugo—'

I interrupted her. 'No.'

'But—'

'No.'

Otis smiled nervously. 'I think Hester is right. You could give him a call and see if—'

'No!'

He flinched. I drew in a deep breath. 'I'm sorry, that was harsher than I intended. We don't need help from the likes of Hugo Pemberville. We're freelance. We're not beholden to anyone else and we're not going to be.'

The last thing I wanted was Hugo to know how much I was struggling in my new career. While I appreciated every single success, no matter how minor, I was certain he'd laugh at my meagre accomplishments. And for complex reasons I didn't fully understand and couldn't articulate, I didn't want him to see me as a failure. Besides, I hadn't spoken to him for weeks and our paths might never cross again – we didn't exactly move in the same circles. 'We can do this ourselves.'

Otis nodded. 'Yes, Daisy. Of course we can. You're right.'

Hester rolled her eyes. 'No, Daisy. We can't. You're wrong.'

I wet my lips. Cumbubbling bollocks. Perhaps I should listen to her.

'Okay,' I conceded, prepared to compromise. 'I promise I won't take on any more small lost-and-found jobs for the time being. I've saved enough to tide us over for a few weeks, so we won't undertake any hunts unless both the reward and the treasure are substantial. I'll extend my advertising to the classifieds in at least one national newspaper, and I'll see who else I can contact at the British Museum for leads.' I paused and eyed both brownies. 'Is that good enough?'

Otis looked relieved while Hester blew out air loudly. 'Finally. No more selling yourself short, Daisy. You're a skilled treasure hunter who should be searching for extraordinary items. From now on, we seek nothing less than a chest full of precious jewels and shiny gold,' she said firmly.

Chance would be a fine thing. Fortunately, for the sake of my sanity and Hester's mood, there was a knock at the door which prevented me suggesting there was a world of difference between optimism and fantasy.

I kicked off my wet trainers, ignored the damp discomfort of my socks, ambled down the corridor and opened the front door. Then I stared. Oh. While I hadn't been expecting anyone in particular, I certainly hadn't anticipated the caller being a child. In my experience, people under the age of twelve were strange and unpredictable and it was wise to avoid them whenever possible.

'Hi.' I tried not stare too obviously at the girl. Her limpid brown eyes were astonishingly large, and she was swamped by the huge puffer jacket she was wearing. I glanced beyond her for any sign of a parent or guardian, but she appeared to be alone.

'Are you the hunter elf lady?' she asked with a faint, audible wobble.

There was an odd prickle on the back of my neck. 'Yes,' I said cautiously. 'Who are you?'

'Sophia.'

I gazed at her and she gazed at me. The silence stretched out for several seconds while the prickle turned into an itch. 'Do you need some help, Sophia?' I asked finally.

'I live down the street.' She waved vaguely to the right. 'I want to hire you. I have a job that needs doing.' She might be no more than four-feet high but she sounded like a Mafia boss ordering a hit.

I smiled. 'How old are you?'

'Nine.'

'Do your parents know you're here?'

'There's only my dad, and no, he doesn't know. He wouldn't like it. He thinks you're weird and he told me to stay away from you.' She delivered the information in a matter-of-fact voice.

'Your dad is right,' I said cheerfully. I scratched the back of my neck with my nails. Did brownies get fleas? Was that why I felt so itchy? 'I *am* weird and you *should* stay away from me. Nice to meet you though, Sophia.' I started to close the door.

'Wait!'

I hesitated.

'I still want to hire you.' She swallowed. 'I *need* to hire you. I need a treasure hunter.'

Oh, man. 'That's very kind of you, Sophia, but I'm afraid I'm busy.'

Although she was obviously nervous, her response was instant. 'No, you're not. You finished that job for Mrs York and I've seen your advert in the shop window down the street that says you'll hunt for *any* sort of treasure, so you can't be that busy.'

Was this kid keeping tabs on me? I should have known that forking over a whole twenty quid to advertise my skills in the corner-shop window would bite me in the arse sooner or later.

She held out a crumpled five-pound note. 'I can pay you.'

'I can't take your money, Sophia.' I tried to sound as gentle as possible. 'You should go home to your dad and ask him for help.'

Her cheeks turned scarlet. 'Stop! Stop patro – patro– patro—'

'Patronising you?'

Her jaw tightened. 'Yeah. That. I want to hire you to get my treasure back. You're a treasure hunter.' She glared. 'So hunt for my treasure.'

'What treasure is it?'

'My doll.'

Help. I scanned the street again. It was devoid of people. 'Um...'

'A doll might not be treasure to you but she's treasure to me. She's the last present my mum gave me before she died.'

My stomach sank to my boots. Shit. 'Where did you last see it?'

'In the cemetery at the end of the road.' She crossed her arms over her chest. 'I was visiting Mum's grave and I took *Nancy* with me,' she stressed the name, as if she were insulted by me calling her doll an 'it'. 'Nancy's my doll. I put her down while I went to get some water for the flowers and when I turned around, she'd gone. Somebody took her. I need to get her back and you can help me.'

'Um...' I tried to think of a polite way to decline. It would have been easy if she were an adult.

Sophia threw the balled up five-pound note at my chest. Without thinking, I grabbed it before it tumbled to the ground and her face immediately transformed into a bright grin. 'Brilliant! Thank you! I'm at number seventy-two. Flat four. You can knock on the door when you've found Nancy. You'll know her when you find her. She has a pink heart sewn on her chest.' She twisted away and marched down the street, her hair swinging in the light breeze.

Nuh-uh. No way. 'Wait! Sophia!'

She didn't turn around. 'I'll be home from school every day at four o'clock!' she called. 'Don't come after six or my dad will see you.'

No sooner had the last word left her mouth than she started to run with the pelting speed that only professional sprinters, expert shapeshifters and pre-pubescent kids could manage. I was left clutching the grubby fiver and staring after her with the definite sensation that I'd been completely conned by a child.

I sighed, stepped back, closed the door and headed for the kitchen where Otis and Hester were already making a mess. 'So,' I hedged. 'You remember what I said about only hunting for substantial treasure from now on?'

A tiny frown creased Otis's brow. 'It was only two minutes ago. Of course we remember.'

'You promised,' Hester reminded me.

Not in so many words. 'Mmm,' I grimaced. 'Well, about that...'

CHAPTER
TWO

Edinburgh is the sort of city where you can turn a corner and trip over an old cemetery. They're all over the placc, often where you'd least expect them. Many no longer accept new burials or cremations and are filled with scattered headstones and graves that are hundreds of years old.

Saughton Cemetery, not far from where I lived, was one of the less dramatic sites but it still organised burials. It was a peaceful spot occupied not only by the dead but by any number of crows, magpies and scurrying mice who mostly stayed out sight. I'd walked past it a thousand times but I'd never passed through its gates until now.

'Where's the grave belonging to the child's mother?' Hester enquired.

I shrugged. 'I don't know.'

Otis flew ahead. 'Was there anybody else nearby who might have taken her doll?'

'I don't know.'

'Is there anything, anything at all, that you *do* know?' Hester asked

I considered the question. 'The blob of toothpaste that sits on your toothbrush,' I said slowly, 'is called a nurdle.'

'Oooh,' Otis said. 'That's interesting.'

Hester only stared at me. I grinned. 'Come on,' I said. 'The graves to the right look more recent, so we'll start over there. Sophia's mother can't have been buried here for long.' I turned, and with both brownies joining me, checked the inscription on each headstone as we passed.

'At least tell me that you know the child's last name,' Hester demanded. I didn't look at her. She hissed, 'Daisy!'

'She said the doll vanished when she went to get water for some flowers,' I said helpfully. 'Look for a grave with fresh flowers on it.'

'This is ridiculous,' Hester muttered.

I turned my head. Although her words were familiar, her tone was different to usual; there was an angry tension to her voice that I'd rarely heard. Hester had made a sport out of complaining, especially in recent weeks when I admit there had been a lot to complain about. But this sounded more serious than that.

I watched her for a moment or two. Her tiny shoulders were stiff and her wings were vibrating more than necessary. Ah. She might use funereal black as a fashion choice, but I reckoned that Hester was feeling distinctly uncomfortable. 'What?' she snapped. 'Why are you staring at me?'

'You're not a fan of cemeteries, are you?'

She sniffed loudly. 'The dead creep me out.'

'Do you want to wait by the entrance?'

'I'm not afraid!' She half-yelled the words, suggesting that she was very much afraid. It was a sentiment that I could empathise with; while I found the cemetery a peaceful place, I knew what irrational fear felt like. I was much the same in small dark spaces.

'Hester,' I began.

She shook her head violently. 'No. I'm staying. Let's find this damned doll and get out of here.'

'You're alright, Hes,' Otis soothed.

'I know I'm alright!' Her voice dripped with the desperate rancour of the terrified. She jerked her head to the left. 'There's a grave over there with fresh flowers on it. Come on!' She took off, flying at high speed away from us.

Otis winced then started to follow her. I bit my lip before doing the same.

The headstone was plain but there was something elegant about its simplicity. However, while the flowers –a collection of red roses, white lilies and some pretty fern-like foliage – were indeed freshly laid, this wasn't the grave of Sophia's mother. Not unless her mother had been an eighty-two-year-old man called David.

Hester's hands were curled into fists. 'Fuck.'

I opened my mouth to repeat that she could wait for us outside the cemetery walls but before I could say a word, there was a guttural shout from my left followed by the sound of pounding footsteps. Hester shrieked and flew behind the headstone.

'Oi! Stop that! Stop desecrating the graves!'

I dropped my hands to my sides to indicate that I was doing no such thing as Otis zoomed in front to defend me. A burly man wearing a high-vis jacket and overalls appeared from behind a row of trees, marching in our direction with his shoulders swinging and his jaw set.

As soon as he saw us, he came to a stuttering halt and his face slackened. 'Oh. Sorry. I thought you were somebody else.'

I waved a hand airily. 'That's okay. I'm just having a look around. I live nearby.'

He nodded then stared at Otis. 'Is that ... is that ... is that a brownie?'

'Good day,' Otis said.

The man jumped.

Hester raised her head from behind the curved edge of the stone. 'Attack!' she screeched. 'Attack him now before it's too late!'

'It's fine, Hester,' I said quickly.

She drew in a breath. I gestured towards her to keep quiet before she started bellowing unnecessary insults or kill commands.

'I've never seen a brownie in real life before,' the man whispered.

Otis executed a perfect bow. 'In that case it is a real pleasure to make your acquaintance. I'm Otis. This is Daisy. And that's my sister Hester hiding behind the headstone.'

'I'm not hiding!' she yelled.

'I'm Will. Nice to meet you all.' He continued to switch his stare between Otis and Hester, shaking his head in wonder.

I stifled a smile and eyed him curiously. 'So who did you think I was?'

Will pulled his gaze away from the brownies and a dark expression crossed his face. 'There's been a witch lurking around here lately taking things from graves, messing with the dirt. It's not right. It shouldn't be allowed.'

Suddenly I was very interested. 'A witch?' A cemetery seemed a strange place for a witch to hang out in. Their skills tended towards adapting living material to their own purposes, usually leafy plants and herbs. A witch had no use for the dead. But a witch who was taking things from a graveyard sounded exactly like the doll-stealing culprit I was looking for.

'Aye, a strange bloke with strange powers. I've got nothing against witches per se – I've used their services from time to time myself when I've needed to. But this particular witch is...' he paused to suck in air through his teeth '...unnatural.' He swept his eyes up and down my petite frame. 'You should steer clear of him if you see him.'

Excellent. I smiled brightly. 'Do you know where I can find him?'

'Didn't you hear me?' His left eyebrow was starting to twitch violently. 'He's clearly not right in the head. He'll do someone like you an injury.'

Uh-huh. I knew what Will saw when he looked at me: a small vulnerable female with messy red hair who couldn't fight her way out of a paper bag if her life depended on it. I didn't take offence. Like most people, he only took notice of the obvious.

So I gave him obvious: I raised my hands and made a show of tucking my hair behind my ears to reveal my pointed elvish heritage. Then I glanced casually at Gladys, the slender, sentient, short sword hooked onto my belt and half-hidden by the tail of my coat.

Will blinked and stepped backwards. 'You're an elf?'

I nodded. I didn't bother telling him that I was a low elf with fewer powers and ability than a high-born individual, or that I didn't actually possess any sword-wielding skills. He didn't need to know everything.

'I didn't realise.' His eyes took on an eager light. 'Can you do magic?'

'Yep.' Before he asked for a demonstration, I took control of the conversation. 'So this witch. Where will I find him?'

'I don't know. He comes here on foot so he can't live far away. I think his name is Mud McAlpine.' He shrugged awkwardly. 'I only know because he talks about himself in the third person and that's what he calls himself. It might not be his real name. He's a weird guy. I don't know where you'd find him, other than here.'

Otis smiled. 'Daisy is the best treasure hunter in the country. She'll find him.'

Will's jaw dropped. 'You're a treasure hunter?'

It was nice to be admired, even if I didn't deserve it. 'I am.'

His awe increased. 'Do you know Hugo Pemberville?'

For fuck's sake. 'Yes,' I said shortly.

'He's amazing! I love him!'

That was quite the declaration. 'Okay,' I acknowledged, not quite sure what else to say.

'I was telling my husband the other night how skilled he is.'

'Uh-huh.'

'The amount of lost treasure he's found is astounding.'

'I guess.'

'Did you know that he found the Loch Arkaig gold all on his own *and* he managed to prevent it from being stolen by a crook?'

My mouth flattened. 'I'd heard something to that effect.'

Will's eyes shone. 'The man is a true hero. I can't wait to see what he does next.'

I gave in to temptation. 'Between us,' I confided, lowering my voice, 'poor Hugo has a terrible fungal condition at the moment that's unfortunately put him out of action. It's very sad.' I sighed, gesturing vaguely towards my crotch. 'I've seen it. It's all green and mouldy and...'

Otis stared at me, utterly aghast. 'Daisy, stop that!'

I folded my hands together. 'You're right. Too much information.' I raised my eyebrows at Will, who was looking morbidly fascinated. 'Anyway, back to Mud McAlpine. Why is he taking things from the cemetery?'

'I have no idea. He's nabbed all sorts – flowers, solar lights, teddy bears. It's disgusting. He's preying on people's grief. I've spoken to the police several times, but I don't think they've done anything.'

'Don't worry. I'll have a word with Mr McAlpine. Perhaps I can put a stop to all this business.' I'd certainly try.

'That would be wonderful. With you being an elf and all, he might listen to you.'

Stranger things had happened. I curtsied to Will and nodded to Otis and Hester, both of whom decided to play nice and fly to perch on my shoulders.

'Good work,' Hester whispered as I walked away. 'We get to leave this godforsaken place *and* you've badmouthed Hugo all at the same time. I approve.'

Otis remained in a huff. 'You're supposed to be his friend now. It wasn't nice to say those things about Hugo.'

No, but it had been fun. I hadn't seen Hugo for two months and I might never see him again. It wasn't as if he would ever know what I'd said to a random council worker in a quiet cemetery.

The main thing was that I had a solid lead on who had taken Sophia's doll. I'd have Nancy back in her hands within hours. Then the real treasure hunting would definitely begin.

CHAPTER
THREE

I'd assumed that Mud was a nickname but a two-minute search of the electoral register revealed it was his real name. I hoped for his sake that he'd changed it by deed poll and that his parents hadn't christened him Mud.

Given that Will had been right and the witch did indeed live reasonably close both to Saughton Cemetery and my home, I didn't waste any time before heading to his address: a basement flat in an old tenement building that had definitely seen better days.

I picked my way along the cracked stone path, avoiding the strewn rubbish and towering, waist-high weeds. A small patch of garden to my left was a messy tangle of more weeds, but dotted amongst them there were glimpses of medicinal plants – feverfew, sweet cicely and even some unseasonal clary sage, which I recognised from the time my adopted mum had bought some from a witch to soothe her conjunctivitis. I suspected that this scrap of land had once been well tended by an experienced witch. Whether that was true or not, it certainly was ignored now.

The main door was open, as was often the case with these

tenement buildings, so I went inside, located the stairs and headed down until I found the correct apartment door. Other than Gladys, I was on my own; it had seemed wise to persuade Otis and Hester to stay behind. I didn't want to scare Mud McAlpine off; from what little I knew of him, I reckoned a gently-gently approach would be best.

This was one of those times when hiding my elvish nature and any hint of my magic would likely reap rewards. I was nothing more than a harmless adult helping out a forlorn child. Go me.

There didn't appear to be a doorbell so I knocked quietly, arranging my face into a meek expression. It was as well I did; even though I'd been warned by Will, Mud McAlpine's appearance was still somewhat surprising.

He was tall, with broad shoulders and a wide girth, though something about the way his skin sagged suggested that he'd recently lost a lot of weight. He had a waxy pallor and his eyes were slightly glazed and tinged with red. This was not a well man.

Gladys appeared to agree with Will that Mud was strange and I felt her blade vibrating against my hip as if she were itching to slice him open and taste his peculiar blood. I touched her hilt lightly, hoping she'd stay quiet. This was not a good time for a sentient sword to start singing.

'Who is this?' he asked, his lank, greasy hair shivering as his head jerked from right to left with every word he uttered.

'I'm Daisy Carter.'

'Mud McAlpine doesn't know Daisy Carter.' He looked me up and down. 'What does she want? Mud McAlpine does not sell nasty spider's silk.'

Maybe not, but Mud McAlpine was very observant. Few people noticed the ring of silver in my eyes that indicated I was an addict, and even fewer people knew what it meant. The light was very dim, making me wonder whether he possessed some shapeshifter blood as well as witchy qualities. That would make a certain amount of sense.

'I don't need spider's silk,' I said aloud. 'I'm here for something else. I'm looking for a doll.'

His brows snapped together. 'Mud McAlpine is not a toy shop.'

Perhaps not, but I was starting to think that he was toying with *me*. 'It's a specific doll that I'm looking for. It belongs to a little girl called Sophia. The doll was the last present her mother gave her before she died, and she lost it in Saughton Cemetery. I know you've been there and I hoped that maybe you'd found it.' I linked my fingers together and blinked earnestly. 'I'd really like to reunite them.'

He cleared his throat, gargling phlegm in a horribly off-putting fashion. 'Mud McAlpine does not want this.' But he didn't step away, and he didn't close the front door in my face.

I dropped my voice until I was speaking in little more than a whisper. 'What does Mud McAlpine want?'

'Much more than an elf like Daisy Carter could offer.'

He was definitely far more intelligent and aware than he looked, and the redness in his eyes didn't disguise his gleam of amusement. First things first, however. 'Does Mud McAlpine have the doll?' I asked.

'Perhaps.'

I waited, keeping my body relaxed. His mouth twitched and he nodded, then disappeared inside his flat leaving his front door wide open. I wasn't foolish enough to follow; I stayed where I was until he returned holding a rather bedraggled rag doll by its hair. There was no guarantee that this was Sophia's Nancy, but it seemed likely.

I reached forward to take it but Mud snatched it back. I raised my hands, palms stretched outwards. 'I'm not trying to steal her. I only want to check if she has a mark here.' I touched my chest to indicate.

Mud pulled up the doll's cotton top and showed me a small embroidered pink heart. Yahtzee. 'This doll is not yours,' I said.

Mud smirked and watched me. Hmm. It was still my move, then.

I chewed on my lip. I could unsheathe Gladys and take a clumsy swipe in a bid to free Nancy from his clutches, but I was no swordswoman. I doubted I'd have much success if I tried an attack now, for all that Mud McAlpine's health was failing. I wasn't a damned samurai, I was nothing more than an ex-delivery driver with a penchant for finding things.

Besides, something about the witch aroused my sympathy. Yes, he was strange but he didn't seem dangerous, despite Will's warnings. I didn't want to throw magic at him; the poor guy was already sick and I didn't want to get into a fight over a ragdoll.

But Sophia's huge brown eyes were seared into my brain and I'd come this far. Eventually I came to a decision and took out my wallet. 'Can Daisy Carter pay Mud McAlpine to hand over the doll?' I asked carefully.

'Mud McAlpine does not need money.'

I barely suppressed an irritated sigh.

'But Mud McAlpine will trade Daisy Carter for the doll.' He rocked forward on his toes. 'Bring Mud McAlpine a fresh toe-clipping from a troll and Daisy Carter may take the doll.' He smacked his lips and chuckled heartily.

Seriously? I couldn't help myself. 'Ewww. You're kidding, right?'

He continued to laugh. 'It must be fresh. No more than twelve hours old.'

'Why would you—?' I shook my head in frustration. 'Take

the damned money. It's not even your doll. You nicked it from a nine-year-old girl, for fuck's sake.'

His laughter abruptly stopped. 'No troll toenail, no doll,' he snarled. And with that, he slammed the door in my face.

~

'You should have punched him in the face, broken his nose and wrestled the doll from him,' Hester said. She seriously overestimated my fighting skills.

'After all,' she continued, 'you managed to stab Humphrey Bridger in the back and stop him from stealing several chests of Jacobean gold, even though he was using blood magic to try and gain the upper hand. If you could beat him, you could have managed to get hold of a single toy.'

'Those were very different, very specific circumstances.'

Otis nodded vigorously. 'Don't forget that Daisy could have ended up in jail for what she did to Humphrey. Violence is not the answer, Hester. I think this is a beautiful thing to do. She's helping a little girl and a needy witch all at the same time.'

'Yeah?' She glared at him. 'So why don't *you* ask the troll for a toenail clipping then?'

Otis paled. 'Daisy will do that,' he squeaked. 'She's more persuasive than me. And she already knows this troll.'

I eyed them both. 'Let's stop with the bickering. I don't want to spend a long time here. If we're fast, we can get the clipping from Duchess and be back at the station in time to catch the next train home to Edinburgh.'

Hester nudged Otis. 'It's nothing to do with the train. Daisy doesn't want Hugo Pemberville to know she's loitering outside his house.'

'Castle,' I muttered. 'He lives in a castle.'

'Why is there a troll living near Hugo Pemberville's castle?' Hester asked with mock innocence.

'Because,' Otis said, missing the point, 'Daisy sent Duchess the troll there to annoy Hugo.'

I stopped my bike, climbed off and leaned it against a fence. The least said about that particular episode, the better. 'Let's find Duchess and get this over and done with.'

'Yes, Daisy,' both brownies chorused as they exchanged glances.

'Will you behave yourselves?'

'Of course,' Otis said.

Hester shrugged. 'Maybe.' It was the most I could ask for.

I walked around the corner, doing my best not to gape as Pemberville Castle came into view. I'd seen photos of the place and I already knew it was grand, but I wasn't there to play tourist or admire the random vagaries of inheritance. I was on a mission.

Otis gasped. 'That's where Hugo lives?'

I ignored him.

'There are turrets!' Hester exclaimed. 'How many bedrooms do you think there are?'

I marched forward, still pretending not to hear.

'We could knock on the door. We're in time for afternoon tea.'

'He'll have a butler. There will be cucumber sandwiches. And perfectly brewed tea.'

'And those little macaron things that you see in French patisseries.'

'And—'

I resolutely refused to look at either of them. Instead I cleared my throat and very loudly called, 'Duchess!' I walked to the bridge over the old moat which led to the castle gate.

'Duchess! It's me! Your old friend, Daisy!' There was no answer, not so much as a whisper from the belligerent troll. I tried again. 'Hello! Duchess!'

Still nothing. Maybe Hugo had found an alternative bridge for Duchess to reside under and persuaded her to leave. I drew as close to the edge of the bridge as I dared and scooted down so I could peer underneath it. The stone arch was angled in such a way that I couldn't see much, so I shimmied further forward. *Please be there*, Duchess, I prayed silently. *Please*.

I'd barely moved more than a couple of inches when a voice drawled, 'I knew you couldn't stay away from me for long, Daisy, though I didn't expect you to prostrate yourself in front of my home to get my attention.'

For fuck's sake. 'I'm not here for you.' I sniffed, refusing to get up or look at Hugo Cumbubbling Pemberville. 'I'm looking for Duchess.'

'She's not there.'

Shit. I'd hoped this was going to be easy. I sighed with frustration, pulled away from the edge of the bridge, got to my feet and dusted myself off. Alas, I could only do so much: there was a long smear of smelly wet mud stretching down the side of my old jeans.

In contrast, Hugo was wearing an immaculate three-piece suit complete with starched collar, pristine white shirt and a perfectly folded handkerchief peeping out of his breast pocket. Of course he was.

He offered me a crooked smile, revealing the dimple in his cheek. 'It's good to see you again, Daisy. You should have called ahead to let me know you were coming.'

'I didn't think you'd be here. I assumed you'd be away on another treasure hunt.'

'I'm between jobs right now.' He raised his eyebrows. 'How about you? Have you had much success so far?'

'Lots,' I lied. 'Lots and lots and lots. In fact, I'm on a very important job at the moment. I'm hunting for a very specific and very valuable item.'

Interest flashed in his blue eyes. 'Oh yes? What is it?'

I tapped the side of my nose to indicate that it was a secret; Hugo didn't need to know that I was searching for a doll. Out of the corner of my eye I spotted Hester open her mouth. She was clearly preparing to tell him everything, so I carried on talking before she could reveal the truth. 'Anyway, I need to find Duchess. I need her help. Where has she moved to?'

'Oh, she's still here,' Hugo assured me. 'But at this time of day she's usually inside.'

My mouth dropped. 'Inside?' Duchess? 'Inside *your* home?'

'Oh yes. We've become quite friendly over the last few months. Many people, even trolls, find me charming.' He smirked and pointed at the castle. 'She often comes in to enjoy a spot of afternoon tea.'

'I told you!' Otis said. 'Are there cucumber sandwiches?'

'Sometimes.' Hugo smiled.

'And macarons?' Hester asked.

'Naturally. You should come in and join us.'

Hester and Otis almost fell over each other in glee.

'Daisy?' Hugo asked.

I pasted on my best smile and reminded myself that Hugo and I were supposed to be friends now. Come on, Daisy. Play nice. 'That would be lovely,' I said. 'Thank you.'

CHAPTER
FOUR

Hugo led the way, taking us through the massive castle gate, across a cobbled courtyard and into a huge hallway with a grand staircase that looped upwards. I looked around, noting a burnished oak floor, a sparkling chandelier and at least four suits of armour. Suits of freaking *armour*.

'I'm going to go out on a limb,' I said faintly, 'and assume that you don't do your own cleaning.'

Hugo laughed. 'Oh, you'll frequently find me in a pinny and with a feather duster in hand.'

I tried hard to get that image out of my head. In my imagination, he was naked apart from the pinafore while the feather duster... No. I forced the thought away.

'But you're right,' he continued, apparently not noticing my blush. 'It takes a lot of people to keep this place going. Most of the Primes stay here too,' he said, referring to his group of treasure-hunting colleagues. 'The castle is more than big enough to house us all, and anything is better than knocking around here on my own.' He shot me a sideways glance. 'I'm very aware,' he added in a quieter voice, 'that I'm incredibly privileged.'

'In that case,' Hester piped up, 'you should give Daisy some of your money. She's broke.'

'I am not!' It was true. I had savings. I was doing fine. I didn't need charity from anyone.

Hugo stopped walking and turned to me, a strangely intense light in his eyes. 'Are you doing okay, Daisy?' he asked.

Exasperated, I waved my hands. 'Yes! Hester's only annoyed because I wouldn't buy the diamond earrings she spotted in a shop window last week.'

'They would have set off your eyes perfectly,' she said, folding her arms.

I suppressed a sigh.

Hugo continued to watch me. 'What about...?' His voice trailed off.

'My drug addiction?' I asked cheerfully. 'I'm still loving all that yummy spider's silk. I'm still a junkie.' I felt a sudden wash of guilt for being so gleeful. Hugo had lost his best friend to a spider's silk addiction. My voice softened. 'It is what it is, Hugo. I'm too far gone to come out of it now.'

His jaw tightened. 'But you're managing it?'

I nodded, slightly surprised that he cared so much. 'Yeah, it's not a problem.' Not really. I tried not to think about how I'd lost control of my air magic on the beach the previous day. That had been nothing more than a mere slip of attention; it was unrelated to my addiction.

'Good.' He seemed on the verge of saying something else then shook himself and took a step back. 'Duchess is probably in the garden room. It's through that door there.' He looked at the brownies. 'Why don't the two of you head in and help yourselves to some tea?'

Neither brownie moved. 'What about Daisy?' Otis asked suspiciously.

'There's something I want to show her first,' Hugo said in an overly casual tone.

Curiosity piqued, I nodded to indicate they should do as he suggested. Hugo smiled. 'This way.' He dipped his head towards my ear. 'I think you'll like this,' he murmured.

We walked side by side away from the garden room, first down one hallway then another. I had a good head for directions but I suspected that I'd easily get lost without Hugo by my side.

Neither of us spoke. While I didn't know where he was taking me, I felt oddly comfortable with the silence – no doubt because it was a break from Hester and Otis's incessant chatter. It couldn't have anything to do with Hugo himself; his presence usually invited extreme discomfort.

Eventually we reached a simple oak door and I moved politely to the side while he opened it. He beckoned me inside and flicked on the lights. I gaped. 'What *is* this place?'

'My office,' Hugo said simply.

In the centre of the room there was a vast table with pads of paper, pens, laptops and computers. I counted twelve chairs and there was a screen for a projector and several whiteboards. But none of those drew my focus because the room was also full of all manner of treasure hunting accoutrements.

There were maps pinned to one wall, some of which looked positively ancient. I darted up to the nearest one and examined its curled edges and intricate draughtsmanship. Several points had been marked out in red ink.

'This is a treasure hunter's map,' Hugo said softly. 'We think it's over five hundred years old. All the red sections are where treasure was supposed to be located. Of course, they've long since been cleared but it's fascinating, isn't it?'

I gazed at it. 'It's beautiful. The detail here.' I pointed to a wooded section. 'That's extraordinary.'

Hugo smiled. 'I knew you'd appreciate it.'

I stepped towards some glass cabinets. When I saw what they contained, I blinked. 'Is that...?'

Hugo nodded. 'An ancient, fossilised dragon's egg? Yes. It's been in my family for generations. I have to be honest, I don't think it should be here but I don't know what to do with it. It's not as if I can wander up to the nearest dragon and hand it over. They'd probably incinerate me on the spot if I tried, assuming I could even find one. None of the museums are interested in it, not even the British Museum.'

I stared at it in awe. 'How old is it?'

'Old. I could have it X-rayed and tested, I suppose, but that seems disrespectful somehow. It's not a hunk of cold metal. Once upon a time it was the promise of precious life.'

I reached out to touch it, my fingers grazing its smooth surface. It was cold. I pulled back. I was very glad that times were different now and we no longer stole such objects away from their rightful owners.

Hugo showed me a larger cabinet. 'These are bones that are purportedly from a sea serpent that once guarded the entrance to an underwater cave used by the pirate Anne Bonny.'

'Wow.'

'And over there is an ancient lantern that belonged to a will o' the wisp. My great-grandfather found it.'

I swivelled around. Everywhere I looked, there was something different to see.

He cleared his throat. 'This room is affectionately called the Bone Zone.'

I stiffened. '*This* is your Bone Zone?' I'd heard that name before. 'Somebody mentioned you had a room called the Bone Zone. I assumed it referred to something less ... uh...' I hesitated. 'Literal.'

Hugo didn't take his eyes away from me. 'I know,' he said. 'That's why I wanted to show you the real thing.'

Oh. I swallowed.

Hugo broke eye contact first. 'This room is usually off limits to anyone who's not in the Primes. There's a wealth of information in here and there's a curated library towards the rear. You're welcome to use any of the resources to help with your current hunt.' He held up his hands. 'I promise I won't look over your shoulder. You can have privacy, if you like.'

Nothing in this room would help me get Nancy the doll back to Sophia. I smiled anyway, confused by the offer. 'I appreciate that but everything's under control.'

The Bone Zone door burst open and thudded loudly against the wall. 'Duchess is going crazy again! You have to do something, Hugo!' Becky, the chirpy blonde who was one of Hugo's Primes, looked frantic. She glanced at me and blinked. 'Daisy?'

I waved weakly. Hugo muttered something under his breath then took off at high speed and disappeared out of the door.

Becky stayed where she was. 'Are you joining the Primes?' she asked, her curiosity overcoming her troll-based anxiety.

'No.'

'But nobody is allowed in the Bone Zone unless they're a Prime.' She frowned. 'Ever.'

'I should probably leave then.' I felt vaguely awkward. 'Anyway, I need to see Duchess.'

Horror filled her face. 'Why? That troll is bloody awful. The hoops we've had to go through to persuade her to let us use our own damned bridge – and she still causes problems!'

That sounded more like the Duchess I knew. I smiled faintly and hurried after Hugo.

I heard Duchess long before I saw her: there was a considerable amount of bellowing, crashing and breaking china. Otis and Hester were outside the garden room and their expressions filled with relief when they spotted me.

'Even for a troll, she's horrible!' Hester said.

Otis agreed fervently. 'Where were you?' he asked. 'What was Hugo doing?'

'Trying to impress me.'

Hester was puzzled. 'Why?'

'Beats me.' I shrugged. But there was still a fuzzy warm sensation in the pit of my stomach. 'Stay here,' I told them. 'I'll deal with Duchess.'

I drew a deep breath and entered the room. Hugo was in the far corner, holding up a chair as a shield. Duchess was standing on top of a table, her head brushing the ceiling. She appeared to be alternating jets of sticky troll phlegm with various china cups and dainty sandwich missiles. 'You wet rag of an elf!' she sneered at him. 'You blue-eyed simpleton!'

'What was that you said earlier, Hugo?' I asked over the racket. 'That you and Duchess are friendly now and that she finds you charming?'

He threw me a baleful glance, his earlier bonhomie no longer evident. Given the state of the room and the way Duchess was acting, I couldn't really blame him.

'You know this is all your fault,' he grumbled, as a slice of cucumber smacked wetly onto his forehead. He dropped the chair, peeled it off his face and glared at the troll. 'Either calm down or I will be forced to use magic against you, Duchess.'

'I'd like to see you try, elf!'

'Don't you remember what happened last time?'

Duchess jumped off the table, landing with such force that even the stone walls around us seemed to shake. 'Oh,' she purred, 'I remember, elf man. I remember it very well.'

I folded my arms and watched. Now that I had time to take in my surroundings more closely, there was a definite lingering scent of troll snot lurking beneath the floral air freshener, spilled tea and freshly baked pastries. Hugo had obviously had more trouble with Duchess than he'd been willing to admit. Yeah, I ought to have felt guilty about that but I only felt amused.

Duchess thumped her chest. 'Come on, then! Come at me! Give me your best shot!'

Hugo gritted his teeth. 'Duchess...'

'You're not man enough to take me on!'

I stifled a giggle. Unfortunately, Hugo noticed and sent me a quick glare. Then he muttered something under his breath and goosebumps rose across my skin when his magic started to stir. Uh-oh.

While I was tempted to see how far he was willing to go and what power he'd produce to quell Duchess, I needed her to be in a good mood if I was going to get hold of that toenail clipping. Shame.

I pulled back my shoulders and jumped between them. 'Hi, Duchess!' I said, waving at her. 'You look like you're having fun.'

Hugo growled, 'Daisy, you need to get out of the damned way.'

I ignored his warning and focussed on Duchess, whose huge brow had creased. Her head swung towards me and she scratched her chin. Aware that her eyesight was very poor, I re-introduced myself. 'It's Daisy.' I kept my voice bright. 'Daisy Carter.'

'I know who you are,' Duchess snapped. 'You're the delivery girl. I've been waiting three weeks for a parcel. Have you finally brought it?'

'I don't work for SDS any more.'

Her scowl deepened. 'Then why are you here?'

'To see you!' I stretched my arms wide. 'To see how you're getting on in your new place!'

Duchess rolled her shoulders in a shrug. 'It's alright, I suppose.' She pointed a long finger towards Hugo. 'It has its amusements.'

'For fuck's sake,' Hugo hissed.

I didn't look at him; instead, I nodded vigorously. 'Yes. He's a fun guy and it's great that you can come inside and have tea with him. You must feel very relaxed to be able to leave the bridge. Aren't you worried that the waterwights who used to live there will return?'

Duchess stiffened. 'No.'

'Or that another troll will scoot by to take up residence?'

She glared at me. 'They wouldn't dare.'

'Hugo wouldn't let them,' I agreed.

Duchess threw back her head and roared, making the delicate chandelier to her right shiver. 'I wouldn't let them! It's *my* home now!'

I kept my expression blank. 'Okay.'

'What have you heard?' she demanded. 'Who's coming here to take my home away from me?'

'No-one,' I said quickly. 'I've not heard anything.'

'Just as well.' Her eyes drifted towards the door; I'd planted the seed in her head and now she was nervous.

Hugo walked up next to me until his shoulder brushed against mine. Clearly he'd understood my plan and was prepared to play along. 'Would you like some tea, Duchess?' He bent over to pick up a teapot from the floor where it had fallen during her table-dancing antics. 'I can get the kitchen to make a fresh pot. It won't take long.' He pursed his mouth. 'Ten minutes or so. Take the weight off your feet and we can have a chat while it's being brewed.'

Duchess had already begun to sidle towards the door. 'Where are you going?' I asked, evincing surprise. 'Stay for a bit. I want to hear how things are going.'

'Things are fine.' She moved closer to the exit.

'You look in good health. Your hair is shiny and your skin looks beautiful. Your new accommodation definitely agrees with you.'

'Uh-huh.' She doubled over, preparing to duck through the doorway. 'I'm going home,' she announced. 'I don't want any tea.'

I grinned. 'That's a shame but I understand if you need to go. Tell you what, once you're gone I can call SDS and see if I can hurry along your delivery.'

Duchess paused. 'Yes,' she said. 'Do that.' She sniffed and started to squeeze through the door.

'But,' I called out, 'I'd like something in return.'

'Fucking high elves,' Duchess muttered. 'They never do anything out of the goodness of their hearts.'

'I'm not a high elf, Duchess.'

'Yeah, yeah.' She pushed through the door frame then turned and stuck her head back through to stare at me with heavy suspicion.

'You know you can trust me. I told you about this place, didn't I?' I said innocently.

'Yes,' Hugo said sarcastically. 'Thanks for that, Daisy.'

I nudged him sharply to stay quiet and kept smiling. 'It's your call, Duchess.'

She rolled her eyes. 'What?' she snapped. 'What do you want?'

I knew better than to assume that I had the situation under control; I had to play my cards close to my chest and as cleverly as possible. I tapped my mouth thoughtfully. 'How about a lock of your hair?' I said.

Hugo stared at me.

'Fuck off, elf.' Duchess glared. 'No deal.'

'It'd be a lovely keepsake to remember you by.'

She snarled, 'No chance. My hair is staying on my head where it belongs.'

I did my best to look deflated. It was understandable: Duchess had very little hair. 'That's a shame.' I pulled my phone out of my pocket. 'I could call SDS now. I know exactly who to speak to.'

'No hair!'

I allowed my shoulders to sag. 'Alright.' I returned my phone to my pocket.

'No hair!' she repeated. To give in would be to admit defeat and Duchess wasn't like that, but when she hesitated I knew that she was preparing to compromise. 'I'll give you something else.'

'Hmm. I'm not sure there *is* anything else.'

'What the hell are you doing?' Hugo muttered in my ear. 'Just let her leave!'

'There must be something,' Duchess said. 'I want my parcel.'

I tilted my head and pretended to think. 'How about a toenail then?' Hugo recoiled. To be fair, so did Duchess. 'Not a whole toenail,' I added quickly. 'Just a clipping.'

Duchess opened her mouth and, for a brief second, I was certain she'd agree. Then understanding flashed in her eyes. 'Oh,' she said. 'I see. This is what you wanted all along.'

Damn it. I'd thought I was going to get away with it.

'You thought you could manipulate me.'

Yep, I had thought that. Yet again, I'd been reminded that I wasn't as clever as I thought I was.

'Why?' she asked. 'Why would you want this of me? Are you trying to mock me?'

My eyes widened. 'No!'

'Then why?'

I sighed, then gave in and yielded to the truth – or at least a palatable version of it that my pathetic ego could allow Hugo to hear. 'The reason I'm not working for SDS any more is because I'm a treasure hunter. I'm on the trail of some precious treasure, but in order to get it I need to hand over the toenail clipping from a troll.'

I raised my shoulders helplessly. 'I don't know why. I am asking for your help – and I really will call SDS and get them to make sure your parcel is delivered straightaway.'

Duchess gave me a long look then her mouth twisted. 'No deal, girlie.' With that, she spun around and stomped off. A moment later I heard the front door thump open as she stormed out. Shit. That was not supposed to happen.

Hugo eyed me. 'It must be some serious treasure if it requires a troll's toenail to retrieve it.'

He had no idea. 'Very serious.' Well, it was serious to Sophia.

'Tell you what,' he said, 'I'll help you get the toenail clipping if you let me join in.'

I blinked. 'Excuse me?'

'I've not had a decent hunt since Loch Arkaig. It sounds like you're on the trail of something intriguing. Let me join you and I'll get you what you need.'

'You want to join *my* treasure hunt?'

He smiled easily. 'Why not?'

Because I was trying to retrieve a kid's toy, not locate piles of gold. 'You might be disappointed with the results,' I said carefully. 'It's not going to be a big pay off.'

'It's a risk I'm willing to take.'

He couldn't say I hadn't warned him – and anyway, I doubted he'd persuade Duchess. 'Alright. Get me that toenail clipping and you're in.'

Hugo looked pleased. 'Good. Give me a couple of minutes.' With that, he strode out of the room and after Duchess.

I caught up with them on top of the bridge where Duchess now lived. 'I'll upgrade your quarters,' Hugo said. 'Whatever you want.'

'Candles,' she said instantly.

'Done.'

Duchess sensed she was on to a winning streak. 'And the bridge should be extended so I've got more space.' She spread her huge arms, gesturing at the width.

Hugo nodded. 'That'll take more time, but I can do it.'

'And flowers planted along the verge by a witch who knows what they're doing. I want them to bloom all year round.'

I sucked in a breath. That would cost a fortune. Guilt traced through my veins. 'Hugo, I don't think—'

'No problem,' he interrupted.

Shit.

'And,' Duchess said, with a gleam in her eye, 'I get to kill every third visitor who tries to cross the bridge.'

'I'm going to have to say no to that one.'

I exhaled.

She grinned. 'Fair enough. I was trying to see how far you'd go to spend time with girlie here.'

I stared. What?

Hugo didn't react. 'Do we have a deal?'

Duchess spat on the palm of her hand and extended it. Hugo didn't hesitate: he did the same and they shook. Then he looked down at her bare feet. 'I don't have any nail clippers that are big enough,' he said. 'But I can speak to the gardener and maybe find some shears that—'

Duchess waved him off. 'No need.' She lowered herself to the ground, then pulled one misshapen foot to her mouth in an extraordinarily limber display that any yoga expert would have been proud of. When she started to chew on her own toenail I had to look away; there were some things that nobody should have to see.

Eventually Duchess gave a grunt and spat out a long, thick, curved section of her toenail. It was yellow and crusty, and if I thought about it too much it would have made my stomach heave.

I pulled out a plastic bag I'd brought for this very purpose and quickly scooped the fraction of toenail into it. 'Thanks, Duchess,' I muttered.

'I still want my parcel.'

'I'll call them,' I promised.

She pointed at Hugo. 'And you'd better come up with the goods, too.'

He bowed. 'I'll make the arrangements immediately.' He glanced at me. 'I'll get Becky to make a start while Daisy and I finish up. I'm looking forward to a new treasure hunt.'

I bit my lip. Oh dear.

CHAPTER
FIVE

Hugo drove us to Edinburgh with my bike secured to the roof of his car. Hester and Otis were uncharacteristically quiet during the whole journey. I'd been hoping that at least one of them would have the temerity to tell Hugo exactly what treasure I was trying to retrieve, but it appeared that they were too baffled by his company to mention it. That meant *I* would have to spill the beans.

I directed him to Mud McAlpine's tenement building. Hugo pulled into the nearest parking bay and turned off the engine. I resisted the temptation to leap out of his car and run away as fast as I could and stayed where I was, awkwardly twisting my fingers together in my lap.

'So, um, before we go in,' I said, 'I should tell you what we're hunting for.'

With Duchess taken care of, Hugo's mood had returned to cheerful buoyancy. 'Yes,' he agreed pleasantly. 'You should.'

'It's, uh, a commission.'

'Okay.'

I chewed on my bottom lip. This was painful. 'And I'm

happy to go fifty-fifty with you as this is now a joint enterprise,' I said.

Hester snorted from somewhere towards the rear of the car. I waited, still hoping she'd reveal the truth before I had to. When no words were forthcoming, I knew I had to continue. I reached into my bag, took out my wallet and located some coins, then dropped them into Hugo's hand. 'Two pounds fifty,' I said. 'It's all yours. Don't spend it all at once.'

He stared at the paltry amount of money and then at me. I saw his mouth twitch and I hastily looked away.

'My client is a nine-year-old girl, a sweet kid called Sophia.' I licked my lips. 'She's asked me to retrieve her doll, which was taken from a nearby cemetery.' I still didn't dare look directly at Hugo. 'It was the last gift her mother gave her before she died, so the doll is very precious. It's called Nancy. The witch who lives here took it while Sophia's back was turned. He won't return it unless I give him a troll's toenail clipping.'

Hugo didn't say anything. After several seconds had ticked by, I risked a peek. He was staring out of the car windscreen, his cheeks stained red and his jaw set into a firm line.

'I'm sorry!' I burst out. 'I know you've agreed to terrible terms with Duchess because of this. I know it'll cost you a fortune. I tried to warn you off.'

Hugo's cheeks turned redder.

'I'll pay you back. We can set up a payment plan,' I said. 'Every penny. No matter how long it takes.'

A strange tiny sound escaped his lips.

'I didn't ask you to get involved!' I almost shouted.

This time the sound coming from Hugo was even louder. His shoulders were shaking and I started to think he was in danger of bursting a blood vessel. I only realised what was really happening in the very second he could no longer contain himself. His laughter erupted into peals of hysteria that filled the car.

I folded my arms across my chest. 'It's not funny. It's a serious matter – at least it is to this kid. The doll is her treasure.'

Hugo half-choked. 'And she's paid you a whole five pounds for your services.'

I glared. 'It's not as if she has a job. She probably saved up her pocket money.'

'Daisy Carter, treasure hunter extraordinaire.' He laughed harder.

A couple of matching brownie chortles drifted from the rear of the car and I rolled my eyes. They were supposed to be on my side. Then, out of nowhere, a small giggle escaped my lips. I clamped a hand over my mouth but it didn't work. The giggle grew and quickly became uncontrollable, even though I did everything I could to stop it. Before long, I was laughing as much as Hugo.

'It's really not funny,' I gasped, wiping tears from my eyes.

Hugo shook his head. 'Definitely not.'

'It's just that laughter is contagious.'

'Uh-huh.'

'A couple of months ago, I was hunting for treasure that was worth millions. Now I'm searching for a ragdoll.'

'Your intentions are honourable.'

I clutched my sides. 'They're not. The kid manipulated me into it. I didn't even agree properly.'

'Don't worry.' Hugo chuckled. 'This will go down in the annals of history as one of the greatest treasure hunts of all time.'

I thumped his arm. 'Yeah, yeah.'

'You know that I agreed to pay Duchess thousands of pounds for her toenail just so I could join you?'

'That makes you crazier than I am.'

His blue eyes met mine and crinkled at the corners. 'I suppose it does. Why on earth would a witch want a troll toenail?'

'Honestly, Hugo?' I finally managed to calm myself down, 'I have no earthly idea.'

His grin stretched from ear to ear. 'Well, let's go and find out so we can rescue Nancy the doll and save the day.'

'Whoop whoop!' Hester screeched. 'Let's do this!'

∽

This time I took the brownies along. The four of us trooped down the narrow, unkempt garden path, into the tenement hallway and down the stairs to Mud McAlpine's front door. I rapped on it and moved next to Hugo to wait. 'I'll do the talking,' I said for Otis and Hester's benefit.

It was Hugo who answered. 'You're the boss.' He smiled at me.

I smiled back and we looked at each other for a long moment until Otis cleared his throat pointedly. 'Hello? Are we doing this?'

'Otis!' Hester chided. 'Stop interrupting! They're having a moment.'

My cheeks started to warm and I stepped away to put more space between Hugo and me. Fortunately, that was when Mud opened his door.

He looked in worse shape than before. The pallor of his skin was now a dull, ash grey and his eyes were redder. A strange scent that I couldn't identify lingered in the air around him. It was acrid and unpleasant and strong enough to make my eyes water. 'Mud McAlpine is busy!' he yelled.

I did my best to sound patient. 'Hi, Mr McAlpine. It's Daisy Carter.' I paused. 'Remember?'

He squinted as if trying to place me. As recognition dawned in his eyes, his lip curled. 'Mud isn't stupid. Of course Mud McAlpine remembers. What does Daisy Carter want?'

I held up the plastic bag containing Duchess's toenail. 'I've got what you asked for.'

He frowned. 'Mud McAlpine did not ask for a plastic bag.'

'No,' I said, as pleasantly as possible. 'But there is a troll toenail clipping inside this bag. And it's fresh, as you requested.'

His expression altered in an instant. 'Daisy Carter got one? Really?' He snatched the bag out of my hands and peered inside. 'Daisy Carter is more capable than she looks!'

I did my best not to take offence but Hester was not impressed by the back-handed compliment. 'Oi!' she said. 'Daisy is a very capable person. Nobody else could have gotten hold of a troll toenail at such short notice!'

Mud blinked owlishly as he noticed her for the first time. 'Brownie,' he said. He glanced at Otis. 'Two brownies.' His head turned towards Hugo. This time his mouth dropped open. 'Lord Hugo Pemberville.'

Hugo bowed. 'Good afternoon. Have we met?'

'No, but Mud McAlpine knows who you are.' For the first time he flashed a toothy grin. 'Mud McAlpine is very happy to welcome such a hero into his home. Please come in.'

Seriously? I ground my teeth. 'Mr McAlpine,' I began.

'Yes, yes. Daisy Carter may come in too.' He sighed dramatically, but he was still grinning. 'Come. See what Mud has achieved.' He thumped his way along his hallway, disappearing into a room at the far end but leaving the door open.

Hugo gave an apologetic shrug. 'The price of fame,' he said. He gestured to the doorway. 'Ladies first.'

I walked forward, preparing to follow Mud but I didn't get

far; in fact, I could only push my way three inches into the hall. Beyond that, there was some kind of invisible barrier that prevented me from going any further. My skin prickled. I'd felt this before. There was a salt ward barring my entry.

'Warded,' I grunted to the others before they thought I was simply being weird. 'And it's a strong one.'

Hugo reached out his hand past me but drew it back sharply when he felt the ward. He gave a low whistle. 'Indeed. Why on earth would he need a ward this strong? Why would he need a ward at all?'

Good question. I licked my lips and called. 'Mr McAlpine? We can't enter. We can't get past your ward.'

There was rumble from deeper within the flat. A moment later, Mud reappeared. 'Mud McAlpine forgot! Wait, wait.'

He scurried towards us with surprising speed before lifting up the hallway rug and revealing the salted barrier, then he half-closed his eyes. Witch magic vibrated from his fingertips. He whispered to himself, stood up and scuffed the salt away with his toe. 'Safe now! Lord Hugo Pemberville may come in!'

I nudged Hugo. 'Let's keep him happy,' I said under my breath. 'You go first this time.'

Hugo nodded and stepped past me while Hester and Otis flapped up to take up their usual positions on my shoulders.

'There's something strange going on here,' Otis said.

'Definitely,' Hester agreed.

I motioned to them to keep quiet. 'Keep your wits about you,' I told them. 'Hopefully this won't take long.' My discomfort was growing by the second and I didn't want to spend any longer here than was absolutely necessary. I held my breath and trailed after Hugo, no longer meeting any resistance as I entered the flat.

Mud took us into one of the back rooms. Initially, I assumed it was his living room, but it was devoid of any furniture beyond a single wooden chair. Some natural light seeped in through the low windows but, as the flat was located beneath ground level, there wasn't much of it.

The dim lighting couldn't hide what Mud McAlpine had done with the place. Every inch of every wall was covered with paper – scrawled maps, scribbled notes and pages upon pages of information and diagrams that seemed to have been ripped out from books. Some of those books were on the floor in towering piles that appeared to be on the verge of toppling over if I so much as looked at them too hard.

In the centre of the room was an open space marked out by a ring of unlit candles, strewn roots, leaves, a considerable amount of dirt and what looked like objects taken from Saughton Cemetery. It spoke of heavy magic that I knew I couldn't begin to understand. Elf magic wasn't like witch magic – not even close – but I was aware of the basics of witch powers because I'd taken the time to learn what I could about them. But whatever I already knew wasn't enough; everything about this room was a mystery to me.

Hester pushed away from my shoulder and flew over to the strange circle to examine it. Mud, who'd been rummaging around in a box in the corner, straightened up and whirled around to bark at her, 'No! Do not contaminate the area!'

Hester froze. She didn't reply but she gave me a look that strongly suggested we should get hold of Nancy the doll and get out as quickly as possible. My instinct was to agree.

Mud returned his attention to the cardboard box. Hugo was gazing intently at something on one of the walls. I merely twitched.

'If you give me the doll, Mr McAlpine,' I said, trying not to sound as if I couldn't wait to escape the place, 'we'll get out of your hair.'

He didn't seem to hear me; instead he picked up something

from the box and straightened. 'Mud McAlpine has found it!' He turned around and I stared at the cheese grater he was holding in both hands. Okay, then; nothing strange about that whatsoever.

Hugo pointed at several of the pages stuck to the wall 'These notes refer to the thirteen mythical treasures of Britain.'

My ears perked up at the mention of treasure, but it wasn't enough to dampen my desire to get out of the flat as quickly as possible.

'Yes. Mud McAlpine has been searching for them for many years.'

Otis flapped over to join Hugo. 'But if they're mythical, they're not real,' he said. 'So how can you be searching for them?'

'They might be called mythical,' Hugo said, 'but their title is a misnomer. The treasures exist – or at least some of them do.' His tone had taken on an edge of awe. He turned to look at Mud. 'Have you found any trace of them?'

This time the witch didn't answer. He reached inside the plastic bag, extracted the crusty toenail clipping and gave it a long sniff, then hummed happily to himself and stepped to the edge of the circle. I watched open-mouthed as he started to grate the edge of the toenail, dropping shavings carefully on top of the existing markings and moving around to distribute them evenly around the circle.

'Where's the doll, Mr McAlpine?' I asked. He continued humming. I tried again. 'Mr McAlpine, where is Nancy the doll? Can I take her?'

Something in my voice must have made an impact because he stopped and looked up. 'Mud McAlpine will let you take the doll,' he said dreamily. 'Mud McAlpine does not need it. It does not have what he needs.' He indicated the cardboard box where he'd found the cheese grater.

I didn't waste any time but skirted around the circle to reach the box and find Nancy.

Mud continued talking, although I wasn't sure whether he was addressing us or speaking to himself. 'Mud McAlpine needed innocence. Mud thought that the doll would provide that, but the toy is tainted. Mud found a car instead.'

Confused, I looked around and spotted a small, rusty, Matchbox toy car nestled in an old bouquet of fading lilies. I scratched my head before returning my attention to the box and locating Nancy.

'Innocence,' Mud hummed. 'Death. Sorrow. Joy.'

I abandoned my search temporarily and frowned at Hugo. He shook his head in warning, though I wasn't sure what he was warning me about.

'Light. Dark. Roots. Flowers.' Mud's mouth curved into a wide smile. 'And the magic final ingredient.'

He reached the other side of the circle, just as the last of Duchess's toenail was rubbed into the grater. He looked up and his eyes rested on Hugo. 'Lord Hugo Pemberville will enjoy this.'

As soon as the words left Mud's mouth, there was a loud, ear-destroying bang and the mysterious magic circle started to fill with blood-red smoke.

CHAPTER
SIX

I let out a high-pitched yelp. Hester zoomed towards me, her tiny arms waving frantically in the air. She threw herself into the pocket that she'd so vocally maligned, while Otis burrowed into the folds of Hugo's suit.

I pulled back my shoulders and prepared to run for the door. I'd only recently been introduced to the horrors and dangers of blood magic – and this looked a hell of a lot like it. I had no desire to experience its effects again.

Before I could get close to the exit, Hugo grabbed me, pulling me towards his body. 'It's alright,' he murmured in my ear. 'I know what he's doing. As long as you don't cross into the circle, it's safe.'

'But—'

'Trust me, Daisy. I wouldn't put you in unnecessary danger.'

Something about those words made me pause and I stayed where I was. I couldn't see Mud – he was on the other side of the circle obscured by the smoke. But I could hear him. His humming had been replaced by singing. 'It's working,' he chanted. 'It's working, it's working!'

'What the fuck is going on, Hugo?' I asked.

'I'll explain later. Watch the circle. You won't see this sort of thing very often.'

I wasn't convinced I wanted to see this sort of thing *ever*, but I stayed where I was. If Hugo wasn't scared then neither was I. I had a reputation as a hard-arse junkie to maintain.

Although the smoke had seemed impenetrable, it didn't take long to dissipate. It thinned out, wisping away until nothing more than a few scarlet tendrils remained. The circle wasn't empty; in its centre, lying on the floor, was a rolled-up scroll. In front of it, Mud McAlpine was dancing from foot to foot, his expression filled with pure glee.

'It's powerful magic,' Hugo said. 'Only a witch of the highest calibre could do this. If McAlpine has done what I think he has, that scroll will provide information about the location of at least one of the thirteen mythical treasures.'

'It's about fucking time as well,' a high-pitched voice said from the doorway. The back of my neck started to itch in earnest yet again. 'You have no idea how long I've been waiting for this.'

I jerked with shock, yanking myself from Hugo's grip. 'Sophia? What are you doing here?'

The young girl crooked a smile in my direction, though it wasn't a cute, innocent grin; in fact, her expression suggested incredible malice. 'Thanks for your help,' she said with a curtsey. 'I wasn't sure you'd come through for me but you did what I needed you to do. You're not as useless as you look.'

I gaped at her. Where had the sweet, grief-stricken kid gone? 'Wh – what?'

'This is where you lose,' she said. 'And I win.' Her nasty smile extended to both sides of her face. 'Sorry. Am I patro – patro – patro – patro – patronising you?'

Mud roared, leapt in front of Sophia and reached for her throat. 'No! The fiend shall not have it!'

'Fiend? You mean—' Hugo didn't finish his sentence. He slammed out a burst of air magic and directed it at Sophia's chest. She was thrown backwards, her spine thudding against the wall and sending several of the pinned papers flying into the air.

Mud's fingers tightened around her neck. And that was when Sophia started to transform.

Her skin changed colour, deepening from pale freckles to a lustrous sheen, almost as if she were made out of gold. Her arms and legs bulged, muscles appearing in places where before there had only been skinny limbs, while her hair receded and smoothed into her skull until she was entirely bald. She didn't grow in height but her physical presence was immensely altered, with waves of power emanating from the core of her body. When she blinked, I realised that her eyes had altered in both shape and colour; not only had they narrowed to thin slits that were less than a centimetre wide, but they glowed the same bright red as the smoke that had recently filled Mud's magic circle.

Cumbubbling bastards. A fiend? What fresh new hell was this?

I sprang forward, unsure what to do but certain that I had to do something. Before I could get close, Sophia wrenched Mud's fingers from her throat and thrust out the base of her now-clawed hand. Her nails were at least four inches in length and pitch-black.

Mud's eyes widened and he exhaled a loud oof as he fell.

Hugo shot out another powerful jolt of air magic. The moment I felt it rush from behind me, I conjured up my own burst and combined my power with his.

This time Sophia – or whatever her name was – was prepared for it. She raised one hand in a fist and halted both spells before they could reach her. Then she leapt for Mud's fallen body once more, grabbing a hank of his thin hair to raise his head before shoving it forcefully down onto the floor again. The crack as his skull fractured was truly sickening.

My right hand reached for Gladys, who had been buzzing violently at my side from the very moment Sophia had revealed her true self. I gripped her hilt tightly as I unsheathed her and she vibrated in response; apparently she was the only one of us who was thrilled by this sudden turn of events.

I brandished the blade in the air, swinging Gladys from side to side as if I knew what I was doing. Sophia raised a single hairless eyebrow. 'That's quite some sword. Even for a high elf.'

'I'm not a high elf.' I advanced towards her. I'd stabbed Humphrey Bridger and brought him down. How hard could it be to do the same to a fiend?

Sophia didn't appear even slightly nonplussed. She watched me for a moment then pursed her thin golden lips and flung her hands out, stretching them past the point of Gladys's blade to smack me in the face.

I recoiled as the force of the blow made my teeth rattle. My hold on Gladys slackened and she clattered to the floor. My mouth was filling with blood and my face felt like I'd been punched in the face by a heavyweight champion. Even my ears were ringing. From Sophia's expression, she'd done little more than give me a mild tap.

'Hey! Fiend!' Hugo called out. 'Is this what you want?'

Sophia's attention snapped away from me. I half-turned but blurred vision from the tears caused by her blow made it difficult to focus. I blinked rapidly and wiped my eyes so I could see. When I could, my heartbeat ratcheted up another notch.

Hugo had jumped into the circle and grabbed hold of the scroll. It had partially unravelled in his hands, displaying an inked drawing and a scramble of letters, none of which made any sense.

'Give me it!' Sophia screamed. 'It's mine!'

'Finders keepers,' Hugo chanted. He summoned a plume of fire magic and directed it straight at her head. The fire ripped past her, engulfing her in flames.

She only licked her lips, ignoring the searing heat and acrid smell of her own burning flesh. 'Is that all you've got?'

Hester squeaked, her voice muffled in the depths of my pocket. 'Do something, Daisy! Kill her!'

I bent down and fumbled for Gladys. Sophia was already advancing on Hugo, and I didn't need to look into her eyes to know that there was murderous intent reflected in their scarlet depths. I felt a chill shudder through me. Hugo looked calm and unruffled but she was going to kill him, I was certain of it. She was prepared to do anything for that damned piece of parchment.

Desperation clawed at me. I finally snagged Gladys's hilt and snatched her up, then I lunged at Sophia, determined to stab her this time. But yet again Sophia was one step ahead of me.

The fiend didn't only possess incredible strength, she also had magic. A wall of flame sprang up, extending from the floor to the ceiling and creating a barrier that I couldn't penetrate.

I wasted no time. While all around us smoke alarms started to scream, I reached for water magic to douse the flames. I threw all the water I could conjure at the fire – but none of it had any effect. Sophia was already reaching for Hugo.

There wasn't time to think. I held my breath and launched Gladys into the air, using every atom of power I possessed. I included a burst of air magic to give her flight more force and she rocketed forward through the fiery wall as the extra spurt increased her speed. Some of the flames that were licking towards Sophia's back were caught up in the momentum.

As soon as I saw what was happening, inspiration struck. I

jumped to my right and, when Gladys sliced into Sophia's shoulder before bouncing to the floor again, I concentrated on the dry parchment of the scroll.

It only took a single spark. The scroll burst into flames and Hugo dropped it instantly. Sophia howled, although I didn't know whether it was from physical pain or emotional agony.

She threw herself to the floor, scrabbling desperately for the burning shreds of paper. 'No!' she screamed. 'No!'

Hugo frowned at me. 'I had everything under control, Daisy. You didn't need to do that.'

I wasn't so sure – and this wasn't over yet. Gladys was lying beyond the wall of fire; if I was fast, I could leap through it, scoop her up and attack Sophia again. I'd end up badly burned but I reckoned it would be worth it.

I sucked in a deep breath – and then a flicker of movement caught my eye.

'Mud McAlpine banishes you.' He'd raised himself to his knees. Blood was streaming from his head and his voice was little more than a whisper, but I could feel the magic vibrating in his voice and his hands. Hugo was right. McAlpine was an incredibly powerful witch – and he wasn't dead yet, not by a long shot. 'Mud McAlpine banishes you,' he repeated.

The walls around us shook and I heard distant screams, probably from residents in the other flats in the building. Mud reached into his pocket and extracted a linen bag no larger than the palm of his hand. He took out a pinch of something and flung it out towards Sophia. 'Mud McAlpine banishes you,' he wheezed for a third time.

There was a clap of thunder. My legs gave way and I stumbled to the floor. When I looked up, the wall of flames had gone – and so had Sophia.

FIENDISH DELIGHTS

∼

The room might not have made the pages of a glossy interior design magazine before Sophia's arrival but it was a scene of utter devastation after her departure. The walls were charred and little evidence remained of Mud's research beyond a few barely legible scraps of paper. The wooden chair was in pieces and there was a scorched line across the floor and the ceiling where Sophia's wall of flame had been.

On the spot where she had vanished, there was a red stain. It wasn't blood – I didn't know what it was. Surveying the damage, I shook my head slowly, still confused by what had happened.

'Are you okay, Daisy?' Hugo's voice was rough.

'Yes.' I glanced at him. His tawny hair was mussed and his once-pristine white shirt was covered in a layer of fine ash. 'Are you?'

'I'm fine.'

I swallowed. 'Otis?'

His head popped out of Hugo's pocket and he waved. 'I'm good.'

I breathed out and opened my pocket where I'd last seen Hester. When I saw she wasn't there, my stomach dropped. Then I noticed her next to Mud, peering anxiously into his face. 'Mr McAlpine?' she squeaked. She sounded worried – and that wasn't like her.

I darted over. Mud had collapsed in a heap; the effort of whatever he'd done to expel Sophia had clearly taken its toll. Given the fracture he must have received to his skull, there was also a chance his brain was bleeding. He desperately needed medical attention.

'So close,' he whispered. He seemed to be fading in and out

of consciousness but every time he focused his attention, it was on the tiny scraps of paper that were all that remained of the scroll. 'Mud McAlpine's life's work.'

'An ambulance is on its way.' Hugo reached out and gripped Mud's shoulder. 'Hang in there. You'll be alright.'

'The scroll. Is there...?' His voice drifted away for a few seconds and his eyes glazed over. Then he blinked and started again. 'Is there anything left of the scroll?'

'I'm sorry,' Hugo said, without looking at me. 'It's gone.'

'But Sophia's gone too,' I told him. 'You got rid of her. You saved the day.' I wrapped my arms around my body as terrible guilt shivered through me. 'I'm so sorry, it's all my fault. I didn't recognise Sophia for what she was.'

'Zashtum.'

I tilted my head. 'Pardon?'

'Her name was Zashtum,' Mud whispered. 'She has gone but...' He gestured to his failing body, and his voice cracked with the effort of producing coherent speech. 'Not Daisy Carter's fault. Mud McAlpine didn't re-set the wards. Mud McAlpine knew better.'

'Hush,' Hugo said. 'Don't use up your energy. You don't need to talk.'

Mud wasn't interested in Hugo's advice. He lifted his head and gazed at us. 'Zashtum is not the only fiend. There are others and they all want the treasure. They want the ancient magic for themselves.'

He sighed mournfully. 'The scroll would have revealed its location. Mud could have found it and kept it safe so no fiend could use it. But Mud McAlpine has failed.' A single tear squeezed out of his eye. 'Mud McAlpine has failed,' he said again.

'Can't you conjure up another scroll to find it?' I asked as if the poor man wasn't already at death's door. I was hoping to imbue him with a fighting spirit to energise him enough to keep breathing until the paramedics arrived.

Mud sighed. 'Only … ever … one. It's lost now. Mud is lost.' His face sagged. As far as Mud McAlpine was concerned, the world was ending. He'd clearly thrown every part of himself into the hunt for this mysterious mythical treasure; now it was over and, with nothing left to show for it, his depression was catastrophic.

'I saw it,' I said.

He stared at me.

I cleared my throat. 'I mean, not all of it but I saw some of it. I saw some of what was on the scroll.'

A desperate light flared in his eyes. 'Daisy Carter will tell Lord Hugo Pemberville. Lord Hugo Pemberville will find the treasure for Mud.'

Hmm. 'Or Daisy Carter could find the treasure herself,' I suggested.

Mud's selective hearing skills were extraordinary. 'Promise,' he said to Hugo. 'Promise Mud McAlpine that Hugo Pemberville will look for the treasure.'

Hugo nodded. 'I promise.'

Mud exhaled in relief. 'The fiends cannot have it.'

'They won't.'

He licked his lips. 'Mud McAlpine says thank you.' And with that, he could no longer cling on to consciousness. His eyes rolled back into his head and he collapsed.

CHAPTER
SEVEN

'It's not your fault, Daisy.'

I looked away from Hugo. It felt like my fault. I realised that my hands were shaking and I reached for a spider's silk pill. Now it was Hugo's turn to look away and his body stiffened as I swallowed the drug. He gazed into the distance, tracking the ambulance carrying Mud to the hospital. It was touch and go whether the witch would survive; the paramedics' expressions hadn't been particularly hopeful.

'I probably wouldn't have recognised her for what she was,' he said. 'She'd have fooled me too.'

I couldn't tell whether he was lying or not, but either way it was cold comfort. I was the person who had been tricked by Sophia – no, by Zashtum.

I cursed aloud. She must have planted the doll for Mud to find and used me to ensure Mud broke his wards. Some part of me had known that something was wrong; that strange itch on my neck had been an indication all along. 'What's a fiend? And why the hell was *this* fiend so keen on *this* mythical treasure? And what *is* the treasure?'

'Which question shall I start with?' He ran a hand through his hair. 'Didn't your education cover most of this stuff?'

'I was brought up in a human family,' I reminded him pointedly. 'I didn't go to high-elf finishing school. Most of what I know is self-taught. And I can tell you, much like blood magic, I've never heard of a freaking fiend before.'

There was a flicker of realisation in his eyes. 'Things like blood magic and creatures like fiends aren't spoken about very often, especially not to the wider public.'

I guessed the wider public was me. I crossed my arms. 'Why not?'

'Well,' Hugo hedged, 'you don't see a lot of blood magic around. Or fiends, for that matter. I've never met one before now.'

'Uh-huh.' I tapped my foot and waited.

Mildly exasperated, he sighed. 'Witches draw their power from the natural world. Elves use elemental magic. Sorcerers work with runes. They all use skills they have to be born with.'

I was starting to sense where this was going. 'Let me guess,' I said, with an edge to my voice. 'Anyone can learn blood magic, and the powers-that-be don't want Joe Bloggs to be able to wield that kind of power.' No wonder I'd found next to nothing when I'd researched blood magic after what had happened with Humphrey.

'Something like that.'

Unbelievable. 'So you keep us in ignorance because you don't trust us.'

He winced. 'It's not me. I don't make the rules.'

I raised an eyebrow. 'There are rules now?'

'It's not a rule, Daisy. It's just the way things are done. A little knowledge can be a dangerous thing.'

'Yeah? Well, no knowledge is worse.' I glared at him as if it were all his fault. I knew it wasn't but I was pissed off.

Because I'd been brought up in a human family, I'd been forced to work hard to learn about my heritage and my powers. I hated the idea that there were gatekeepers to information that could possibly save my life.

Hugo spread out his hands. 'The fact that there are very few instances of blood magic being used – and hence very few fiends – means the tactic works.'

My eyes narrowed. 'What do you mean? Are blood magic and fiends connected?'

'Yes,' he said quietly. 'They are. Fiends don't spring from a mystical realm of pure evil – they're not demons. Many are human, a few are witches or sorcerers, and several are elves, bogles, trolls... Anyone can become a fiend. The one thing they have in common is that all of them have been corrupted by magic.' He gave me a long look. 'Specifically, blood magic.'

'Like Humphrey?'

He nodded, his expression grim. 'If Humphrey hadn't been stopped, he would have become a fiend too. Blood magic doesn't let you go – and it always demands more blood and more power. Fiends devour that power and abuse it for their own ends and in turn it takes hold of their souls and wrenches away every shred of morality they ever possessed. Many are hundreds of years old because their power sustains their life force beyond what should be their natural lifespan. The longer a fiend lives, the more warped their body becomes.'

His mouth flattened grimly. 'Judging by her appearance, Zashtum must have been very old indeed. Creatures like that have long since embraced darkness.' He eyed me. 'They are tied into the dark arts. There are rumours that their grip on that sort of magic is so strong that they can control similar beings.'

'You mean—?'

'Vampires. Lich. Any being that treads the line between dead and alive.'

Jeez. I shivered. 'So if she had all that power, why would she be interested in some old treasure? Why would she need to worry about wealth?'

'It was not money she was after,' Hugo told me. 'A fiend's only goal is to find more magic to abuse for their own devices and to sustain themselves for more lifetimes. If she found one of the mythical treasures, she would drain it of its power.

'A fiend doesn't start life as an evil being, Daisy, but that's certainly what they become. Zashtum wanted to find this treasure to become even stronger while extending her life further. And if we really are talking about one of the thirteen mythical treasures, the power it contains would make a creature like her unstoppable. She already possessed incredible strength – I've only heard of one fiend who was strong enough to manipulate his form like she could. He conjured the plague into existence in the fourteenth century for no other reason than his own amusement.'

'So fiends are pretty bad, then.'

'Yeah, pretty bad. Hundreds of thousands of deaths pretty bad.'

I shuddered. 'At least she's gone. Mud banished her.' I didn't know to where, but I hoped it was nasty. I nibbled my bottom lip as I thought of something else. 'If he'd not done that...'

'We'd be screwed.' He met my eyes. 'Nobody in recorded history has ever killed a fiend, and there's no prison in this realm that will hold one for long. For them, it's magical banishment from this world or nothing.'

I absorbed this unsavoury piece of information. I was starting to understand why the fiends' existence was kept secret from most of the population.: they were bloody terrifying. 'He said there were others.'

'Not many, and thankfully they're not organised. They're lone beasts. But,' Hugo added, 'if they also know about this treasure, they'll be like her. They'll risk everything to find something with such potential.'

My jaw tightened. Zashtum had fooled me but, now I knew what fiends were and what they were capable of, it wouldn't happen again. I wouldn't allow it. I *couldn't* allow it. 'What else don't I know? What other dangerous secrets are there like blood magic and fiends?'

'That's it,' Hugo said. 'There's nothing else.'

I sniffed. 'Would you tell me if there was?'

He didn't look away. 'Yes, Daisy. I would.'

I wasn't exactly mollified but I couldn't throw a tantrum at Hugo for problems that were society wide. I changed the subject. 'The thirteen mythical treasures? What are they?'

'They're all Welsh. They've existed since medieval times. Two were located years ago and are kept in strict conditions in the deepest vault at the British Museum – it's the only place safe enough to house them. The rest of the treasures are believed to be lost.'

Hester was beaming broadly. 'We're talking gold, right? Lots of shiny, pretty gold? And maybe some jewels?' She gestured to my ears. 'Daisy could still get some diamond earrings?'

A ghost of a smile crossed Hugo's face. 'Most of the thirteen are utensils or everyday objects.' Hester's expression dropped instantly. 'The British Museum holds the Horn of Bran Galed from the North. It's a wooden cup.'

'A wooden cup?' Hester threw up her hands. 'Who cares about a wooden cup?'

'This wooden cup will fill itself with whatever drink the holder desires.'

Otis looked interested. 'Any drink?'

'Whatever you want.'

'Hot chocolate?'

Hugo shrugged. 'Sure.'

'With marshmallows?'

'Yes.'

'And whipped cream?' Otis's expression was awestruck.

Hugo nodded good-naturedly.

Hester crossed her arms. 'Boring. What's the second one?'

'The Mantle of Tegau Gold-Breast. Essentially it's a cloak,' Hugo said.

'A very old cloak, no doubt,' Hester grumbled. 'In fact, likely so old it will smell worse than the inside of Daisy's pockets.'

'What does it do?' Otis asked.

'If a woman who's been unfaithful to her husband puts the cloak on, it won't fit her. If she's been faithful, it will adapt perfectly to her size.'

'Cool.'

Hester and I glared at him. 'Not cool,' she snapped.

'Is there a version for an unfaithful husband?' I enquired icily.

Hugo suddenly avoided my gaze. 'Not as far as I know.'

I snorted. 'Of course not.' I shook my head in disgust.

'We can walk away now, Daisy,' Hester said. 'It was only Hugo who promised Mud that he'd look for this other mythical treasure. You can tell him what you saw on the scroll and we can go home and leave him to it.'

'This is hero stuff!' Otis yelled. 'Daisy's not going to walk away.'

I looked at Hugo. 'It's your call,' he said. 'We don't know what this particular treasure will be and the search for it will probably be arduous and treacherous. I'll understand if it's too much for you, Daisy. It's considerably more serious than retrieving a doll. More fiends may appear if they learn what we're up to. You should stick to safer ventures.'

'Hugo,' I said.

'Yes?'

'Fuck. Off.' I folded my arms. 'This is *my* treasure hunt. I invited *you* in. I'm in charge. I don't care what you promised Mud McAlpine, this job is mine.'

His mouth twitched and he suddenly looked very pleased with himself. 'We'll have to hunt together, then. I'll round up my Primes. We need every scrap of help we can get. And we can't delay.'

'It's my treasure hunt,' I repeated. 'I'm in charge. You can come along for the ride.'

'We agreed fifty-fifty.' He smirked. 'You wouldn't renege on our deal, would you, Daisy?'

Cumbubbling bollocks. I sniffed. 'I'm not that kind of person.'

'Good.'

Otis rubbed his hands together. 'Great! I can't wait to get started.'

Hugo's gaze continued to hold mine. 'Me neither,' he murmured. 'Me neither.'

~

Four hours later, after a quick stop off to grab a bag and stuff it with clean clothes and the equipment I thought I might need, I was sitting at one end of the large table in Hugo's Bone Zone. He was at the other end with several members of his vaunted Primes between us. Hester was sprawled in the centre of the table, lolling around like she owned the place. Otis, who was apparently feeling somewhat more reticent, had found himself a quiet corner where he could avoid attention.

I leaned back in my chair and examined Hugo's cronies one by one while he brought them up to speed. I knew most of them from the hunt for the Loch Arkaig treasure, but a few of the faces were unfamiliar. It wasn't a surprise that they were all high elves, although they ranged in age; the other thing they had in common was a deep respect for Hugo. Even when they disagreed with him, they were deferential without being obsequious.

'Surely,' Rizwan said, 'the best approach is to do nothing and leave this treasure exactly where it is. If we go looking for it, we risk showing the other fiends where it is.'

'Those other fiends might find it anyway. You can't put the genie back in the bottle. If they've heard of it, they'll be looking for it. We can't sit back and hope that nothing happens.' Hugo linked his fingers together. 'A passive approach is never a good idea.'

No, I thought. Hugo Pemberville was many things but passivity didn't seem in his nature.

'What about the treasure itself?' Becky asked. 'Eleven of the thirteen items have been lost for generations. Do we know what we're looking for now? Is it one of the mythical treasures, or is it *all* of them?'

'I don't know much about the thirteen treasures. I've always assumed that the remaining items couldn't be recovered.' Hugo waved at four members of his team. 'Your task is to stay here and find out more about them, as well as searching for other fiends who might be on their trail.'

A tall, balding elf with a silver cuff on his ear frowned. 'Stay here? I'd rather join in the hunt.'

Hugo shook his head. 'We need to keep the team members on the ground to a minimum, Mark. The more people we have, the more attention we'll draw to ourselves. Sometimes it's helpful to advertise our efforts, but sometimes it makes more sense to be discreet. Remember, we have to do everything we can to avoid other fiends latching onto us.'

I coughed delicately. Everyone turned to me and I felt a shiver of embarrassment. I wasn't used to having so many people focus on what I was about to say. 'You're the celebrity, Hugo. Perhaps you should stay behind and focus on research while the rest of us head out and start the search.'

Instead of snapping at me, which I'd half-expected, Hugo took my suggestion seriously. 'There's no doubt that my face is well-known and that's a concern. But I'm the most experienced treasure hunter, and I'm best placed to defend against an attack if other fiends appear. Even without the promise I made to Mr McAlpine, my presence is a risk worth taking. My magic is strongest.'

He wasn't boasting, simply stating facts, but I still wasn't sure if his words sprang from natural arrogance or if his self-assessment was correct. He hadn't brought Zashtum down; then again, neither had I.

A tiny smile played around his lips. 'If anybody asks, we'll tell them that we're on a training exercise. Specifically, I'll be training you to be a better treasure hunter.'

'You'll be training me?' I said flatly.

'Yep.' He gazed at me with an oddly satisfied expression.

Great: so now I was Hugo Pemberville's protégé. Unfortunately, I couldn't think of a good enough reason to argue. 'I won't pretend to be a Prime,' I said.

'Okay. You can still act as my temporary apprentice, though.' As he grinned, the dimple in his cheek reappeared. 'It'll be fun.'

Would it? It seemed to me that it would be an excuse for Hugo to order me around. But we were in this together and, without a better plan to offer, the best option appeared to be to lean into the role.

I pulled back my shoulders, snapped out a sharp salute and shouted. 'Sir, yes, sir!' Hugo's eyes gleamed.

'Why don't you tell us what you saw on the scroll, Daisy?' Becky asked. 'Where do we start looking?'

I stood, walked to the whiteboard and picked up a marker to scrawl what I remembered so that everyone could see it. 'There was a drawing,' I said, trying to re-create it as best as I could.

'A map?' Rizwan asked.

I added a bit more detail.

'No.' Becky shook her head. 'It's a man waving.'

'How is it a man?' A muscular elf, heavily adorned with tattoos and whose name I'd learned was Slim, pointed at my art work. 'Unless you know of any men with three arms?'

Becky stuck her tongue out at him. He stuck out his tongue at her and there was a ripple of laughter around the table.

Miriam, a female elf in her sixties with a golden ear cuff that signified she was Hugo's equal tilted her head. 'Is it a horse?'

I took three steps backwards and looked at my drawing. Hmmm. I'd not translated the image very effectively.

'It's a tree,' Hugo said.

'It is.' Thank goodness someone had recognised it for what it was supposed to be. 'This will probably be more useful.' I returned to the whiteboard and wrote down three words, taking care to spell them correctly. 'I saw a few different words. None of them are English, but that shouldn't be an insurmountable problem.' I stepped to the side so they could see what I'd written.

'*Coelcerth*,' Miriam said aloud. 'That's Welsh for bonfire.'

'Or pyre,' Rizwan said in a darker tone.

'*Brigyn* is twig or small branch, and *cychwyn* is to start or commence.' Miriam frowned. 'But those words together don't make much sense.'

'I could only see a small section of the scroll – there's a lot I couldn't make out,' I explained.

'So we can't really tell what it means.' She sighed. 'This might be a dead end, Hugo.'

'There's more.' I scribbled down three more words. 'There,' I said, allowing a moment to be pleased with myself before I butchered the pronunciation. *'Cwydd Y Gal.'*

Miriam and Rizwan looked mildly shocked but everyone else was confused. 'It's obviously Welsh too,' Slim said. 'But what does it say?'

'Hester?' I asked.

She stretched languidly and sat up. 'It roughly translates as "Ode to the Penis".'

From the back of the room, Otis called out, 'It's a medieval poem by Dafydd ap Gwilym. It contains some lovely rhyming couplets and majestic alliteration.'

Hester snorted. 'To say nothing of the subject matter.'

Becky scratched her head. 'Um...'

'Intriguing as it sounds, I don't see how this will lead us to ancient treasure,' Rizwan said.

It was time to show that I was more than the sum of my parts. 'I researched it quickly on the way here,' I said. 'The poet is believed to be buried on the grounds of Strata Florida Abbey.' I raised my eyebrows at my pathetic attempt at drawing a tree. 'There's not much left there now beyond a few ruins and,' I tapped the whiteboard, gesturing to the Welsh word for twig 'some old yew trees.'

'It sounds like a good place to start. Maybe we'll get lucky and find the treasure right there.' Becky looked pleased.

Hugo smiled. 'We have a starting location. Saddle up, folks. We're going hunting.'

CHAPTER
EIGHT

Wales, I decided, was very pretty indeed. Rolling hills, picturesque villages, crisp blue skies and sparkling frost across the fields, as if somebody had thrown a layer of icing sugar over the landscape. I should have visited before. It was my kind of place.

'Where are the dragons?' Hester asked, scanning the glittering vista. 'They all live in Wales, right? So where are they?'

Slim's knuckles turned white on the steering wheel. 'You don't want to meet a dragon,' he said darkly.

Becky nodded her head vigorously. 'No dragons,' she said. 'Definitely not.' She shuddered. 'Dragons are a treasure hunter's worst nightmare. Thankfully there are only three left.' She paused before adding ominously, 'As far as we know. They tend to stay out of sight.'

Slim's expression matched Becky's. 'They're vicious, nasty and will attack anyone who goes near their lairs. And if a dragon does decide to go for you, you're not permitted to do anything other than run away. Anyone who harms a dragon, even slightly, will be slapped with an immediate jail sentence. Not for a month or two but for *years*.'

That was understandable given how few of them remained. I hadn't realised there were only three left, but I knew they'd been hunted to near extinction in the nineteenth and twentieth centuries so I couldn't blame them for hating us. All the same, I suddenly felt an absurd desire to see one. Yep, I possessed a curious nature that often got me into trouble.

Hester crossed her tiny arms, her wings buzzing as she flapped them in irritation. 'I'd like to find a dragon.'

'Not this trip, Hes,' I said. Alas.

The Jeep in front of us, containing Hugo, Miriam, Rizwan, and a vast quantity of treasure hunting equipment that I couldn't imagine would ever be necessary, indicated left. Slim smacked his lips in satisfaction. 'Finally. The abbey is up ahead.'

I sat up straight. It had been a long drive from Scotland and the simple act of sitting in the back of a car had exhausted me. Now we were finally there, though, I felt a surge of adrenaline. Given the possibility that more fiends would become involved, the stakes for this hunt were incredibly high, but I was still thrilled at the chance to search for some real treasure. Frankly, I couldn't wait to get started.

Slim drove into a small car park and reversed into a space. Unless there were other visitors who had arrived on foot, we were the only people there. I jumped out of the car, both brownies took up position on my shoulders and we looked around.

Unsurprisingly there was very little of the abbey left: a few walls and an impressive archway through which I could see the gentle slopes of low-lying mountains beyond. If I pushed myself up on tiptoe I could also see a graveyard and a small church, but there wasn't much else.

'Henry VIII has a lot to answer for,' Hugo commented wryly as he joined me. 'Imagine what things would be like if he'd not ordered the dissolution of the monasteries. Our landscape could have been very different.'

I gazed at the ruins, trying to imagine what they might have looked like in their heyday. From the remaining archway, it was clear that it would have been an extraordinary building.

'Yes,' I said. 'Do you see—?' I stopped mid-sentence as goosebumps rose across my skin and I stiffened. I could hear faint musical chimes – but there was nobody there. I couldn't work out where the sound was coming from.

'You can hear it. I wasn't sure if you'd be able to,' Hugo said.

'Hear what?' Otis asked.

'Shhh,' I told him. I tilted my head and listened harder. It was an eerie, though not unpleasant, sound that drifted across the broken walls as if the ruins themselves were imbued with musical notes. 'What is it?'

Hugo watched me. 'Given the dampening effect of the drug on their magic, most spider's silk users couldn't hear it.' He gave a short laugh. 'Most elves couldn't hear it, either. You're more sensitive to power than I expected. This area isn't only steeped in history, it's steeped in magic too.'

He was right: I couldn't only hear the notes of ancient magic that stirred the place, I could feel it too. This was hallowed ground in more ways than one.

'Are you alright, Daisy?' Hester asked. 'You're looking pale. And you appear to be swaying from side to side.'

I forced my body to still. 'I'm fine.'

Hugo's mouth tightened. 'Do you need a dose of spider's silk?'

'No.' I managed a smile. 'It's the power of this place. It's...' I shrugged. 'I guess it's getting to me.'

Hugo didn't say anything but a thoughtful look came into his eyes. 'What?' I asked.

He shook his head. 'Nothing. Come on. The others are

setting up camp. Let's do a quick sweep of the abbey and the graveyard before the sun sets. There's not much more than an hour of daylight left and I'd like to get an overview of the area.'

I glanced over my shoulder at the other four. Becky and Miriam were already hiking away from the ruins, lugging various bags and equipment; Slim and Rizwan were rummaging in the back of Hugo's jeep. It felt like Hugo and I were swanning off on a leisurely stroll while everyone else did the hard graft.

'We all have work to do,' he said softly, as if he were reading my mind. 'We need to establish the lay of the land and make sure it's safe before night falls.'

I bit my lip, then nodded sharply.

'Safe?' Otis squeaked as we moved closer to the ruins. 'Why wouldn't it be safe?'

'Boogeymen,' Hester said, smirking at him.

I rubbed my arms. 'No.' My voice was quiet. 'We like to pretend that we control magic and have tamed it to our will, but places like this prove that magic is a wild thing. Our control is illusory – and temporary. There's no telling what might happen here if we're not careful and alert.'

'Can't you see the graveyard, Hes?' Otis asked, with an uncharacteristically sly edge. 'It's over to the left.'

'Graveyard?' Her demeanour altered drastically. 'Nobody told me there would be a graveyard!'

It was time to nip this in the bud. 'Can the two of you join the others and help set up camp?' Hester was flying towards Rizwan and Slim before the words had left my mouth.

'*I'm* not scared of a graveyard,' Otis said.

'No, but Hester could probably do with some reassurance.'

A flash of guilt crossed his face and he took off after his sister. I felt Hugo watching me and glanced at him. 'What?'

The corner of his mouth crooked up. 'You're good with them. That's all.'

'The Primes are your people.' I shrugged. 'Hester and Otis are my people.'

He was silent for a long moment. 'I should never have misjudged you when we first met.'

I snorted. 'That goes without saying.' Then, before the conversation became too serious and awkward, I pointed to the arch. 'Come on. We've got a job to do.' And I strode towards the ruins.

∽

It didn't take long to explore what was left of the abbey, even though Hugo and I took our time to examine every nook and cranny. I wasn't certain what we were looking for, although I had a vague, unsubstantiated confidence that I'd know it when we found it.

There was nothing that immediately suggested itself worthy of closer inspection. The good thing was that there were also no signs of anything untoward: no disturbing trail marks or hints of nasty beasties.

The swirl of magic was at its strongest beyond the ruined archway, where presumably the centre of the abbey had once stood, but it felt benign and there was no sense of anything dark or mysterious. Eventually, we abandoned the ruins for the graveyard beyond. By that point the sun was already dipping low and the light was growing dim – it was December, after all, and the days were frustratingly short.

We walked up and down lines of gravestones, the frost-laden grass crunching beneath our feet, but it was obvious that we both knew where we were heading. Close to the small church stood a large yew tree. Dafydd ap Gwyllim was supposedly buried beneath a tree, and given that I was sure it was a yew tree etched onto the scroll in Mud McAlpine's flat, it had to be the most promising place to explore.

Despite the fading light, I wasn't in a rush to reach it; strangely, neither was Hugo. Taking our time, we circled the rest of the graveyard until only the yew tree itself was left to investigate. 'Last but not least,' I whispered.

'You feel it too, don't you?' Hugo said. 'That thrum of excitement that says we're getting somewhere, that we're on the right track and our hunt will prove worthwhile.'

'Doesn't everyone who does this sort of thing feel that way?'

He laughed. 'No, definitely not. Some hunters are in it for the money.'

'That's me,' I said. '*All* me.'

'Some hunters are in it to solve a puzzle.'

I considered that. 'Also me.'

'Some enjoy the glory.'

Hmm. Alright. A part of that was me too.

Hugo leaned closer. 'All of those things are good, but for me it's the thrill of the hunt that I truly enjoy. Once I have the treasure in my hands, it's something of an anti-climax.' His blue eyes glittered. 'Tell me you don't feel that way, too.'

'This is only my second real treasure hunt. But yes, I feel the thrum,' I conceded.

'I knew it.' He smiled. 'Time for the tree, Daisy Carter.' He stepped back and walked towards it.

I watched for a second or two then I marched after him, moving quickly until I'd passed him. Nice try, Hugo, but I would reach the yew tree first.

As soon as I'd drawn in front, Hugo quickened his step in an attempt to overtake me. Nope. Not happening. I hastily sidestepped and blocked him. He chuckled. 'You know I could simply throw you out of the way?'

'I'd like to see you try,' I scoffed.

I felt a ripple of power before the faintest wisp of air magic ruffled my hair and tickled my nape. In response, I conjured up a few droplets of water, drawing on the moisture clinging to the frosty ground to help. When I heard Hugo's intake of breath as a fat, icy drop landed on his nose, I grinned.

He responded by sending a stronger breeze of chilled air in my direction, making me stumble slightly and veer off course. He snickered and started to march past me. I shook my head and pulled on a larger surge of water magic – but as soon as I reached for it and flung it at him, I knew I'd mis-stepped.

It might have been the strong aura of magic clinging to the abbey behind us; it might have been an inadvertent result of my stumble. Either way, instead of sending a tiny splash of water towards the top of Hugo's head, several gallons coalesced in a bubble above him. I squeaked with alarm and threw my arms wide in a vain attempt to halt the inevitable. Half a second later, the water crashed down, soaking him from head to foot.

'What the fuck!' He jumped, spluttered and whirled to face me. His clothes were dripping wet, his hair was plastered to his head and rivulets of cold water were running down his face. 'Bloody hell, Daisy!'

Oh no. 'Shit, I'm sorry,' I babbled. I leapt towards him and raised my hands, using my cuffs to ineffectively dry him off. Hugo gritted his teeth and moved away, indicating that I should leave him alone. 'I didn't mean to go that far. It's like I said before, magic is a wild thing. We can't truly control it.'

He glared at me. 'You knew what you were doing.'

Except I didn't. I honestly didn't.

Hugo shook himself, sending a wave of drops flying in all directions. He shivered and peeled off his jacket then his wet shirt. I shrugged off my coat and held it out to him. 'Here,' I said. 'You can put this on.'

'It won't fit.'

'Hugo, I—'

He growled. 'It's fine. Just leave it, Daisy.' He glanced up at the tree. 'I'm going back to get a change of clothes. It's too cold to stay out here like this, and anyway it's getting too dark to see much. We'll investigate the damned tree tomorrow.'

Filled with contrition, I bit my lip and nodded. We walked out of the graveyard, through the abbey ruins and towards the distant lights where the others were setting up camp. This time Hugo strode in front of me and I didn't attempt to catch up.

And when I returned to Otis and Hester, I ignored the shocked expressions of the others, searched for my bag and hastily swallowed two spider's silk pills in quick succession.

CHAPTER
NINE

Dinner was an awkward affair. Slim and Becky had cooked up a storm on the camp stove, producing a hearty stew that I'd have been thrilled to eat anywhere, let alone perched on a small camping chair in the middle of chilly, rural Wales.

But Hugo, who had disappeared into his tent to get changed as soon as he'd returned, barely looked me in the eye. He conducted cheerful, lengthy conversations with the rest of the group; if I could sense there was an edge to his voice, then the others certainly could too.

I ate my meal in silence. Did he really believe I'd deliberately attacked him with gallons of water? To be fair, I had form...

Once everyone was done eating, Hugo collected the dirty bowls. Huh: he wasn't too posh for dishwashing. I stood up to help but he waved me away, insisting that he'd sort them out.

'I wouldn't take it personally,' Becky said, as he disappeared into the darkness with the bowls balanced on top of each other. 'Hugs gets like that when he has something on his mind.'

That something on his mind was probably that I was an untrustworthy junkie. 'Mmm.'

'He likes you a lot.'

I was no longer sure about that. 'Mmm,' I said again. Then, because I couldn't help myself, 'How do you know?'

'He made it very clear to all of us that you're leading this hunt as much as he is. Hugo normally never works with anyone who's not already a Prime, and he doesn't trust outsiders easily. Especially,' she added, 'when those outsiders are—'

'Rebecca!' Miriam interrupted her with a hard look. 'Enough of that.'

'It's okay,' I said. 'She can say it. I'm a drug addict. It's not a secret.' I shrugged. 'Not to anyone here.'

All four of them exchanged glances. I eyed them. What the hell. 'If you want to know anything about me, all you have to do is ask.'

'Hugo told us not to be nosy.'

I ought to have guessed he'd done that, given that during the journey here the conversation had consisted of random treasure hunting chatter and the weather. None of the Primes had been unwelcoming towards me, but they'd been reserved.

I grinned slightly. 'I thought posh high elves like you were too well-mannered to do something as uncouth as be nosy.'

'Oh, honey,' Miriam said with a smile, 'we're not as posh as you think. And we're nosier than most.'

Slim laughed. 'Miriam, you have a gold cuff in your ear. Your favourite musicians have been dead for three hundred years and you've probably got an emergency tin of beluga caviar in your bag.'

'It's true, I do,' she admitted. 'And none of you are getting any of it.'

'Miriam is by far the poshest,' Rizwan said. 'But we're definitely all nosy.'

'I know you are,' I told him. 'You went around to my parents to investigate me during the Loch Arkaig treasure hunt.'

He had the grace to look embarrassed. He focussed on his shoes. 'Sorry about that.'

'It's water under the bridge.' I waved a hand airily.

'Or,' Becky asked with a sly wink, 'is it a troll under the bridge?'

Everyone laughed. Slim shook his head. 'Honestly, Daisy, the look on Hugo's face when he found out about Duchess was only matched by the one when he learned that you were the one who'd sent her to Pemberville Castle.'

'It was priceless,' Miriam agreed. 'We should have filmed it.'

'You know,' Rizwan remarked, 'don't tell Hugs, but I really like Duchess. She's fun to have around.'

Miriam leaned in. 'I think Hugo likes her too.'

'I'll admit, I have a soft spot for her,' I said.

Slim looked at me. 'What about Hugo? Do you have a soft spot for him too?'

Hester zipped forward to insinuate herself into the conversation. 'Oh, Daisy really does—' I glared at her and she pretended to zip her mouth closed.

'Yeah,' Becky said, without an ounce of shame. 'We really are nosy, aren't we?'

Miriam patted my hand in an odd, motherly fashion that left me more awkward than reassured. 'We have a vested interest in Hugo's welfare. You see, Becky was right – he likes you a lot,' she said. 'Far more than he lets on.'

This conversation was going places I definitely did not want to be. Desperate to get off the topic, I racked my brains for something to divert them, but small talk wasn't really my forte. 'Let's go back to my drug addiction,' I said quickly. 'That's a much safer topic.'

Rizwan drew in a breath. 'What does it feel like? What does it really *feel* like when you take spider's silk?'

'It feels like none of your fucking business,' Hugo growled.

Every one of us jumped guiltily, even Otis who hadn't said a word throughout the chat. Hugo loomed over our small group, his jaw set and his eyes hooded. I swallowed and stood up. 'I told him that he could ask me anything, Hugo.'

He gave me a long, measured look. 'Not that.' He put down the clean bowls. 'Come on. It might be dark but it's still early.'

Confused, I tilted my head. 'So?'

'Are we going to a nightclub?' Hester asked eagerly. 'Cocktails? Dancing?' She pirouetted in the air. 'Partying the night away?'

'Hes,' Otis said, 'we're in rural Wales. Where do you think the nearest nightclub is?'

She pouted at him and raised her fists, preparing for a mock fight. Becky and Slim tried not to laugh, but I didn't think Hugo noticed.

'We are going to start Daisy's training,' he said. A muscle ticked in his jaw. 'Before it's too late.'

~

More bemused than anything, I followed Hugo to a patch of open ground near the campsite. When he reached the centre, he turned around and gazed at me, his hands shoved in his pockets and his stance deceptively casual.

'I understand that training is our cover story,' I said, 'but nobody is around. It's dark. We don't have to put on an act. There isn't an audience.'

'You're the one who keeps complaining that you didn't receive a magical education like the rest of us. It's time we addressed the gaps in your knowledge.'

'Is this because of what happened by the tree?' I glanced at his hair which was still damp and curling around his ears more than usual. 'I already apologised for that.'

'You lost control of your magic, Daisy.'

'It was an accident, that's all.' I spread my arms. 'You got a bit wet, and I'm sorry about that. But no real harm was done.'

He stepped towards me. 'You have more power than a low elf normally has, yet you can't control it. That makes you dangerous. What if it's not a few buckets of water next time? What if it's fire? Or an earthquake? Or—'

It felt like he was criticising me. 'I'm in control.' I hesitated. 'Most of the time.'

'And where does that control come from?' he asked simply.

I didn't answer. We both knew where my control came from: I used spider's silk to dampen the effects of my magic.

'I'm not dangerous,' I said finally. 'Not any more. What happened by the tree was an aberration.' Even as I said it, I felt the lie dripping from every word. I cringed, then I lifted my chin and sternly told my ego to take the hit. 'But I'm always happy to learn more.'

'Good. Because the longer you take that fucking drug, the less effective it becomes. You'll be forced to take more and more until it destroys you and everyone around you.'

My natural urge to defend myself was still strong but I knew deep down that Hugo was right. This time I remained silent.

When he realised I wasn't going to argue further, he visibly relaxed. 'Anyway, it's not only your magic we need to focus on.' He gestured at Gladys, who remained sheathed by my side. 'You have no idea how to wield that thing. If you're going to carry her around, you ought to learn.'

I raised an eyebrow. 'I hadn't realised that you were an expert swordsman on top of everything else,' I said, with only a tiny hint of sarcasm.

'I'm not – but Miriam is. She'll teach you those skills.' His eyes gleamed in the glow of the moonlight. 'But for now let's work on magic.' He pointed down at the ground. 'Make a hole three inches wide and three inches deep.'

Piece of cake. With a lazy grin, I directed a burst of earth magic downwards. Almost instantly a cloud of dirt flew upwards and damp grass exploded into the air with it. 'There,' I said. 'Easy.'

Hugo clicked his fingers and raised up a small, hovering ball of fire to illuminate my achievement. I beamed in satisfaction. He frowned. 'I said three inches. Does that look like three inches to you?'

The hole was about half a foot. I shrugged. 'I rounded up.' I winked. 'Isn't size everything?'

Hugo didn't smile. 'Control, Daisy, that's what we're working on. Instead of bulldozer, think tablespoon.' He focused on the ground, using his own magic to smooth it over and return it to its original condition. 'Again.'

I did as I was told. I hadn't got this far on my own without being a fast learner who was prepared to fail numerous times in order to achieve success.

'Too small,' he barked. 'Again.'

I drew in a breath and focused.

'Better,' Hugo said. 'But the depth is wrong. Again.'

I gritted my teeth, then I threw everything I had at the spot at my feet, pulling back when the hole was the right size. When I gazed at the results, I beamed broadly. 'There! I did it!'

'Too untidy. The edges are ragged – it looks like it was created by a toddler.'

'It's three inches,' I argued. 'It's what you asked for.'

'Only perfection is acceptable,' Hugo told me. 'He pursed his lips. 'Close your eyes.'

I gave him a suspicious frown but did as he said. I sensed

him draw closer and stiffened slightly when he moved behind me.

'May I place my hands on your shoulders?'

'Uh, yeah.'

His touch was light but it still made me shiver. 'Now,' Hugo said, 'pay close attention.'

I felt his warm breath on the nape of my neck. I could hear the distant chatter of the others from around the campfire but I blocked them out and concentrated on nothing but the sensation of his hands. When I felt the vibrations of his magic, I couldn't prevent a gasp.

'Take a look,' Hugo said softly.

I opened my eyes and squinted. There in the ground was a perfectly formed hole. And yes, as far as I could tell it was three inches by three inches. But it wasn't the end result that made me inhale sharply, it was the way Hugo's magic had *felt*. There had been steely strength behind it but also a delicate touch that dampened the effect to a pointed whisper of power.

I knew that my magic was nothing like that; I was like a bulldozer in comparison to the finest chisel. 'Show me how to do it like that,' I said.

I couldn't see his face but I knew he was smiling. 'As the lady commands.'

CHAPTER TEN

I'd never considered sleeping bags and cramped tents conducive to a good night's sleep, but I was so exhausted after the session with Hugo that I was out for the count immediately.

I slept like the dead until morning. I took my time stretching before I dressed, aware of an unfamiliar ache that had settled in my bones from my efforts the night before. It wasn't only the bursts of magic that had affected me; once Hugo was satisfied with my attempts to create a perfectly formed hole in the ground, he'd moved onto meditation. That had been harder to accomplish than the magic; emptying my mind and concentrating on my breathing definitely didn't come naturally.

But I could already feel the benefits. More gallingly, I was painfully aware that these were basic techniques that could have taught me how to control my magic more effectively if I'd learned them at a young age. I'd never have had to resort to spider's silk.

I could regret the past all I wished but I couldn't change it. I could only work with what I had now.

As soon as I stepped out of the tent, Miriam accosted me. 'The sun won't be up for another hour,' she said in a stern tone that was nothing like the kind one she'd used the night before. 'And Rizwan is on breakfast duty so it'll be ages before anything is ready. He is not a morning person.'

I heard a few clunks and a muttered curse from the campfire area. Fair enough. 'Good morning, Miriam,' I said politely.

She frowned at me as if there were no time for such niceties. 'Good morning, Daisy.' She pointed at Gladys. 'Get out your sword and come with me. We've got work to do until it's time to eat.'

I'd been hoping for at least twenty minutes of staring vacantly into space with a cup of coffee before I had to do anything. 'Er ... can we start in half an hour?'

'We start now!' she barked.

Okay, I guessed she meant business. Hester, who was perched on my shoulder, stifled a yawn and sidled up to my ear. 'Take my advice, Daisy, and run away now. Very fast. It's far too early for this.'

Otis, on the other hand, bounced around in the air in front of me. 'Brilliant! I want swashbuckling drama! Samurai skills! Blade work that will beat even the most skilled of swordsmen!'

Miriam placed a heavy stone in each of my hands. 'We will begin with a run.'

'What are the stones for?' Otis asked.

'Throw them at her, Daisy!' Hester hissed. 'You can knock her out and still get away!'

'You will carry the stones at all times during the run,' Miriam said. 'We need to put some muscle on you.'

Hester launched herself off my shoulder. 'I'm going back to bed,' she muttered.

Otis watched his sister for a moment. 'I'd better go with her.'

'Oi!' I protested. 'I thought you were excited about this training!'

'I am.' He smiled. 'Work hard!' Then he hastily flapped away as if he were afraid that Miriam would hand him rocks to carry, too.

'Come on, Daisy,' she ordered. 'Chop-chop.'

Great. I sighed. Lucky old me.

∼

Despite the cold winter morning, I was a hot, sweaty mess by the time Miriam allowed me to stop. I'd run around, drilled basic sword positions and finished with a sparring routine where she'd knocked me on my arse several times.

It didn't help that Hugo had ambled over to watch. I wasn't usually clumsy and I didn't normally mind a small audience, but there was something about the way his eyes tracked my every movement that gave me the jitters.

At least Gladys seemed to enjoy herself; she hummed and buzzed in delight the whole way through. That made me feel somewhat guilty. She deserved a better owner than me.

As soon as the session was over, Miriam returned to her usual twinkly self. She nodded at Gladys. 'She really is an extraordinary blade. It's astonishing that she accepted you so readily – most sentient swords can be picky about their owners.'

'To be fair,' I mumbled, 'she'd been stuck in the deepest part of a dark cave for centuries. She'd probably have accepted anyone. Beggars can't be choosers.'

Miriam gave me a long look. 'I always took umbrage with that phrase. Just because you don't have many options doesn't mean you can't be empowered to choose for yourself or be allowed to maintain your morals and beliefs in the face of adversity. You can be backed into a corner and still forge your own path. It might be more difficult, but there is always another way.'

Hugo came over and handed me a mug of coffee and a bacon roll. 'You can see why I like Miriam so much,' he said wryly. 'She always challenges the status quo.' He offered a smile. 'She challenged me over my behaviour towards you.'

Miriam also smiled. 'Everyone needs someone like me in their lives,' she said serenely. 'Where's *my* breakfast, Hugo?'

'Coming right up, ma'am.' He spun around in the direction of the campfire.

She glanced at me as he left. 'He's a good boy.' I couldn't disagree.

We joined the others. I gulped my coffee and munched the roll, pausing only to wipe the clinging sweat from my forehead. I wasn't the only one who was eating quickly; with the birds twittering overhead and the sun rising, it was clear there was only one thing on everyone's mind. The expectation that we were about to uncover an ancient treasure was high, and conversation was at a minimum. Every single one of us was itching to get to the yew tree and investigate it properly.

For the first time in a long time, I felt the joy of kinship and shared goals. There was a lot to be said for working in a team.

Rizwan, who'd recovered from the trauma of cooking breakfast, cleared away the dishes at high speed, while Becky bounced from foot to foot, and Slim and Miriam slung heavy looking backpacks on their shoulders. Even Hester seemed excited as she emerged from the tent with a zippy whistle. Otis was spinning eagerly at her side.

'You know we're heading to the graveyard, Hes?' I asked.

'It's for the greater good and I'm mentally prepared,' she said. 'Bring it on.'

'You don't have to come.'

She glowered. 'I'm coming. I want to find the mythical treasure. I don't want you lot uncovering any smelly magical cloaks or stupid enchanted cups without me.'

I stifled a smile.

As everyone looked at Hugo, he looked at me. 'Shall we?' he asked.

Anticipation fizzed in my veins. 'Yes.' Hell, yes.

Six of us marched and two of us flew. This time we skirted the abbey ruins and made a beeline for the ancient yew tree high up near the wall of the old graveyard. I paused only briefly to appreciate the melody of magic swirling up around me, then I quickened my step. Mythical treasure, here we come.

Now that it was daylight, the yew tree looked ancient and unkempt. From a distance, it appeared to be listing slightly to one side, as if unable to maintain its own weight. Up close, however, it was obviously the heavy branches that gave that impression. As an evergreen, it didn't appear particularly fazed by the onset of winter; its leaves remained glossy and green, even though its wide trunk was gnarled and knotted.

I doubted it was lost on any of us that the yew tree was a symbol of immortality. It certainly seemed a fitting spot to conceal old treasure.

A low wall had been built around the base of the yew, perhaps to protect its exposed roots from damage or maybe to show that this tree in particular deserved special recognition. A large stone was inscribed *Dafydd ap Gwillem*. 'It appears that we're in the right place,' Hugo said.

We circled around the tree and inspected it carefully. 'If the treasure is here, presumably it's buried beneath the tree,' Slim said. We all frowned at the ground; if that were the case, it would take careful engineering to retrieve it.

'Or it could be concealed through magic,' Becky suggested.

'And unless we know what that original magic entails,' Rizwan contributed, 'we'll struggle to uncover it.'

'We also have to consider what else Daisy saw on the scroll.' Miriam tapped her mouth thoughtfully. 'Bonfire. Twig. Beginning.'

Otis buzzed in sudden alarm.

'Don't worry,' I told him. 'We're not going to burn the tree to the ground on the off-chance it will reveal the treasure.' And if anyone suggested otherwise, I'd slap them. Hard.

'Definitely not,' Miriam said, shocked at the suggestion.

Slim reached up and stroked one of the yew tree leaves reverently. 'Never. The research team at home have discovered that one hundred and fifty years ago there were thirty-nine yew trees here. Now there are only two, this one and that smaller tree to the east. We can't risk doing anything to damage them. There's as much power, if not more, in those trees than there is inside any of us. They deserve our respect.'

Otis relaxed. To be honest, so did I.

'What do you think, Daisy?' Hugo said. 'Shall we start with a magic questing circle to see if anything lies beneath the roots?'

A whattitty-what? I frowned, before dredging through my memories of all those hours I'd spent teaching myself about elf magic and poring through unfamiliar textbooks. 'We link hands and use our combined senses and power to search for hidden objects that displace and disrupt the elements?'

'Yep,' he said cheerfully. 'It will take a few hours of concentration to avoid damaging the tree, but the end result will be worth it. It'll be a good opportunity to practise the feather-light control we were working on last night.'

I half-nodded, vaguely understanding. Everyone else immediately moved around the tree. I stayed where I was.

'Daisy?' Hugo queried.

'Or,' I said, 'we could go the quick route and use earth magic on its own.'

Hugo looked at me patiently. 'We can't uproot the tree or disturb the ground it lives in and risk hurting it.'

I was confused. 'I don't mean that, I mean we cast out a net of simple earth magic designed to search. It'll be a lot faster.' Suddenly everyone was staring at me.

'What do you mean?' Rizwan asked.

'You know.' I gestured helplessly, puzzled as to why they didn't think this was the easiest way. 'Use earth magic to sense what's unnatural and what doesn't belong. It'll tell us if there's anything buried beneath the tree that shouldn't be there.'

When all I received in response were five blank faces, I persisted. 'I know this is a graveyard and there are bodies buried here, but they've been here long enough to become part of the earth itself. They shouldn't affect what we're doing, especially if we focus on this section.'

Slim squinted at Hugo. 'Would that work?'

'Of course it would work,' Otis said, flapping towards him.

'Yeah, what's wrong with you?' Hester waved her arms. 'That's how Daisy found the necklace Otis and I had been conjured into. It doesn't work somewhere like a beach or a city park where you can expect to find lots of litter and items that don't belong, but it should work here. This is a rural place and most of what's here belongs to the land. And you,' she sniped, 'are all idiots!'

I frowned at her.

'Sorry,' she muttered. 'I'm not as mentally prepared for the graveyard as I thought I was.' She rolled her eyes. 'But I'm not wrong. They *are* idiots.'

Hugo stared at me. 'I've never heard of that technique before, and I've certainly never tried it. Did you read about it somewhere?'

'No,' I mumbled. 'It's just the obvious thing to do.'

It was Miriam who smiled first. 'The benefits of not having a formal magic education. You're not constrained by the knowledge of how things were done in the past, so you find your own methods.'

I honestly couldn't understand why the idea of using earth magic that way was so unfamiliar to them. It wasn't rocket science, it was a simple technique.

'It always bothered me that you found the brownies' necklace so quickly,' Hugo said. 'I thought you'd gotten lucky.'

It hadn't felt quick to me: I'd plodded around that valley for hours before I'd found it.

'If this works, it could change what we do forever,' Rizwan said.

An uncomfortable thought occurred to me. 'Are you lot making fun of me? Or trying to make me feel better by pretending I know something that you don't?'

'No!' Becky looked shocked. 'Honestly, Daisy, this is new to all of us.'

Weird. I pointed at a bare patch of land beyond the graveyard wall. 'Try it over there. It's really not difficult. You feel a bit of pain when something is revealed, but it's not intense and it doesn't hurt for long.'

Abandoning the yew tree, we clambered over the wall into the field. They all seemed eager to try this supposedly new-fangled way of using earth magic. Go figure.

'They're idiots!' Hester whispered loudly again to Otis.

'At least you get to leave the graveyard for a while,' he said.

'It doesn't count,' she replied. 'I can still *see* the graveyard. In fact, now it's worse because all those dead bodies are behind me where I can't keep an eye on them.' She whipped around and glared at the silent headstones, as if expecting zombies to crawl out from beneath them.

'Once you're dead you're dead, Hester,' Otis said patiently. 'There's no magic in the world that will change that. You don't have to worry.'

'I'm not worried!' she shrieked.

He shot me a pleading look. I cleared my throat. 'I need the two of you to stand guard at the car park. This is a public spot and I've already been accused of desecrating graves once this week. Some advance notice of anyone else arriving would be useful.'

As Rizwan yelled and jumped six inches into the air, Hester froze in terror. 'I can feel it!' he shouted. 'It's working!' He darted across the field and dug into the ploughed earth before plucking out a bent piece of metal.

'Yes. Let's guard the car park,' Hester said. '*Now.*'

The brownies took off at high speed. I watched them go, idly wondering whether zombies could talk – if they actually existed. Surely if they could walk and eat brains, they could hold a conversation too.

'I can't wait to learn what else is going on in that brain of yours,' Hugo said.

I turned around. He was gazing at me with warm approval. It was probably wise not to tell him I was wondering what the walking dead would want to chat about.

'It's clear,' he continued, 'this training business is going to work both ways.'

I managed a smile. 'Win win.'

CHAPTER
ELEVEN

I stood slightly apart, letting the others try the supposedly new technique on the ground around the old yew tree. Rizwan cracked his knuckles, Becky stretched and Miriam's mouth puckered in concentration, but it was Slim who started. He tensed his shoulders, pushed out his hands and twisted his wrists. I watched, genuinely interested in his movements.

'It's an old affectation,' Hugo murmured. 'Slim used to be embarrassed by it, but now it's his signature move and he's proud of it.'

'You bet your arse I am,' Slim said. He screwed up his face. 'It feels like something is down there but...' His grimace deepened. 'There's a block of some kind. My magic can't penetrate the ground properly.'

'Let me try!' Becky bounced up.

Unlike Slim, she didn't throw her hands out but, in the split second before her magic burst out, her nose twitched. My fascination grew. Did every elf have a physical quirk like that? Did I?

She nodded. 'I see what you mean. There's some sort of

barrier.' Her eyes shone. 'That means there's definitely something there, right?'

'Try that spot,' Slim said, directing her to the north side of the yew.

Becky shuffled around and focused her powers. Her nose twitched again. 'It's clear,' she said. 'There's nothing beneath this spot.' She pointed to the opposite side. 'Whatever has created the barrier must be under there.'

Rizwan and Miriam both gave it a shot. Rizwan tapped his foot, matching the beat to the pulse of his magic; Miriam's tell was less noticeable but it was there all the same. At the moment the power left her body, her breath quickened and hissed from between her teeth. 'Whatever is creating that barrier is at least a foot deep.'

'And it feels powerful,' Rizwan added. 'We're definitely on the right track.'

Hugo glanced at me. I knew he was about to suggest that I step up next but I wanted to watch him try first. I'd seen him perform magic feats several times and I'd never noticed any particular tell. Now I wanted to pay more attention. I indicated he should go first.

He shrugged slightly and directed his magic to the ground. I stifled a chuckle. When his power flashed out, the dimple in his cheek appeared, even though his mouth didn't move.

'Is something funny?' he demanded.

'Nope!' I smiled innocently. I would definitely have to video myself using magic and work out what my quirk was. I smoothed my expression. 'What can you sense?'

'I can feel the same as everyone else.' Hugo was still frowning suspiciously at me. 'There is something that's preventing my magic from going deeper – there must be something buried there. We need to pinpoint the exact spot so we don't disturb the ground any more than we need to.' He toed the spot. 'Daisy? You're the expert. It's your turn to see what your magic tells us.'

I flicked out a tendril of probing earth magic. Within seconds I felt the obstruction the others had described – but it wasn't what I'd expected.

Regardless of whatever magic tell I possessed, Hugo recognised that something was up. 'What is it?' he asked. 'What's wrong?'

I chewed on the inside of my cheek before sending a second more powerful surge of magic downwards. Only when I was sure did I meet his eyes.

'Something is down there,' I said. 'I agree with that. But it's not a conventional ward. It's not salt or iron, and it doesn't hurt. Usually when I use earth magic this way, I feel a flash of pain that indicates something is there that doesn't belong to nature.' I shook my head. 'I don't feel it this time. I don't think this is the mythical treasure we're looking for. It's something else.'

Hugo gazed at me for a moment. 'Well, there's only one way to find out.' He knelt down and rummaged in the bag at his feet before extracting a small shovel and handing it to me. 'Let's dig.' He raised an eyebrow. 'Unless you have another technique we can use that will uncover what's down there without harming the tree roots?'

Alas, no. 'Unfortunately we'll have to do this the hard way,' I said. And given the cold temperature and frosty ground, it would be very hard indeed.

∼

I wasn't wrong. In teams of two, we spent hours digging

and scraping away at the packed earth, taking turns to minimise any damage we caused as well as conserve our strength. Even so, my arms were aching and blisters were forming on the fleshy part of my thumbs.

Otis appeared at one point, his expression suggesting that Hester had sent him to find out what was taking so long. He took one glance at our grubby, sweaty faces, mumbled something to himself and flapped back to the car park.

Despite the strenuous work, our mood remained upbeat. I couldn't shake the growing feeling that whatever was beneath us had nothing to do with treasure, but equally I couldn't dampen my enthusiasm for the act of treasure hunting. Whatever was buried down there would be intriguing. As long as we kept working, we'd hopefully dig it up before the daylight dimmed yet again.

It was Slim and Miriam who hit paydirt. Miriam let out a crow of exultation when Slim's narrow shovel clunked against something that most definitely wasn't dirt. I sprang up from where I'd been sitting with a bottle of water.

'Whatever it is, it's bloody large,' Becky breathed.

Rizwan's expression was awestruck. 'Daisy was right. It's not a ward, not in the traditional sense. But can you feel the magic throbbing from it? Is that—?'

'Fire magic,' Hugo said. 'Or at least some form of it.'

A shiver of anticipation ran down my spine. I couldn't begin to imagine why there was something buried in the ground that had fire magic clinging to it, but I was desperate to find out what it was.

The discovery revitalised us and we worked faster, carefully brushing away clinging tree roots but hauling clumps of hard earth from everywhere else. Eventually Hugo and Slim were able to tug the object out, yanking it from the earth's hold after goodness knew how many years.

It was at least half a foot in length and very heavy. They carried it between them away from the tree before setting it down on a scrap of bare land, then Rizwan conjured up water magic to clean away the last of the dirt and reveal what we'd discovered.

Huh. It was stained from the years it had spent in the ground, its colour a deep brown despite Rizwan's efforts to wash it. And it certainly wasn't treasure, at least not in the traditional sense.

'Is that—?' Becky asked.

'Yep,' Hugo said.

'From a—?' Rizwan said doubtfully.

'Yep.'

Miriam frowned. 'It can't be.'

I knelt down and touched the enamel surface lightly. The sense of fire magic was stronger now, making it warm to the touch. 'It is,' I said. 'It's a dragon's tooth.'

'An incisor, to be exact.' Hugo pointed to the root. 'Look. It's rotten here. You can see the decay inside.'

'Can you tell how old it is?'

'No, but I've got dating equipment at the castle that will tell us more.'

'It doesn't look that old.'

'It's been buried underground. It could be hundreds of years old – the earth will have preserved it.'

Slim scanned the sky, as if half-expecting a dragon to appear from behind the nearest hill. 'Or its owner could still be lurking around.'

'Whichever dragon owned this is long gone now,' Miriam reassured him.

'You hope,' Becky said with foreboding.

Rizwan shook his head. 'You *pray*.'

Unless a fire-breathing beast actually appeared in front of

me, I wasn't going to concern myself. The tooth was fascinating, and there was no telling whether someone had deliberately placed it at the foot of the tree or if it had ended up there by accident, but it wasn't what I was there for.

I stood up and returned my attention to the tree. The old dragon magic that still clung to the tooth had blocked our earth magic from sensing what might be buried beneath it. Now the tooth had been removed, it should be easier to search.

I strode up to the hole we'd created, drew in a breath and remembered what I'd learned from my training session with Hugo the previous evening. Then I flicked out a carefully controlled surge of earth magic.

Nothing happened. I couldn't sense a single thing.

I tried again, boosting my power to a higher level while taking care not to disturb either the visible or the concealed tree roots.

Still nothing.

I ground my teeth in frustration. Third time lucky.

Even though I extended my range on the off-chance that the dragon's tooth had been blocking more than this particular spot, nothing was revealed to me. If Dafydd ap Gwillem was buried here, his remains had long since been swallowed into the earth, together with whatever else he was buried with.

My magic sensed nothing beneath the yew tree. No modern-day litter. No old Roman coins. No unnatural detritus. And definitely no mythical treasure.

∼

'I hate an anti-climax,' Slim muttered as we trudged to the campsite.

Rizwan agreed. 'I was hoping this would all be done and dusted by Christmas.'

I shot the pair of them a surprised look. In my opinion, one setback didn't constitute a failure, it just made the final success all the sweeter. Before I voiced my thoughts, though, my attention was caught by the sound of raised voices drifting from the car park. Uh-oh. That sounded like Hester in full fury mode. My stomach clenched and I started to run.

'I've told you already!' Hester yelled in a high-pitched voice. 'The graveyard is out of bounds!'

I raised my eyes heavenward. Then I ran faster.

A family of four – mum, dad and two wide-eyed kids – were standing by the gate that led from the car park to the abbey and the graveyard. The children, who couldn't have been more than ten years old, were obviously fascinated. The smaller of the two kept snatching his hand out in an attempt to catch Otis, who was flitting back and forth from the family to Hester to calm things down.

The woman was shaking her head in amazement. She had her phone out and was recording Hester's squalls. I supposed that brownies were rare enough for their presence to be deemed film-worthy. Her partner had no interest in that. His cheeks were stained scarlet and his chest was puffed out; when he started wagging his finger vigorously at Hester, his mouth curled in a snarl. I cursed to myself.

She wouldn't react well to finger wagging. Nobody ever did.

'My great-grandfather is buried there! You can't stop me from visiting my family's resting place!'

'I can do whatever I want,' Hester sniffed. 'The graveyard is out of bounds. Come back next week.'

I bolted for the space between the pair of them, while Otis exhaled in relief. 'Thank goodness you're here, Daisy.'

'I will not allow a creature the size of my thumb to dictate what I can or can't do!' the man bellowed.

I raised my hands, indicating both surrender and my desire to calm the situation. 'My sincerest apologies, sir. I asked my friend Hester here to keep an eye out for any visitors and let me know if someone appeared. She must have misunderstood. Of course you can go to the graveyard whenever you want.'

He ignored me. 'I will spit roast you and eat you for dinner!' he snarled at Hester. That was something of an over-reaction. And Hester wouldn't provide him with much more than a single mouthful.

'Daddy isn't going to hurt them, is he?' the smaller child asked. 'I want to take them home. You said we could get a pet. Let's take them, both of them.'

Otis flinched but Hester curled her tiny hands into fists, baring her teeth. 'Why, you little scrote. Pet? I'll pet you, you—'

'Enough!' I ordered before matters escalated further.

'Is there a problem?' Hugo asked smoothly, inserting himself into the tempest.

'Yes, there's a problem,' the man snapped.

His wife stared at Hugo, then immediately swung her phone towards him. 'Alan,' she said.

'I'll tell you what the problem is,' her husband continued, not listening to her.

'Alan!'

'Not now, Miranda!'

'That's Hugo Pemberville,' she hissed.

'I don't care if it's Lord Lucan. I—' He stopped mid-sentence and his mouth fell open as the penny finally dropped. 'Hugo Pemberville!'

Hugo smiled. 'It's a pleasure to meet you. I'm so sorry about all this. There's been a terrible misunderstanding.'

Although the man's cheeks remained red, his manner

altered drastically. He rushed forward, his hand outstretched. 'I'm a huge fan!'

Hugo shook his hand. 'That's so very kind.'

'You're here hunting for something, aren't you?' Alan's eyes widened. 'You're looking for treasure, right?'

'We're only doing some preliminary investigations,' Hugo said. 'And training a new apprentice.' He pointed at me and I did my best to look like an enthusiastic trainee, although I was as impressed by him as the family. Hugo had morphed instantly into full PR mode; his smile was professional, his voice was smooth, and he gave every impression of being delighted to chat to a complete stranger in the middle of a dark car park in the middle of December.

'Please forgive my small colleagues here. They misunderstood their instructions,' he said.

'I didn't!' Otis glared.

'Of course, of course. It's no problem at all.' Alan was now smiling.

'You can visit the graveyard at any time. It's certainly not out of bounds,' Hugo continued.

'We don't want to interrupt your great work.'

'You're not interrupting anything. Honestly.'

'Can I have your autograph?'

'You certainly can.' Hugo clasped his hands together. 'If you'll do me a small favour.'

The man bounced on his toes. 'Anything!'

'We're trying to keep a low profile. I'd really appreciate it if you didn't post that video on social media.' He gestured to the woman who was still clutching her phone and filming every second.

'Oh no! We wouldn't do that! Don't worry.' Alan punched Hugo's arm lightly. 'You can trust us!'

'Thank you so much,' Hugo smiled. Becky appeared and

handed him a pen and a piece of paper in a way that suggested this was far from the first time he'd been asked for an autograph. He scribbled his signature. 'It's been lovely to meet you.'

'Mummy? Can we take the tiny fairies home with us?' One of the children asked.

Steam was still coming out of Hester's ears. 'Fairies? We're brownies! We're fu—'

I grabbed hold of her and drew her close. 'Let the nice people go quietly,' I told her.

She buzzed angrily as I stepped aside. The faster I got Hester away from them, the better.

Hugo murmured a few more niceties before also moving away. As soon as we were out of earshot, he asked Becky, 'What are the chances they won't post that video online?'

'Almost zero.'

Hugo sighed. 'Yeah, that's what I thought.'

CHAPTER

TWELVE

Despite the long day of digging and earth magic, I spent the better part of two hours training with Hugo and Miriam before we sat down to eat dinner by the campfire. As I raised a spoonful of hearty lamb stew into my mouth, Slim held up his phone. 'It's already gone viral. Half the country knows we're here.'

Cumbubbling bollocks. I swallowed my mouthful and eyed Hugo. 'Is it worth it?'

'Is what worth it?'

'Touting yourself on television and maintaining a celebrity profile. Is it worth it?'

His expression darkened. 'I'm not a celebrity.'

Could have fooled me. I shrugged. 'Okay, then.'

'Treasure hunting doesn't happen in a void,' Miriam said. 'We need leads, odd scraps of knowledge. Rumours passed down through generations that aren't written down anywhere, but which might lead to something extraordinary if they're followed up.'

'Not to mention sponsorship,' Rizwan said.

'And funding,' Slim added.

'It's a necessary evil,' Becky finished.

Ah. I sensed this was a discussion they'd had many times before.

'It's annoying,' Hugo conceded. 'But the benefits outweigh the disadvantages.'

I nodded. 'Should we expect a large crowd tomorrow?'

'There might be a few people, yes.'

'That's not going to help us keep a low profile and avoid the notice of curious fiends.'

Hugo frowned. 'I'm aware of that, Daisy.'

Otis nudged Hester. 'This is all your fault.'

'It is not!'

'It is!'

'It is not!'

I intervened. 'I swear I will track that family down and hand you over to them if you don't stop squabbling.'

'Bitch.'

Otis glared at Hester. 'Don't be mean to Daisy.'

'Only telling like it is.'

I raised my hands. 'Enough!'

Slim stared at his phone again. 'There's something else,' he said. He paused, reading what was on his screen, then alarm flickered in his eyes and he shut off the phone. 'Never mind. It's not important.'

Miriam squinted. 'What was it?'

'Nothing.'

'Go on, Slim,' Becky urged.

His expression shifted and he scratched his neck. Hugo gestured towards him with his fork. 'Go ahead. How bad can it be?'

'It's only a silly rumour. It's not worth mentioning.'

'Tell us!'

Slim coughed. 'Fine!' He rolled his eyes. 'For fuck's sake.

There's a rumour on some message boards that Hugo is undergoing some medical issues.'

'What sort of medical issues? I'm perfectly fine.'

I felt a tickle of foreboding.

'It says that you have a fungal infection. That's all.'

Oh no. I started shovelling the last of the food into my mouth; I needed to eat quickly and retreat to the safety of my tent as quickly as possible.

'Like athlete's foot?'

'Sure,' Slim said. 'Like athlete's foot.' His gaze slid away.

Becky finished her meal, placed her plate on the ground and dug into her pocket for her phone. I was already on my feet, collecting up the plates so I could scurry away to wash the dishes before pleading exhaustion so I could bed down for the night.

'Ohhhh.' Becky smirked. '*Not* like athlete's foot.'

'You have to tell us all what it says now,' Miriam told her.

'Apparently poor old Hugo has a groin infection. There's mould. And it's green. He's in terrible pain and hasn't been able to have intimate relations for months.'

I definitely hadn't said anything about that last part.

'What?' Hugo sounded more astonished than offended. 'How do people think up this sort of horseshit?'

I coughed and took his plate. If I started whistling casually, would that look suspect? I avoided looking anyone in the eye, but I did stare pointedly at Hester and Otis to warn them to stay quiet. Frankly, it was a miracle that they did.

I grimaced guiltily and took off at high speed with the pile of dirty crockery. I'd already said far more than would ever be necessary.

Oops.

If anyone suspected my culpability in the rumour about Hugo, they didn't say anything. I sneaked off to my tent, snuggled into my sleeping bag and fell asleep almost immediately.

Given the day I'd had, I'd expected to be out for the count until morning, but when I woke up I knew instinctively that it was the middle of the night and dawn was many hours away.

Hester and Otis lay curled up together, snoring gently in tandem. I frowned and turned around to get comfortable again, but when I closed my eyes I heard a twig snap outside my tent, followed by a long, low guttural moan. In an instant, I was completely, one hundred percent awake.

At first I didn't move; it was possible that one of the others had gotten up half-asleep for a midnight stumble to the loo. Unfortunately, it didn't take long to work out that wasn't the case because there was another moan and some strange huffing noises. I could hear them in stereo on either side of the thin canvas tent walls. Either a flock of nocturnal sheep suffering from a nasty cold had wandered onto the campsite or there was something else out there. I was betting on something else.

As quietly as possible, I edged out of my sleeping bag. I didn't waste time getting dressed though I spent a few precious seconds hauling on my boots. Going barefoot would cause more problems than it would solve.

My heart was thumping, but I remained as calm as I could as I slowly unzipped the tent to peer outside without alerting whatever was out there. It was extraordinarily dark: the moon was hidden behind a layer of thick cloud, and there was little light pollution out here in the Welsh countryside. I fixed my gaze on the shifting shadows...

When I realised what was out there, my blood chilled. Vampires. At least three, possibly more.

I crawled back into the tent and went with my instincts, reaching first for my bottle of spider's silk and swallowing a pill, then grabbing Gladys. I was still less than proficient with the blade – two training sessions with Miriam hardly made me an expert – but I felt more confident using her than I had a few days ago. And given that the best way to tackle the fanged posse outside would be to dispatch them one by one instead of trying to fight the whole group at once, using Gladys instead of resorting to magic seemed like a wise decision. Tempting as it was, I didn't think there was time to alert the others; they'd be groggy and if they made any noise, the vampires would be on us in seconds.

I'd dealt with their bloodthirsty kind before, but only one-on-one and with the helpful addition of street lighting. In darkness, the vamps held all the advantages – and once a vampire latched onto a target it didn't quit. I didn't want to play hero all on my own, but I didn't seem to have much choice.

Holding my breath, I stepped out of the tent, every move slow and deliberate. There was one vamp to my right and, from the snuffling, another behind it. I raised my head, trying to pierce through the darkness.

Cumbubbling bollocks. One, two – no – three more vampires were up ahead, circling around the cold ash of the campfire. They must have smelled the remnants of our dinner. I swallowed hard before edging left so I could circle around the entire group of five fanged fuckers and come up behind them unnoticed.

I stayed on the balls of my feet, trying desperately to remain quiet. When I sensed the creatures' heads swinging in my direction, I froze. Vampires were stupid; unless they drifted too close, they'd probably assume I was just a strangely shaped tree.

Eventually, after what felt like an eternity of creeping, I positioned myself at the rear of the group. The closest vamp, who was still lurking to the side of my tent, was a good fifteen metres away from the others. One by one, Daisy, I told myself. You've got this. You've killed a vamp before.

I remembered my long-ago admonition to Eleanor to arm herself with some effective vamp-repellent spray. I didn't have any with me; I hadn't thought I'd need it because vampires were city dwellers. One of these days, I'd learn to take my own advice.

I started to move forward. Now I was behind the group, I felt more confident that I could move silently, but I was worried by the way in which my breath was visible in the cold night air. Surely they'd sense it? I grimaced and held my breath as I tiptoed up to the vampire's back. For all sorts of good reasons, I'd have to make this quick.

Gladys often hummed when she grew excited, but she knew that this was not the time to murmur a happy tune. I tightened my grip on her, focused on the nape of the vamp's neck and lunged with as much force as I could muster. Her tip slid into his flesh and I thrust it upwards into his brain.

The vamp's body went rigid and for a second he didn't move. Then he pitched forward. Oh no. I hadn't thought that part through. I grabbed the back of his ragged shirt, snatching at the fabric. It gave me enough time to manoeuvre my other hand to the cold flesh of his chest so I could control his collapse and avoid his body making a loud thud as it hit the ground. One down. Four to go. In theory, anyway.

Despite wiggling a sharp blade around his skull and whisking his brains as if they were scrambled eggs, I knew that the vampire at my feet wasn't properly dead. To kill him for certain and ensure he'd never rise again, I had to either set his body alight or chop off his head. I couldn't do the former for risk of alerting his pals; I couldn't do the latter because there wasn't time to saw through sinew, flesh and bone. I had to hope that I'd done enough to keep him down until I'd taken care of the other four vamps. This was a good time to cross my fingers tightly and hope for the best.

The trio of vampires by the campfire were still sifting through the ash and occasionally licking their fingers while the fourth one, a female, was meandering towards Rizwan's one-man tent. From the way she'd raised her head, she had guessed that a warm body was in there and she was only seconds away from flicking into full predator mode.

I wiped Gladys' blade clean on my pyjama-clad thigh and advanced, but at that moment the breeze changed direction and carried my scent to her. She stiffened and swung towards me, her lamp-like eyes wide.

It was too late to pretend to be a tree. A wide smile broke across her ravaged face, she opened her mouth and her tongue lolled out like a dog's. I was certain she was going to alert her companions to my presence, but it seemed she was too confident in her own skills to do that. She wanted me for herself. She licked her lips, displayed her fangs to me like the weapons they were, and leapt.

I didn't know what to do. In theory, I would have brandished Gladys using the sword swipes and thrusts that Miriam had taught me. In practice, I panicked and waved the blade in front of me in the vain hope that the vampire would throw herself on it.

She was far faster and lither than I'd expected, and the height she'd gained in her initial jump forced me to crane my neck upwards and squint. I sliced Gladys up to the left in a clumsy effort to stab the vampire's chest but I didn't move quickly enough. In a heartbeat, she was on top of me, knocking me backwards so my spine smacked into the ground and her body sprawled on top of mine. Knowing I was about to feel her fangs biting into my jugular, I tensed, unable to do anything that wouldn't draw the attention of the remaining vamps.

Except nothing happened. I waited – and waited. Eventually I realised that the vampire on top of me wasn't moving. She wasn't even twitching.

I wiggled my fingers and my toes but she didn't react. Then, while my brain tried to compute what had happened, she rose up.

As I adjusted my grip on Gladys and swung her hard towards the vampire, there was a low hiss of warning. A moment later Hugo appeared from behind her, gesturing at me to keep quiet. I dropped my hand in the nick of time while he yanked a dagger out of her back. He must have stabbed her as soon as she'd jumped and somehow neither she nor I had noticed. That was embarrassing – but I was more relieved not to be dead.

Hugo laid the vamp's body on the ground while I scrambled to my feet. Miraculously, the remaining vamp trio hadn't noticed the scuffle. They appeared to have located some lamb shank bones in the bag of rubbish to the right of the campfire and were focused on ripping it apart.

I mouthed a heartfelt thank you to Hugo. He grinned, made a show of tossing his hair, and blew me a kiss. I rolled my eyes. The man was wearing thermals: if he thought he looked sexy right now, he was wrong. Nobody, not even Hugo Pemberville, looked sexy in neck-to-ankle thermals. Then again, I was wearing my favourite fuzzy pyjamas with bunny rabbits on them, so I couldn't talk.

I indicated the prostrate body of the male vampire behind me. Hugo glanced over and his jaw tightened, then together we turned to face the final three. I wasn't alone in this fight any more and that counted for a hell of a lot.

Hugo nudged me and mimed a magical attack, gesturing with a flick of his fingers to use fire. I pulled a face. Ordinarily that would be a good plan but there were still three vampires and only two of us. If we set them alight and they stumbled into one of the tents and self-combusted where our snoozing colleagues lay, we'd have problems. It would be safer to incapacitate them and use fire on their bodies afterwards.

I did my best to say as much to Hugo without actually speaking. Unfortunately, charades weren't really my forte and all I did was confuse him. I gave up, crouched down, picked up a small sharp stone and mimed throwing it towards the road on the opposite side of the campsite. The vamps would follow and their backs would be turned to us. I'd take out the one on the left and Hugo could attack the one on the right. If we did it swiftly, we could then combine our efforts to bring down the middle vampire.

Hugo frowned and twisted his hands into a series of indecipherable signals. I stared, utterly baffled. His frown deepened and he started from the beginning again, albeit more slowly. It didn't help.

I was about to give up and go after the vamp trio on my own when a loud noise ripped through the night air.

At first I thought it had come from the vampires; it took a few seconds to realise that the noise was coming from Becky's tent. Oh no. I stiffened. Then it happened again. Bloody hell — that woman snored like a freight train.

This time, the remaining vampires couldn't help but notice. They abandoned the rubbish bag and swivelled towards the snores. All three of them screamed with delight and sprinted for her tent.

We abandoned any attempt to make a coherent plan. Hugo inhaled and immediately focused on his water magic, trying to conjure up a powerful jet that would knock the vampires off course – but there wasn't enough moisture in the air for it work effectively. However, the plume of water made them hesitate, which allowed me time to run straight at them with Gladys held out in front of me. This time her blade screeched aloud with war-like intensity; the time for staying quiet was over.

All three of the fanged fuckers rushed me without looking at Hugo, even though at that moment he was the greater threat to their existence. Yeah, they were stupid. I grinned; with their focus on me, I could easily draw them away from the tents and the rest of the group.

I threw back my head, screamed like the very best damsel in distress and ran from the campsite towards the dark shadows and wider space of open road to the right of the abbey ruins. I didn't need to look back to check that they were following me – I could hear them.

'Right!' Hugo shouted. 'Veer right!'

I did as he said. A split second later, a howl ripped through the air and I knew that Hugo's magic had finally caught up with at least one of them. There was no chance to celebrate, though. Unable to see the ground in front of me, I caught my foot in a small hole; instead of hurtling forward at high speed I hurtled downwards, banging my knee painfully on a small rock. Worse, I dropped Gladys.

One of the vamps roared with delight and sprang on top of me. I heaved myself up and tried to shake him off, but he was clinging on with all his might and his teeth were snapping at my neck. As soon as I felt the tip of his fangs scrape my skin I reacted, throwing myself backwards so this time it was the vamp who was trapped. He released his hold on me just enough for me to wriggle free.

Panting hard, I snatched up Gladys and launched myself into a two-pronged attack, swiping her blade hard at his exposed neck and following it up with a burst of fire magic, using the vamp's own dirt-stiffened rags as kindling. He screeched in agony as flames licked his body and dark blood poured from his neck wound.

Even then he wasn't prepared to give up, and he flung himself at me yet again. Out of the corner of my eye, I saw Miriam roar at the final vamp and throw a small blade directly at him. Rizwan and Slim were at her back – almost everyone in the camp was awake now and on the attack.

Then the burning vampire was on me, seemingly ignoring the fact that his flesh was on fire.

I jumped back, twisted Gladys and used the long edge of her blade this time. She sliced through both the flames and the vamp's right arm, and the whole limb thudded uselessly to the ground. But the cumbubbling bastard still kept coming. I suppose that answered one question: vampires definitely didn't feel pain.

He was so close now that I was likely to go up in flames, too. I hissed under my breath then changed tactics and forced out a thrust of earth magic, creating a tiny quake under his feet. His body juddered and he collapsed to his knees.

Unfortunately, he wasn't the only one who was struggling. A wave of light-headedness assailed me. Not now – I didn't need this now. I sucked in a breath and, before my legs buckled, shot out another more powerful plume of fire.

This time the vamp didn't simply burn, he exploded.

The force lifted my body and threw me backwards. Before I had time to panic as I sailed through the air, a gust of air snatched me and stopped my flight. I knew that magical touch and I raised a grateful hand in Hugo's direction.

A moment later the burst of air magic gently lowered me to the ground. I raised my head, checked that all the vamps were accounted for and none of our people were dead or bleeding. Only then did I allow my traitorous body to get the worst of me.

My stomach lurched and I vomited up everything in my stomach. Ick.

∼

I expected the campsite and the surrounding area to look like a disaster zone. It made sense, given I felt like a human disaster zone, but other than the bodies of the fallen vamps and a few scorch marks everything seemed intact. Even my stomach appeared to have settled, although I still felt annoying waves of dizziness attack me every few minutes. I gulped down a half litre of water and located a Mars bar in the camp supplies. There. That should help.

'Are you alright?' Hugo sounded gruff.

I nodded mid-chomp, waving at him to indicate that I was fine. Becky, who'd finally woken up, brushed her sleep-tousled hair out of her eyes and shook her head, half in horror, half in awe. 'Five vampires,' she said. 'Five fucking vampires.'

Miriam and Slim appeared beside us. 'We've checked the perimeter,' Miriam said. 'There aren't any more.'

'This is why we need to start bringing a witch or a sorcerer with us,' Slim muttered. 'We need to set up wards around our camp. We could all have been killed.'

Hugo nodded, his expression grim. 'We'll talk about it. I promise.'

I wiped my forehead. 'The main thing is that we're all fine. We survived.'

Rizwan, who looked desperately pale even in this light, pointed at my neck. 'You're bleeding.'

'It's only a scratch,' I told him.

'Thanks to me,' Hugo said.

Yeah, yeah. 'My hero.'

He smirked. Before he grew too pleased with himself, I continued. 'But what the hell were those hand signals supposed to mean?' I asked him. 'I'm not SWAT. It looked like you were putting on a puppet show without any puppets.'

He raised an eyebrow. 'It's not my fault that you couldn't understand. My gestures were perfectly clear.'

As if. I snorted in mock derision.

'I don't know why you're taking umbrage with me,' he went on. 'I should be the one having words with you.'

'What? I'm the one who acted as bait and drew those vamps away from the tents. Plus, I saved our sorry arses by waking up when I did! There were five of those fuckers!'

'I woke up too,' he said pointedly. 'And I saved *your* sorry arse. Frankly, you're lucky they didn't rip you apart.'

Miriam's knuckles tightened around the hilt of her sword, Slim cleared his throat nervously, his eyes flitting around him, and Becky shuddered.

Hugo glanced at them then returned his attention to me. 'Anyway, I wasn't talking about the vampires. I was talking about the rumour that I have some sort of fungus that's affecting my sex life.'

I snapped my mouth closed.

'Yes, Daisy. I saw your expression when that emerged. That rumour started because of you, didn't it?' He stepped towards me. 'Tell me, were you trying to knock out your competition?'

Huh? 'My competition?'

'For my affections. Because you don't have to worry on that score. If you want me that badly, I'm more than happy to oblige. All the other ladies can wait in line.'

Unbelievable. 'I didn't make up that story because I wanted to be the only one to get in your pants!'

His eyes glinted. 'So you *do* want to get into my pants.'

'That's not what I said!'

'Um, guys?' Rizwan squeaked. 'I hate to be the one to break this up, but the vampire over there is starting to move again.'

I cursed then stomped over to the first vamp who'd been felled. His dark eyes were blinking up towards me, first in confusion and then with hungry desire as he registered that I was food. I flicked out a searing surge of fire to finish him off. When I glanced over my shoulder, Hugo was doing the same to the second vamp. Good.

'I'm going back to bed,' I sniffed. I wrapped my arms around my body and trudged away.

Unfortunately, I knew exactly why Hugo had turned the conversation away from the vamp attack to something ridiculous – if utterly embarrassing for us both.

It was still the middle of the night. The team's anxiety was palpable, so he had wanted to change the subject and avoid voicing the obvious. Vampires didn't usually roam in hordes, they were almost never found in the countryside, and there was no earthly reason why they'd have ventured to our campsite unless someone, some *thing* – or, most likely, some damned fiend – had sent them to find us.

CHAPTER
THIRTEEN

Hester was hyperventilating. 'The undead? The undead were here last night? And they nearly killed us?'

'If it helps,' I told her, 'they probably wouldn't have bothered with you. You're too small.'

She stared at me. 'Is that supposed to be comforting?'

'Everything's fine,' I said. 'It's been taken care of.'

'Has it? *Has* it? How do you know? There's an entire graveyard out there! What if all of them rise up?'

'They've been dead too long, Hes,' Otis said. 'You know vamps don't work like that.'

She put her hands on her hips and glared at him. 'Then where did the army of vampires come from last night?'

'It wasn't an army.'

Her bottom lip jutted out. 'It might as well have been. You should have woken us.'

If anything, her reaction only reinforced my gratitude that both brownies had slept through the attack. 'It's daylight. You're safe now,' I reassured her.

'Until the sun goes down later today.' She scowled. 'As that damned ball of fire is wont to do.'

Becky walked up. 'That pesky sun,' she said, with a small smile. She glanced at me. 'Hugo's called a team meeting.'

I sighed; I could guess why. I smiled back at her. 'We're on our way.'

I joined the others around the cold campfire. It appeared that nobody had the stomach for breakfast this morning. The sleep-deprived faces suggested that everyone had struggled to get back to sleep during the night.

Hester glowered and plonked herself on my right shoulder with a loud huff. Otis gave the group a small sheepish wave of hello.

'First of all,' Hugo asked, 'is everyone okay?'

'No!' Hester said. The rest of us nodded. I reached up and used my pinkie to give her a tiny hug. She hesitated, before wrapping herself around it tightly. 'Thank you.' Her voice was muffled but heartfelt.

'How's your neck, Daisy?' Slim asked.

I tilted my head so he could see. 'It's fine. No nasty vamp infection, no loss of blood. Thank you for asking.'

He exhaled. 'Thank you for saving us all last night.'

I met Hugo's eyes; this wasn't the time for our usual competitiveness. 'It was a team effort.'

'We play well together,' he said softly.

Yeah. The mutual compliments proved we were in serious mode now. I licked my lips. 'There doesn't appear to be anything underneath the yew tree – not any mythical treasures, anyway.'

'This whole area is imbued with ancient magic. There might still be something that's hidden from us,' Hugo said. 'But we don't have any way of either confirming or denying it.'

'We know that there used to be many more yew trees around here,' I offered.

Slim nodded. 'Thirty-nine.'

'So we might not be looking in the right spot.'

'And,' Hugo said, 'the research team told me this morning that there's a chance Dafydd ap Gwillem isn't buried here. Despite the stone marking the spot, it's only educated guesswork that his body is underneath it.'

Miriam added, 'Not to mention that Daisy only saw a fraction of what was written on Mud McAlpine's scroll. Dafydd ap Gwillem might have nothing to do with this treasure.'

I nodded dejectedly. She was right.

A car horn honking loudly made us all jump. I glanced up and saw a campervan pull into the car park. Two people were hanging out of the window and waving at us frantically. 'Hugo! Hugo Pemberville!' they yelled.

I rolled my eyes. Great.

'We don't know where the vampires came from last night. It might have been a fluke.' Hugo raised his hand to acknowledge the van but otherwise ignored it. 'But there have been stories for years that fiends can control vampires. It's possible that the attack last night was premeditated because of our search for the treasure.'

A second car appeared. Then a third.

'And now we've got members of the general public to contend with,' Rizwan said. 'Some of them will try and camp here. If we're attacked again, their lives will also be at risk.'

We all exchanged dark glances before Hugo gave me a meaningful look.

It was inevitable. 'We don't have enough concrete information.' I grimaced and amended my statement. 'We don't have *any* concrete information. We can continue looking for a needle in a haystack that might not even be here and draw more attention to ourselves or—' My voice trailed off.

'Or,' Hugo finished, 'we can spend more time on research and come back here if we need to when we're more confident about what we'll find, and when it's safer to do so. We are not quitting. We're being smart and making a temporary tactical withdrawal.'

'Agreed,' Rizwan said. 'It's the only way forward for now.'

'Agreed.'

'Agreed.'

'Agreed.'

Hester released her grip on my finger. 'Agreed!'

Otis nodded. 'Agreed.'

'Daisy?'

I sighed. I didn't like it but it was the best move for now. 'Agreed.'

'Christmas isn't far off,' Hugo said. 'We'll see what the research team come up with then re-group after New Year. We all know that treasure hunting can be dangerous but any risks have to be calculated.'

There was another honk of a car horn. 'Hugo! Babe! Marry me!'

That fungus rumour clearly wasn't doing him any harm. I smiled slightly, suddenly feeling less guilty. Then I got to my feet. It was time to pack up and get out of there.

∽

I tossed my bag into the boot of the car. 'If you could drop me at the nearest train station, that'd be great.'

Hugo's forehead creased. 'You're not coming to Edinburgh?'

'It's almost Christmas,' I reminded him. 'I'm going to spend a few days with my folks then head up north. I'll be back by New Year. You're not continuing this treasure hunt without me, have no fear on that score.'

'I wouldn't dare,' he murmured. 'But there's no need for you to catch the train. I can drop you off at your parents' house.'

'It's out of your way. And I like the train.'

'I don't mind. Without a reservation, you'll probably have to stand all the way to Yorkshire. We've got two vehicles, Daisy. Everyone else can pile into the first car and I'll take you in my Jeep.' He smiled, indicating it was a fait accompli, and turned away to shift around the bags.

I twitched, discomfited. I wasn't sure why I didn't want Hugo to play chauffeur but somehow the idea unsettled me. I told myself to stop being so silly. Hester and Otis would be thrilled. They enjoyed travelling in comfort.

Feeling prickly and unwilling to watch Hugo sort out the luggage while I stood idly by, I turned and glanced at the abbey ruins and the graveyard beyond. Only the topmost branches of the old yew tree were visible from here.

I gazed at them for a moment before telling Hugo I'd be back shortly, then jogged to the tree. We'd smoothed over the evidence of our efforts the previous day and only a discerning eye would spot that the ground had been disturbed. It was just as well: more and more of Hugo's fans were appearing, and the last thing we needed was a posse digging around the tree in a vainglorious bid to find their own treasure.

I sucked on my bottom lip and thought about what I'd seen on Mud McAlpine's scroll before looking around to check that nobody was watching. When I was sure, I pushed myself onto tiptoe and broke off a small twig. I fiddled with it for a moment or two then shrugged and used a tiny burst of fire magic to set it alight.

The twig smouldered for a few seconds before burning. Nothing else happened beyond it singeing the skin on my fingers. I wasn't surprised – but I took another few seconds to break off a second, larger twig and stuff it into my bag. You never knew.

～

Less than fifteen minutes later, Hugo and I had said our farewells to the rest of the group. Miriam pointed me towards several online links that contained exercises to continue my sword work, and added the stern admonishment that she'd know if I didn't practise. Everyone else gave me hugs and warm wishes. It was a far cry from the cold reception I'd received when I'd first met the Primes a few months ago.

We sped away in Hugo's Jeep with Hester sticking her tongue out at the graveyard as it disappeared from view. 'I wouldn't get too complacent,' I told her. 'There's a good chance we'll be back if we can pinpoint the exact location of the treasure.'

'I make a point of never worrying about tomorrow,' Hester said. She waved her little arms in the air. 'I'm all about the here and now.'

Otis tutted. 'Planning and preparation aid success.'

Before they descended into another round of sibling bickering, I turned to Hugo to change the subject. 'What are your plans for Christmas?'

'Quite a few of the Primes stay at Pemberville Castle. There will be lots of wine, I'll make an attempt at cooking, and there will probably be a cheesy Christmas movie and some silly hats involved.'

I tried – and failed – to imagine Hugo in a party hat. 'What about your parents?'

'They're abroad – I think they're in France right now. They don't spend a lot of time in this country any more.' There was something in his tone that suggested it wasn't a subject he wanted to get into.

'New Year will be spent at the Royal Elvish Institute,' he said. 'They host a grand gala every year.' He glanced at me, momentarily taking his eyes away from the twisting road. 'You should join us.'

I pulled a face. 'I'm a low elf. My kind is not usually welcome there. It's a bit too posh for the likes of me.'

'You know,' Hugo said wryly, 'you possess a large dose of inverted snobbery, Daisy.'

'How many other low elves are you inviting to this grand gala?'

'I don't know many low elves.'

'There you go then.'

'Perhaps we both need to widen our experiences and attitudes.'

I considered that. Yeah, he was right. 'I'm prepared to try if you will.'

He grinned. 'Done. Whether we're twenty-one or eighty-one, we can always learn to be better.'

My spider's silk addiction meant I had no earthly hope of ever getting close to eighty-one but there was no point saying that out loud. Especially not to Hugo.

'I'm sorry about the fungus rumour,' I said. 'It wasn't something I planned. I'm not your nemesis any more, and I wasn't being mean. Not that that's any excuse. I shouldn't have done it.'

'Daisy,' Hugo said, in an odd tone, 'we are long past the nemesis time of our relationship.' He hesitated. 'I appreciate the apology but, given our friendship is relatively new, I'm not sure it's enough.'

I raised an eyebrow. 'You'd prefer grovelling?'

'Do you know how to grovel?'

'As you've pointed out, I should widen my experiences.'

The corners of his mouth turned up. 'How about you owe me a favour instead? To be delivered in the time and manner of my choosing?'

Whoa. Agree to owe a high elf a favour? Any favour? That was a big ask; in fact, that was a huge ask.

'Nothing that will go against your morals. Nothing that will hurt anyone. Just…' he grinned '…something someday that will please me.'

'That sounds incredibly dodgy,' Otis piped up from the back.

'He's not wrong.' I eyed Hugo.

'And I thought you were starting to trust me.' Hugo sighed in a melodramatic fashion. 'If you're afraid, you only need to say so. I'll withdraw the suggestion.'

'I'm not afraid.' I sniffed. 'Fine. I, Daisy Carter, owe you a favour.'

A slow, delighted smile spread across his face. His tongue darted out and I was certain that he was literally licking his lips in anticipation.

Uh-oh.

CHAPTER
FOURTEEN

My mother insisted on inviting Hugo in for a cup of tea. Minutes later, that became a meal. Then my father suggested that he stay for the night. 'We've got the space. You can take the spare room at the back. Unless you and Daisy would rather share a bed—'

'No!' My protest was loud enough to echo around the living room.

Hester and Otis, who by now had introduced themselves to my somewhat bemused parents instead of hiding away like last time, giggled.

Hugo smiled genially. 'I should get home,' he said. 'But dinner before I go would be wonderful.'

My mum and dad beamed. 'Brilliant,' Mum said. 'I'm so glad that you finally have some elf friends, Daisy. It's good to spend time amongst your own kind. She was adopted, you know, Hugo. We're human.'

I loved my mum very much but she was truly a fan of stating the obvious.

Hugo nodded. 'I'm aware.'

'We don't know any elves – this is quite a rural area and

there aren't any nearby, either low or high. Daisy's birth mother lived up north and we were told she died. We don't think she had any family to speak of, so we can't look up any elven connections that way.'

Any second now she'd be telling Hugo that I'd wet the bed until I was seven, that my teenage diary was in a box in the loft and he'd be welcome to read it before he left.

Hugo looked at me. 'I'm sorry about your birth mother,' he said softly.

'I was a baby,' I said. 'I don't have any memory of her. I was lucky to be adopted by such a loving family.' I reached across and hugged Mum. She hugged me back while my dad smiled proudly.

'Daisy had a sad beginning,' he said. 'But I think we've made up for it since.'

'She's obviously lucky to have you.' Hugo leaned forward. 'Forgive me for asking, but are you sure that her mother was a low elf? Daisy has a lot of magic. It's ... unusual.'

'Oh, we're sure,' Mum said. 'She was left as a foundling at Freemark Hospital with a note stating that her mother had died and her remaining family couldn't look after her. The note emphasised that Daisy's mother was a low elf. The police tried to find her and double-checked the information they had, but no high elves knew who she could be and no elven babies were missing from any high-elf families. Neither were there any recently pregnant high elves who fit her mother's profile. Obviously there are far fewer high elves than low ones, so it was easy for the police to confirm that Daisy didn't belong to any of them, and we checked it out ourselves later. Unfortunately, despite everyone's best efforts, we don't know much beyond she was a low elf living in Edinburgh and she couldn't look after Daisy. We completely understood when Daisy decided to move to Edinburgh herself. Even though it's very far away,' she added with only a tinge of sadness.

'When I first moved there,' I said softly, 'I wondered if I might bump into some family members – it's not a big city. But I never found anyone – not anyone who wants to be found.' I looked at Hugo, suddenly wishing the sympathy in his eyes wasn't quite so intense. 'I've long since made my peace with it,' I said firmly.

Mum lifted a plate in Hugo's direction. 'More cake?'

Fortunately the conversation changed course and I stopped feeling quite so uncomfortable about Hugo learning so much about me. Before dinner, Dad hauled him off to his shed to show him his collection of model aeroplanes, which Hugo had made the fatal mistake of sounding interested in.

As soon as he'd gone, Mum couldn't help herself. 'He's very handsome.' Yep. Still stating the obvious.

'We're only friends, Mum.'

She pretended not to hear me. 'He's clearly smitten with you.'

I was a spider's silk addict; friends or not, I was the living embodiment of Hugo's deepest fears. 'I think you're reading too much into our relationship.'

'So there is a relationship?'

I rolled my eyes. 'Not the sort you're thinking about.'

'You look good together.'

'We're friends.' And getting to that point had been a struggle. 'But our differences are greater than our similarities.'

'Opposites attract.'

I could feel a long, exasperated sigh coming on. 'That's not actually true.'

'Well,' she shrugged, 'as long as you practise safe sex.'

Unbelievable. 'Mother...'

She winked at me. 'I'll say no more, Daisy. My lips are sealed on the subject.'

I knew she was lying, *she* knew she was lying – even Hester and Otis knew she was lying – but to call her out on it would only have extended the conversation. Instead, I pinned my mouth shut and helped her set the table. I knew she only wanted the very best for me, but she didn't know about the spider's silk and she didn't know my days were numbered because of it. There were some things I couldn't tell my parents, not because I didn't love them but because I did.

It was late when Hugo finally said his farewells. I walked him to the door and waited while he shrugged on his coat. 'It's a long journey back up north,' I said. 'You can stay if you want to. You don't have to drive through the night.'

The corner of his mouth crooked up, revealing his dimple. 'Thank you for the offer, but I don't mind the journey and I ought to get back.'

'Okay. Drive safe.'

'Anyone might think you cared, Daisy.'

I pulled a face at him and he laughed. He stepped towards the doorway then lifted his head as his eye caught something. I followed his gaze and frowned when I saw the sprig of mistletoe hanging there. Hmm. I was certain it hadn't been there when we arrived.

'Traditions are important,' he murmured.

I gazed at the offending decoration. 'I don't think a piece of mass-manufactured plastic is what our forebears had in mind.'

'All the same, Daisy, it would be very rude not to.'

Fine. I moved closer, stood on tiptoe and kissed his cheek. 'There.'

Hugo ran his tongue over his lips. He gazed at the mistletoe again before meeting my eyes. This time when he spoke the teasing edge had gone from his voice. 'You know there is something between us, Daisy. You feel it like I do.'

I blinked. I'd had the feeling this conversation was coming, I just hadn't expected it would happen now. Or on my parents' doorstep.

'It's been some time since that kiss we shared outside Smoo Cave. And it's been some time since I've faced up to the surprising truth that I want you.' He lifted his chin and I recognised the glint of challenge in his expression.

Hang on a minute. I folded my arms and took a step back. 'The *surprising* truth? You really know how to make a girl feel good about herself.'

Hugo didn't miss a beat. 'You haven't struck me as the kind of person who enjoys platitudes or white lies. Of course it's surprising that I want you, and you must be surprised that you feel the same way about me. If you'd prefer me to tell you that we're kindred spirits whose destinies are entangled with each other, or that my heart sings because I've finally found my true soul mate, you'll be disappointed. I have many flaws but I'm not a liar. I'm telling you the truth, and the truth is that I want you. And I know you want me too.'

If I could have written down all the reasons why nothing should happen between Hugo and I, it would have been a very long list indeed. Not to mention I was still stung by that '*surprising* truth'. 'We both know it's the hunt that thrills you, not the reward. You've said as much yourself.'

'You're putting words into my mouth. That's how I feel about treasure, not people. Besides, you're as much a fan of the hunt as I am. So,' he said smugly, 'instead of telling me how you think I feel, why don't you tell me how *you* feel?'

I looked into his blue eyes. What the hell; maybe it *was* time to admit the truth. 'Sure,' I said. 'I *do* want you.'

Hugo's grin returned.

'But,' I added, 'only in the physical sense of the word and in the same way I want the talented Mr Ripley or the Goblin King.'

'Who?'

'David Bowie's character in *Labyrinth*.' It was my turn to smile. 'You're a good-looking guy and you know it, Hugo. Sure, I'm physically attracted to you, but I'm not a teenager. I don't live my life according to my baser desires – if I did, I'd eat chocolate ice cream for every meal. But chocolate ice cream wouldn't satisfy me for long.'

I didn't bother reminding him that I was also a spider's silk addict. He hadn't forgotten.

'I'm not asking for your hand in marriage, Daisy.' He raised his eyebrows. 'I might be chocolate ice cream. I am definitely *not* vanilla.'

'Vanilla is my favourite,' I said for no other reason than to be perverse.

Hugo's voice was suddenly soft. 'Liar.'

I half-laughed and stepped away. 'It's not a good idea.'

'Bad ideas are under-rated.'

I shook my head, both amused and exasperated. 'You have a long journey ahead of you, Hugo. You should go.'

'Daisy—' He ran a hand through his tawny hair.

'I'll see you in the new year,' I said firmly.

'Don't fight the inevitable.'

'Goodbye, Hugo.'

He paused for a long moment. 'Goodbye, Daisy,' he said finally. 'Don't forget to keep up your training exercises.' Then he turned on his heel and left.

I thought I was fine; I thought I had myself under control. But ninety seconds after Hugo's Jeep departed and was swallowed up by the night, I couldn't stay calm any longer.

Magic burst out of me, erratic, wild and entirely uncalled for. My knees buckled and I fell forward. Cumbubbling bollocks.

That wasn't good at all – and it was one of many reasons why Hugo and I could be nothing more than friends.

∾

Mum and Dad were still talking about it on Christmas Day morning. 'It's extraordinary,' Dad said. 'An earthquake! In these parts!'

Mum sipped her mimosa; it might be morning but it was Christmas, which apparently made drinking alcohol absolutely permissible. 'I know they happen here from time to time but I've never experienced one before. I thought the house was going to come down around our ears!'

Neither Hester nor Otis said a word. I swallowed uncomfortably. A few pictures had fallen off the walls and several slates off the roof of the house, but fortunately there was no other damage and nobody had been hurt. I'd checked in with all the neighbours to be sure; it was the least I could do.

'Here,' I said, thrusting a parcel into Mum's hands in a desperate attempt to change the subject. 'Open your gift.'

Dad handed me a slim, gift-wrapped parcel. 'You too, Daisy. It's a "one of a kind". Betty down the street makes them and sells them on Etsy, but she assured me that nobody else has one like this.'

I unwrapped the box to reveal a pretty pendant necklace, a dangling crystal bauble entwined with copper. 'It's beautiful.' I fastened it around my neck. 'Thank you.'

They both beamed at me. Hester twirled in the air, showing off her new black cloak with tiny diamante beads fixed to the collar, and Otis doffed his jaunty baseball cap. 'Did you make these yourself, Daisy?' he asked.

I snorted. My sewing skills extended to wonkily hemming full-size trousers – and only if I concentrated very hard. Fortunately the internet offered a wide range of doll-sized clothes that were perfect for the brownies. Nobody should have to suffer seeing me brandish a needle.

Dad held up the model aeroplane kit I'd given him. 'I'll enjoy making this in the new year.'

'Model aeroplanes aren't the only thing you should be making.' Mum wagged her finger. 'What are your new year's resolutions?'

He groaned. 'Can't we enjoy Christmas before we start thinking about new beginnings?'

Hester gazed dreamily at the glowing fire, which had been lit to celebrate the occasion. Like the morning mimosas, it was a rare occurrence. 'Do you know,' she said, 'that if you gaze into a fire at the exact moment the clock strikes midnight on New Year's Eve, you'll see the person you're going to marry?'

'That's a stupid superstition that doesn't work,' Otis told her. 'I tried it. For several years running.'

She shrugged. 'I guess that's because you're never getting married.'

'A New Year's Eve fire is for cleansing the past and embracing the new,' he said huffily. 'Your version is nothing but an old wives' tale.'

'Why is it always an old wives' tale?' Mum asked, speaking to nobody in particular. 'Why do women get blamed for superstitious stories and not men?'

'Because women like to talk a lot,' Dad answered instantly. 'Usually about nothing of consequence.' He paled, realising abruptly that he'd spoken aloud. 'Er, I'll go and peel the potatoes, shall I?'

'You do that. And fetch me another mimosa,' Mum ordered.

'And then you can learn your place by scrubbing the kitchen floor. In silence. Because you're a *man*.'

Dad's mouth twitched. So did Mum's.

'What about you, Daisy?' she asked. 'What would you like your father to do as penance for his foolish words?'

I didn't answer. I was too busy grinning.

'Daisy?'

I raised my glass to them both. 'Merry Christmas,' I said. 'And here's to new beginnings in the new year.' And, I added to myself, here's to the thing that might help us find Mud McAlpine's damned mythical treasure.

I'd be attending a certain Hogmanay party after all.

CHAPTER
FIFTEEN

I dressed up. I didn't possess a vast wardrobe of sparkly glad rags, but there were a couple of functional dresses that would pass muster at a Royal Elvish Institute party. In the end, I grabbed a simple black number with a plunging neckline that I'd worn on a whim to a staff night out when I'd worked at SDS, and which had been consigned to a coat hanger ever since. The necklace from my mum and dad would distract from all the boob on display. Hopefully.

'Do you know, Daisy,' Hester said, 'we've been with you for months now and this is the first time we're going to a party? It's heresy that it's taken this long.' She looked me up and down. 'You should snip a few inches off that hem and show more leg.'

'I'm not going to do that.'

'At the last party I went to, flashing your bare ankles was considered shocking,' she continued, as if she hadn't heard me. 'Now you can wear whatever you like and nobody cares!'

That wasn't actually true; I could think of many outfits that would horrify the high-elvish community if I wore them.

'Less is more, Hes,' Otis frowned. 'Or rather more is less.

Perhaps you should put a cardigan over the top of your dress, Daisy. And button it up.'

I wasn't going to do that, either. 'You two should stop being so judgmental about what I wear.'

Hester twirled in the air. 'But you want to look sexy for Hugo!'

I ground my teeth. 'I do *not*.'

'She doesn't want him, Hes,' Otis argued.

'She does want him. She's just too afraid to admit it.'

'All he wants is sex.'

'So?' Hes challenged him.

'He can't cope with her addiction.'

'That's his problem. Not Daisy's.'

'If Daisy has sex,' Otis said earnestly, '*good* sex, she'll need at least four spider's silk pills beforehand to stop her magic from destroying half of Edinburgh during the throes of passion. We all know what's been happening to her lately. And we all know that Hugo will provide very good sex because—'

Aaaaargh! 'Enough! Hugo and I will remain professional and friendly.' I hoped. 'There will be nothing more.' I glared at the brownies. 'And there will be no more discussion on the matter.'

They exchanged looks. 'Sure, Daisy,' they chorused.

I had a sinking feeling it was going to be a very long night.

∾

My favourite pair of grumpy, recalcitrant bouncers were on the door of the Royal Elvish Institute, standing beneath an elaborate garlanded centrepiece, while strains of music could be heard from inside. To be fair to the doormen, they were only grumpy towards me; they were perfectly polite to everyone else.

'Huey! Duey!' I waved at them. 'Long time no see!'

They folded their arms across their broad chests with pleasing synchronicity. 'My name is Lewis,' said the doorman on the right. 'And he is called James.'

I clapped my hands. 'Finally we're on a first-name basis! You'll be inviting me around for tea and cake soon.'

They simply stared at me. Oh well. Baby steps.

As I started to climb the steps. Lewis and James moved in front of the door to bar my way. 'We need to check whether your name is on the guest list before we can permit entry,' Lewis growled.

I knew my name was on the list because I'd suffered enough humiliation at this place not to check beforehand. Hugo and I may have parted on awkward terms, but he'd still had the foresight to add my low-elf name to the list of attendees.

I waved a hand airily at them. 'Sure. Go ahead. Check.'

James sniffed and picked up a tablet lying on a small table by the door. 'What's your name again?'

They knew who I was. 'Daisy,' I said. 'Daisy Carter. You might have forgotten but I'm the one who saved your sorry arses when Humphrey Bridger turned rogue and tried to murder several people.' I pointed beyond the front door. 'It was in that room. You were there.' I smiled helpfully.

He stopped the pretence of scanning through the guest list and sighed heavily. 'Fine,' he muttered. 'You may enter.'

Lewis glowered. 'For tonight.'

'Thank you, lovelies!'

James frowned at the terrible imposition of my presence. 'Just go in.' His lip curled as he glanced at the large bag on my shoulder. 'You can check that in at the cloakroom.'

I would do no such thing, though I didn't tell them that. Instead, I simply curtsied. 'Happy New Year.'

'I hope your testicles shrivel up and die,' Hester added, from her perch on my shoulder.

'Enjoy your party time out here in the freezing cold,' Otis said. Hester gasped at his uncharacteristic audacity. 'What?' he asked. 'They were being dreadfully rude.'

'I'd have been disappointed if they weren't,' I murmured. There was something oddly reassuring about the doormen's consistency.

I straightened my shoulders and joined the party.

At my behest, Hester and Otis drifted away, flitting between guests in search of tasty canapés and champagne. There were more people than I'd expected, so it wasn't going to be easy to locate Hugo and the Primes. I circled the large drawing room then went into the dining room, which had been transformed into a ballroom.

There were well-dressed elves everywhere and I noted that they all boasted ear cuffs – bronze, silver or gold. There was the usual smattering of humans, witches and sorcerers who all appeared rich and well-connected, at least to my unrefined eyes. There were even a few more unusual creatures – but the place was mainly full of high elves. Hardly surprising.

Catching a glimpse of blonde hair out of the corner of my eye and expecting to see Becky, I turned to my left. I should have looked where I was going because the corner of my bag collided with an outstretched hand holding the stem of a wine glass. The chilled fizzy contents spilled down the front of my dress and I drew in a sharp breath.

'My deepest apologies!' A tall dark-haired man in a tuxedo, who looked far more alarmed and shocked than I felt, delved hurriedly into his pocket and extracted a pristine white handkerchief. He leaned forward to dab at my chest before suddenly thinking better of it and passing the handkerchief to me.

'It was my fault,' I said, doing what I could to mop up the sticky mess. 'I wasn't looking where I was going.' I held out the stained, crumpled handkerchief. 'Er, sorry about the mess.'

'Please, do not apologise. And keep the handkerchief – it might come in useful later.' As he smiled, I registered the sudden recognition flaring in his eyes.

'Thanks,' I said awkwardly.

'You're Daisy Carter, aren't you? You're the one who helped stop Humphrey Bridger.'

'Yeah.' I nodded. 'That was me.'

'Extraordinary.' He looked me up and down. 'We shouldn't underestimate elves like you.'

Uh-huh. Something in his tone made me realise exactly what he meant by *elves like you*. 'I was away when all that went down,' he continued. 'If I'd been here, I'd have taken care of Bridger myself. If I'd stabbed him, he wouldn't have stood back up again – though my magic would have been more than enough.'

Wankstain. I smiled prettily and met his eyes. With a jolt, I saw the ring of silver around his pupils: he was a spider's silk user. High elf or not, he wouldn't have as much magic as he thought.

He nodded towards my bag. 'Does that contain what I think it does?'

I doubted it.

'Because if it does,' he continued smoothly, 'there must be enough in there to supply the needs of everyone in this building. How much for ten?'

'I'm not a dealer.'

'You can trust me.'

Uh-huh. 'Still not a dealer.'

'Because if you were, you'd use all your own product. Am I right?' He laughed. 'What's the bag for then? So you can steal the silver?' He laughed harder, genuinely amused at his own humour.

He'd been the picture of politeness until the moment he'd realised who I was – or rather what I was. Spotting a passing waiter, I snagged a glass of wine; I'd throw it in his face if he said anything else untoward. Then I noticed Hugo watching me from the other side of the room with a dark expression.

'You know,' the man said, blithely unaware of anything other than himself, 'I have a private room upstairs. The two of us could retire there and get away from all this noise. I've fucked a few low elves before – I know what your kind enjoy.' He reached out and I had the horrifying thought that he was about to stroke my arm as if I were some kind of pet. Or attempt something worse.

I manoeuvred myself to the side and jerked the edge of my bag so it poked into his thigh perilously close to his groin.

'Steady on!' he protested.

I smiled. 'That's Gladys. Gladius Acutissimus Gloriae Et Sanguinis, to give her full name, but I call her Gladys for short. She's an ancient sentient sword gifted to me by a creature known as the Fachan after I bested him in battle.' Okay, that last part was a lie. 'She can be ... touchy, and so can I. I suggest you move away before one of us decides you're becoming a problem.'

'Psycho bitch!' he hissed, his urbane mask slipping. In an instant, he'd disappeared into the crowd.

I should have stabbed him, I thought idly, although the truth was that Gladys was safely locked up at home. I wouldn't bring a sword to a party, not even this party.

'Hey, Daisy.' I turned and saw Rizwan grinning at me. 'I thought I'd see if you needed any help with Alan D'Engle. He has something of a reputation. I should have known that you wouldn't need rescuing.'

I grinned back before looking over to where Hugo had been. He was no longer there. 'I need to speak to Hugo,' I said. 'And you – all of the Primes, in fact. I have an idea about what to do next to find the mythical treasure.'

'Can't it wait until after the party?'

My grin widened. 'Actually,' I said, 'it can't.'

~

It took longer than I'd anticipated to round up everyone and get them away from the partying, food and alcohol. 'I've cleared the library on the second floor,' Rizwan said. 'It's got what you need.'

Hugo frowned. Everyone else seemed interested. 'Lead the way!' Miriam burbled, raising her glass. 'We should do more treasure hunting with champagne in our hands. It's much more fun.'

We trooped up the stairs past numerous paintings and display cabinets. I'd thought that the ground floor of the Royal Elvish Institute was swanky, but it was even grander once you went up a flight or two. I smirked; maybe I should swipe some silver after all.

'Thinking about Alan D'Engle?' Hugo enquired, catching my expression.

In a way. I shrugged.

'A party crammed full of guests and the first person you find to talk to is a spider's silk user,' he said.

'How do you know he was the first person I spoke to?'

His voice dropped to a murmur. 'I knew you were here the moment you entered the room.'

'Lord Pemberville!' A waiter came scurrying up the stairs after us. 'Here you go. Exactly as you requested.' He bowed before holding out a silver tray: in its centre was a silver bowl, a small spoon and a few scoops of ice cream. My mouth went dry.

'Wonderful.' Hugo took the bowl. 'Thank you so much.'

Miriam peered at him. 'Is that chocolate ice cream?' she asked. 'In December?'

Hugo dipped his little finger into the bowl and licked it slowly 'Not only is it chocolate ice cream, it's got sprinkles.' He didn't look at me – he didn't have to. 'There's plenty more where this came from. You're welcome to order some for yourselves.'

I cleared my throat. 'Do they have vanilla?'

Hugo finally looked at me. 'Tragically, no.' He raised a mocking eyebrow.

I pinned my mouth shut and marched faster up the stairs. 'Is there a rush, Daisy?' he called out.

I straightened my shoulders and replied without turning my head, 'Yes. So toss that ice cream and get a move on.'

His laughter drifted after me. I had no idea what everyone else was thinking about our exchange – I was too chicken to check.

CHAPTER
SIXTEEN

Despite Rizwan's attempts to clear the room, a bickering couple were standing in the centre throwing both books and insults at each other. The holiday season often brought out the worst in people.

Miriam, who was by far the most calming influence in our group, and Joe, one of the research team, managed to defuse the situation before gently escorting them outside.

I strolled to the fireplace in the corner, dumped my bag onto a table and waved at the others to join me. Once everyone had assembled – with more than a few inebriated shuffles and grins – I laid out my theory.

'From what I saw on Mud McAlpine's scroll, we know there's a possible connection to the Welsh poet Dafydd ap Gwillem. We've got the three words that roughly translate as bonfire, twig and commence.'

Becky raised her glass in a mock toast. 'And there's that scribble of the yew tree.'

I nodded. 'We didn't have much luck at Dafydd ap Gwillem's supposed burial site but it's still the most likely location because of the tree and the other clues.'

Slim squinted. 'But there's nothing there – nothing that we could find anyway.'

'Although there might be some ancient magic concealing what's buried there,' Hugo conceded. 'It would make sense.'

'Even if there is, we don't know what that magic might be,' Slim said. 'So we have no way to counter its effects.'

Mark, a tall elf from the research team, raised his hand. 'We've spent hours poring over old documents relating to the graveyard and the sort of magic that might be used to hide a powerful piece of treasure there. So far we've narrowed it down to twenty-three possible spells, none of which we can check. Mud McAlpine remains gravely ill in hospital, so we can't find out what else he knows. And as for the graveyard?' He sighed. 'It might be the poet's final resting place, it might not. We don't even know if Dafydd ap Gwillem's body has anything to do with the treasure. Everything is conjecture.'

Hugo gazed at me. 'Do you have an idea, Daisy?'

I answered honestly. 'I have more conjecture.' I checked the time. 'But conjecture that can be proved in less than ten minutes.'

I was met with a sea of confused faces. 'The New Year bells are going to ring very soon. It's a time for fresh starts, resolutions.' I paused. 'New beginnings.'

Something glinted in Hugo's eyes. 'And New Year has often been linked with fire.'

Becky snapped her fingers. 'There's that place up north! Stonehaven, right? Where the townsfolk swing fireballs to ward off evil spirits for another year?'

Mark said, 'In Latin America they burn effigies to cleanse and bring good luck. In Russia, people write their wishes on scraps of paper, burn them and drink the ashes when the countdown begins.'

Miriam re-joined the group. 'So we burn something?'

'A twig.' Hugo was still watching me. 'That's what was written on the scroll.'

'Any twig?'

I reached for my bag, rummaged inside and pulled out the slender branch I'd pretended was Gladys only minutes earlier. 'How about a twig recently snipped from the yew tree above Dafydd ap Gwillem's alleged burial site?'

Grins broke across every face in front of me.

'It beats slobbery kisses with strangers when the clock strikes midnight,' Rizwan said.

'Speak for yourself,' Hugo murmured but he was smiling, too. 'That might work. That might definitely work.'

Glasses were disposed of and champagne bottles ignored, as were the raucous sounds coming from downstairs. Instead we all watched the clock and waited, the tension growing by the second.

'That was intelligent thinking, Daisy.' Hugo sidled up to me while everyone else shuffled their feet and murmured quietly. 'On all counts.' His blue eyes gleamed with anticipation. 'You should join the Primes full time. There will always be space for you.'

'I'm freelance,' I reminded him. 'This collaboration is a one-off.'

The corners of his mouth crooked up. 'If you say so.' He paused. 'You know, you look lovely tonight.'

My eyes narrowed. 'What are you after?'

'I'm merely stating a fact. The dress suits you.' His eyes dropped and I registered a sudden flicker of confusion. 'But that necklace...'

My back stiffened. 'It was a present. I like it.'

'As do I. It's beautiful, but it also looks very familiar.'

'It's a one-off design.'

He stared at it for a moment longer. 'How strange.' He pursed his lips then reached for his bowl of ice cream, which now contained nothing but a puddle of chocolate.

'It's melted,' I told him. Obviously my mother's tendency to state the obvious had rubbed off during the time I'd spent with her.

Hugo scooped up several creamy droplets with the spoon and lapped at them delicately. 'One day soon,' he said quietly, 'I'm going to make you melt, too.' He licked his lips and raised the bowl in a toast.

I frowned, trying to ignore the flip-flop of my stomach. He smiled back, displaying his dimple.

'It's time,' Becky said. 'It's almost midnight.'

Hugo turned to the Primes. 'Excellent. Let's find out if Daisy's theory is right.'

We crowded round the fire. The flames were low and it would soon need some more fuel, but it was sufficient for our purposes. The long twig I'd taken from the graveyard yew tree was dry enough to burn quickly even in these dying embers. 'We'll only get one shot at this, so let's get the timing right,' I said.

Several members of the group pulled out their phones to display clocks that would be accurate to the second. I moved as close to the fire as I could and held out the twig so I could drop it into the embers at exactly the right time. I sensed that everyone was holding their breath. I certainly was.

'One minute,' Hugo said. 'Get ready.'

A few poorly timed fireworks were already exploding outdoors with bangs and screaming whizzes. I held my nerve and my arm steady, waiting for the exact moment. Then, from downstairs, the chant of the countdown began.

'Ten! Nine! Eight! Seven!'

I sucked in my breath and looked up at Hugo. He winked at me.

'Six! Five! Four! Three!'

'Ready,' he said.

'Two! One!'

There was an explosion of noise from all directions. The fireworks outside started in earnest, and cheers and shouts erupted from downstairs. And everyone inside the library yelled at me. I released my hold on the yew-tree twig. It fell into the fire and the flames quickly surrounded it. I stared at the flickers. Come on, I urged it. Do something. Show us *something*.

And then it did.

It started slowly, a single tangerine orange tendril stretching upwards, abandoning the fireplace for the space in front of it. I moved back and collided with Hugo. As I stumbled, he grabbed hold of me and pulled me further away. While the sounds of the partying showed no signs of abating, in this room everyone was silent.

The frond of fire rose further, questing higher until it hovered above our heads. I watched it, my fingers curled into anxious fists. There was no telling what it might do – it might even attack us. I was ready to spring a gallon of water magic on it if need be.

I needn't have worried because the fire had other ideas. Now it had the freedom and space to move, it quickened, twisting one way then another, arching into a shape. Within seconds, what appeared in front of us was no longer a flame that had escaped its natural confines but a very obvious – and very intricate – rune.

'A sorcerer,' somebody hissed. 'We need a damned sorcerer!'

Rizwan and Becky were already speeding for the door to search for one in the throng of partygoers downstairs. I reached for my phone, as did several of the other Primes, and quickly snapped several photos but when I looked at the results, there was nothing but a blur. From their faces, the others were having the same problem. This particular magic obviously didn't blend with modern technology.

I abandoned my attempts to take a photograph in favour of committing the rune to memory. It curved in a snaking spiral before arching out three times. There was a flick, a dot and several slashes that intersected. I ground my teeth: it was desperately complicated and I knew that any slight deviation in my memory would alter its effect if I tried to reconstruct it. And once the yew tree twig was consumed by the flames, the rune would probably vanish.

The library door burst open and Rizwan and Becky reappeared, hauling a surprised and rather nervous-looking man between them. Becky sent an apologetic glance to Hugo and I felt his body stiffen. 'This was the first sorcerer we could find,' she said.

Belatedly, I recognised him – although it was his gangly form and jumpy demeanour rather than his face that I remembered. It was Gordon Mackenzie, the sorcerer who'd unlocked the underwater rune for us at Smoo Cave months before. At least he'd know what he was doing, though I was aware that there some odd tension between him and Hugo. Unfortunately, I didn't know why.

'This isn't right! You can't just drag me out of a party!' Gordon's cheeks were red and his hands were shaking, but even so he was doing a good job of standing up for himself.

I decided this wasn't an occasion when Hugo was the best person to take charge. I cleared my throat. 'Gordon, we need your help. Please.'

He squinted at me. 'You're Daisy Carter. What gives you the right to—?' He faltered mid-sentence as his gaze finally snagged on the rune. His mouth dropped open and his spectacles slid down his nose. 'Oh my God.'

He shrugged away Becky and Rizwan before moving as close to it as he could. 'It's exquisite. The curlicue here – the way it sweeps.' He shook his head in amazement. 'I've never seen such a perfect specimen.'

'Do you understand it?' I asked. 'Does it do something? Unlock somewhere?'

Gordon didn't seem to hear me. He extracted a notebook and started sketching the rune, the tip of his tongue visible between his lips as he concentrated. 'It's a key,' he said. 'A beautiful, old key. It's extraordinary. Only a true master of sorcery could create such a thing. It both conceals and protects.' He didn't take his eyes away from it. 'How did it come to appear here of all places? Surely this is not where the lock is located?'

'No.' I watched as he drew furiously, copying the difficult rune line by line and curl by curl.

Slim edged nearer to the fireplace. 'The twig is all but gone. It's nearly burned up.' He was right: it was already mostly ash. The rune was also starting to disintegrate and the hovering flames were becoming less and less distinct. It would vanish in seconds.

'Hurry,' I urged Gordon.

He didn't look at me; his attention was wholly on the flickering rune and his notebook. 'Almost there,' he muttered. 'Almost there.'

There was a loud crack. The space that had been occupied by the rune suddenly filled with pure white smoke. I checked the fireplace: the twig had gone – and so had the rune. If we wanted to see it again, I suspected we'd have to prune more twigs from the Welsh yew tree then wait twelve months until the next New Year.

'Did you get it?' Miriam asked Gordon hopefully.

A tiny smile crossed his face. 'I did.'

'Thank you,' Hugo said briskly. 'If you'll kindly give us your sketch, we'll let you return to the party.'

Gordon's eyes fixed on a point over Hugo's shoulder. 'I can give it to you,' he mumbled, 'but it won't do you any good. It's old magic, complicated old magic. There are only two other sorcerers who can reproduce that rune to do what you presumably need it to do. Neither of them are in this country.'

'How very convenient,' Hugo muttered. He raised his head. 'In that case I would like to hire your services to reproduce the rune for us so we can use it to unlock what we're looking for.'

Gordon looked directly at Hugo for the first time. 'Not every treasure should be found,' he said quietly. 'Whoever placed this rune made it complex for a reason. They did not want anyone to unlock its mysteries. Some things are better laid to rest.'

Hugo's voice took on an edge. 'Advice that we should listen to more often, but in this case we need to find the treasure in question. It's imperative that the rune is reproduced in the right location.'

Gordon was already shaking his head, refusal written all over his face. I cleared my throat. 'You say that you're the only sorcerer in this country who can manage that rune.'

'I'm not boasting.' His voice quavered only slightly.

'I don't believe you are.' I drew in a breath. 'But what about fiends? Could a fiend replicate that rune to unlock whatever is hidden?'

Gordon's skin, already pale, turned pure white. 'A fiend? You can't mean...'

We all stared at him. Gordon glanced from one of us to the next, registering the truth in our eyes. 'Yes,' he said finally. His shoulders dropped in defeat. 'A fiend that's old enough and powerful enough could manipulate that sort of magic.'

Zashtum was gone, but given Mud McAlpine's dire words

and the vamp attack we could expect at least one other fiend on the trail of the treasure. We had to get to it and secure it before that happened.

'We need you, Gordon,' I told him.

He swallowed hard. 'Alright.' His voice was little more than a whisper. 'Alright.'

CHAPTER
SEVENTEEN

We waited another day before returning to Wales. Despite our desire to finally uncover Mud McAlpine's mythical treasure, searching on New Year's Day was never an option. It was a public holiday; friends and families would be out enjoying the fresh air, and relatives of those buried in the graveyard would be taking advantage of the holiday to pay their respects. It made sense to wait until normal routine was restored. Hopefully Hugo's fans would also have decided that he wasn't returning and left the area too.

Given the state of Hester and Otis, it was a good thing there was a delay. Hester had decided to take a dive into a punchbowl during the party and, when some of the guests had complained, Otis had gone in after her. I was certain his plan had been to haul her out but it didn't quite work out that way. I didn't know how much alcoholic punch he'd swallowed accidentally, or how much Hester had drunk deliberately, but they both spent most of New Year's Day moaning loudly and clutching their heads. And they both now had a faint purple tinge to their skin.

In theory, the silver lining was that they still felt ill the next day as we travelled south and the rest of us were spared their usual bickering. In practice, I wished it were otherwise. The atmosphere in the Jeep, which contained Hugo, Gordon, Slim and me, was uncomfortable to say the least. The conversation was monosyllabic. Hugo and Gordon sat ramrod straight, refusing to look at each other. Slim wouldn't meet my eye and the air crackled with tension.

By the time we crossed the border into England, with a long way still to go until we reached Wales, I could stand it no longer. 'I spy with my little eye something beginning with R,' I said.

Hugo, his hands on the wheel, rolled his eyes. 'Road.'

I grinned. 'Your turn.'

'I spy with my little eye,' he said, albeit reluctantly, 'something beginning with C.'

Slim leaned forward. 'Cows.'

'No.'

'Clowns.'

'Do you see any clowns, Slim?'

I snapped my fingers. 'Clouds.' Hugo nodded. 'My turn again!' I straightened up. 'I spy with my little eye something beginning with U, T, F, N, R.'

Nobody said anything. I waited for a beat then filled in the blanks. 'Unbearable tension for no reason. So what gives?'

Slim hissed a warning under his breath while Hugo and Gordon stayed quiet. 'Hello?' I asked.

Hester raised her head weakly. 'Yeah, spill the beans. Even I can work out something is wrong, and I'm at death's door.'

The awkward silence stretched out, but sooner or later somebody would break it. Normally, I'd have kept my curiosity to myself – everyone deserved to keep their secrets – but this particular secret could jeopardise our treasure hunt if this tension continued.

It was Gordon who sighed heavily and started to explain. 'Several years ago I was hired to do a job that Hugo didn't approve of. That's all.'

'What you do is your business.' Hugo's knuckles were white as he gripped the steering wheel more tightly. 'You are free to choose whatever job you want.'

Gordon snorted but didn't say anything else. For goodness' sake. 'That's not a lot of information to go on,' I protested.

'Never a truer word was spoken,' Hugo muttered.

Gordon sat up. 'Just because there's not a lot of information doesn't mean it's not worth investigating.'

'How long has it been since you started? Seven years? What have you actually discovered in that time?'

I blinked. The last time I'd heard Hugo sound so bitter was when he'd discovered I was a spider's silk addict.

'Not much,' Gordon answered.

Hugo sniffed. 'Well, then. You should stop taking Grace's money and let the matter lie. Lady Rose is dead. Nobody knows what happened or who killed her – but my family certainly had nothing to do with it.'

My eyes widened. Whoa.

'I can confirm that I have found no evidence that suggests your family was connected with her disappearance,' Gordon said.

'See?'

'And no evidence that exonerates them either,' he added bravely

Otis and Hester were now fully awake, their hangovers forgotten. 'What are you talking about?' Otis asked, wide-eyed. 'Who's Lady Rose?'

'Why did Hugo's family kill her?' Hester whispered.

'They didn't,' Hugo snapped. A muscle ticked in his jaw. 'The Assigney family own the land next to Pemberville Castle. Our families have never been ... friendly. Thirty years ago Rose, the sole heir to the Assigney fortune, disappeared. One day she was there, the next day she wasn't. Nobody knows what happened to her.

'My parents had tried to reach out to her in the weeks before her disappearance to smooth things over and bury the hatchet. They'd visited her a few times but she wasn't interested in speaking to them. They kept trying, however. They were the last people to see her alive.'

Whoa again. 'So there's a suggestion that your mum and dad killed her?' No wonder they tended to stay out of the country.

'It's a stupid rumour.'

I wondered if there was any truth in it. As if he were reading my mind, Hugo growled, 'They did not do it.'

'For the record,' Gordon said, 'I was hired by Rose's great-aunt, Grace Assigney, to find her – dead or alive. I was not hired to establish the guilt or innocence of any party.'

I was starting to understand. 'But your involvement and your investigation has stoked the rumours and stirred up bad feelings.'

'Not deliberately. Lady Rose deserves to be found. When she is, we can establish what happened to her and that could put your family in the clear once and for all.'

'There's been no trace of her for thirty years,' Hugo said. 'She's gone. The work you've done over the past seven years has been pointless.' He paused. 'Unless you've discovered something you're not telling us?'

Gordon was silent and I turned around to look at him. 'I've found nothing,' he said eventually. 'Only a series of dead ends.'

'Because there's nothing to find,' Hugo said. 'And there never will be.'

My stomach clenched uneasily. So even high elves had skeletons in their closets. I managed not to say that out loud; it wouldn't have been a wise move.

'I spy with my little eye, something beginning with S,' Slim said in a small voice.

Thank goodness he'd changed the subject. 'Sky?' I guessed.

'Nope.'

'Seatbelt?' Otis asked.

'You win.'

Otis smiled, though unfortunately nobody else did.

～

It was dark by the time we pulled into the now familiar – and thankfully deserted – car park. The abbey ruins stood stark and silent, framed by the moon which, for once, was unobscured by clouds.

I was beyond grateful that the long, uncomfortable journey was over. I grabbed Hugo as soon as we climbed out of the Jeep and pulled him to one side. 'I'm sorry,' I said. 'I shouldn't have gone prying into your life.'

Frustrated, he ran a hand through his hair. 'It's not your fault, Daisy. You'd have known about it if you'd been brought up amongst elves – it's been the subject of speculation for many years. I've mostly escaped being blamed because I was barely a toddler at the time but...' He sighed. 'Mud sticks, you know.'

Yeah, I did know. 'I'm sorry,' I repeated.

'Don't be.' He forced a smile. 'Besides, we're even now. I

know your background and you know mine. That's got to count for something, right?'

I didn't smile back. 'You shouldn't blame Gordon. It's not his fault. He's only doing his job.'

'Unsuccessfully.'

I touched his arm. 'Hugo…'

'Leave it. Lady Rose is ancient history now. We've got our own ancient history to worry about – and this one could involve some modern-day fiends. We should get a move on.' He strode off towards the old graveyard.

I bit my lip then followed.

As a group, we'd already decided that we wouldn't camp out for the night and we wouldn't wait for daybreak. We knew where we were going and what we were doing, and we couldn't risk drawing any more attention either from the living or from the dead. This time it was important to work quickly; with luck, we'd be driving out of Wales by the time dawn broke.

There were a few scuff marks around the old tree, suggesting that some of Hugo's cannier followers had worked out what we'd been interested in and had attempted some digging of their own, but most of the earth was undisturbed. They'd obviously not had any more luck than we had on our first visit. That was something.

This yew tree would endure for many more years after we had gone, and none of us would be responsible for its death. I reached up and pressed the palm of my hand against its rough bark, silently promising that it wouldn't come to any harm. Hester and Otis solemnly followed suit and a moment later the others joined in.

When Hugo glanced at me, his eyes were warm and the awkwardness from the journey had ebbed away. He understood; everyone did. For some reason that meant more to me than I could put into words.

Eventually we all stepped back. Miriam gave a satisfied jerk of her head. 'I can't sense any vampires. I think we're in the clear.'

'What about ghosts?' Hester asked.

She smiled. 'No ghosts.'

'Zombies?'

'No zombies.'

From Hester's expression, she still wasn't reassured. She'd already told me several times and in no uncertain terms that she refused to lurk around the car park again.

She and Otis flapped towards me and settled in their usual positions on my shoulders. Hester's body vibrated with tension but she was holding herself together admirably. 'You've got this,' I whispered.

'So have you, Daisy,' she whispered back.

We all turned to Gordon, who was twisting his fingers together nervously. He swallowed hard. 'Er, could I perhaps have some light?' he asked.

Within three heartbeats, six bobbing balls of fire were illuminating the tree and making great shadows flicker and dance around our feet. Given the moonlight it was probably overkill, but I supposed every little helped.

Gordon started to circle slowly around the base of the tree, examining every crevice, while the rest of us waited with bated breath. 'Where is due north?' he asked finally.

As if he'd been expecting the question, Hugo pulled an elegant gold compass from his pocket and snapped it open. 'There,' he said, pointing.

Gordon didn't look at him but he did move to the correct spot. 'You should all move back a few metres, just in case.'

We did as he asked. A light, chilly breeze picked up, rustling through the leaves on the tree and ruffling my hair. I turned up the collar of my jacket.

Gordon's hands started to move. A greenish glow sparked from his fingertips as he sketched out a perfect replica of the rune we'd seen in the library at the Royal Elvish Institute.

I felt the buzz of his power. Regardless of how Hugo felt about him, there was no denying Gordon's level of magic. What he lacked in confidence, he made up for in magical strength. I'd caught a glimpse of what he was capable of during the hunt for the Loch Arkaig treasure, when he'd opened up the underwater rune that led to a hidden cavern at Smoo Cave, but this was on another level. The ground beneath my feet vibrated with the force of his enchantment while the air hummed with magicked vitality.

'Forget Hugo,' Hester said in my ear. 'This guy is the one you want to get close to. He's got all the power.'

I hushed her, though my admiration didn't decrease. Gordon's frown deepened as he concentrated, and his hands flicked faster and faster. Sparks flew, crackling and vanishing almost as soon as they appeared. The atmosphere thickened and my throat clogged with magic.

A single drop of sweat ran down Gordon's forehead, then he threw back his head and roared. I jumped, shocked that such a loud noise could come from any man, let alone rail-thin Gordon Mackenzie. I didn't have long to think about it, though, because a second later the ground in front of the yew tree opened up to expose a tangle of roots.

'I can't maintain it for long,' Gordon wheezed. 'You have to move fast.'

We didn't need telling twice. We rushed forward and crouched around the smooth edges of the hole. I caught a glimmer of something – a box perhaps – and thrust my hand downwards before instantly regretting my rash move as pain flashed through me.

I hissed and drew back. I'd thought that the salt ward

surrounding Mud McAlpine's flat in Edinburgh was strong but it was nothing compared to the protective magic in place here.

Hugo saw me grimace. 'We all have to work together. We won't be able to retrieve it otherwise.'

'Work quickly.' Gordon's voice was strained.

I nodded. 'On a count of three. One, two,' I held my breath, 'three.'

This time we all reached into the hole and grabbed the cold shiny object that lay beneath one of the larger roots. I felt the pain again, but the team effort made it more manageable. Clenching my teeth, I pushed the object away from me to try and free it from the root it was snagged under. Miriam helped me as Slim gently lifted the root to create more space. Hugo, Becky and Rizwan pulled at it, intense concentration etched deep into their faces.

'Just a bit more,' Becky gasped. 'Another inch and we'll have it.'

I pushed harder. Power juddered through me until my very bones seemed to be scalded by the effort.

'Almost got it,' Hugo muttered.

Gordon's breath caught. 'Hurry. For God's sake, hurry.' He was starting to shake.

It took one final combined effort to quash the magical resistance still afforded by the residual power that was concealing the object. Then it was free, rising up from the earth in Hugo's hands as if it couldn't wait to breathe fresh air again.

Miriam snatched at my arm to haul my hand out of the hole. A second later, Gordon's magic gave way and he collapsed as the earth fought back and reclaimed the space. I barely had time to blink before the magically induced hole vanished.

I sucked cold air into my lungs before I checked the tree to make sure it was unharmed. Then I turned to Hugo and the simple, though quite large, silver box in his hands. His face was pale – he'd found the effort of retrieving the box as difficult as the rest of us – but his eyes glowed with anticipation. I knew my expression matched his.

'If this turns out to be nothing more than a smelly old cloak,' Hester said, 'we will all be disappointed.'

'It won't just be a smelly old cloak,' Otis told her. 'It'll be a smelly old *magic* cloak. Or an enchanted wooden cup.'

Hester sniffed. 'How thrilling,' she said flatly, though she still flew away from the safe spot on my shoulder to get closer to Hugo.

He dusted off the last of the clinging dirt. The box looked unremarkable; it had no inscription and no decoration. However, when Hugo indicated that I should touch it and I stretched forward to brush my fingertips against its surface, I gasped. It might appear innocent, but there was no denying the buzz of deep magic surrounding it.

'Here.' He pushed it into my hands. 'This is your hunt, Daisy. You started it. You should open it up.'

For reasons I couldn't explain, a tremor ran through me as I accepted the box. It was much heavier than I'd expected.

'Open it!' Hester urged.

Otis wrinkled his nose. 'Be careful! It might be dangerous!'

I nodded. Carefully holding the box in front of me as if it might somehow attack me, I thumbed the catch and flipped open the lid. When I saw what was inside, my jaw dropped.

It wasn't an old cloak or a wooden goblet: nestled inside the box were a lot of tiny statues, half made of silver and half of gold. Everyone, including Gordon, crowded around to peer at them. There were thirty-two of them. 'Chess pieces,' Miriam breathed. 'They're chess pieces.'

I picked one up and turned it over in my hands. She was right: it was a rook. It was exquisite, carved out of gold with a level of detail that I'd never seen on a piece of metal before.

'There's a chessboard underneath,' Rizwan pointed out, looking into the gap the rook had revealed.

'The research team indicated this might be one of the treasures,' Hugo told us. 'If it's set up accurately, you can play a game without the need for another player.'

Hester scratched her head. 'So it's a board game for people with no friends?' She pulled a face. 'At least it's made out of silver and gold, I suppose.' She looked up at me. 'You could always melt it down.'

'Chess is the game of kings, Hes!' Otis protested.

She glanced at him. 'Nerdy kings.'

'Those pieces are larger than we are!'

'Everything is larger than we are, Otis.'

I returned the rook to its spot and looked at Hugo. 'We've got what we came for. We should get back to the car park and head for the British Museum as quickly as possible. This needs to be put in a secure vault before anyone catches wind of it.'

'It's exuding strong magic,' Miriam agreed. 'We need to get it to safety before any fiends sense it.'

Hugo smiled. 'We can be in London within six hours if we leave now. There's no need to stop on route. Mud's treasure will soon be safe.' He reached across and, without warning, pulled me into a hug. 'You did it, Daisy,' he murmured in my ear. 'You found it.'

'*We* found it,' I said. My words were muffled by his shoulder but my glee was unmistakable. 'We all did this.'

'Do you hear that?' Hester asked, interrupting the moment. There was panic in her voice.

I pulled away from Hugo. 'Hear what?'

'That sound.' She shot an alarmed look around the graveyard but it remained silent.

I tilted my head and listened. Hester was right – there was an odd noise. It wasn't coming from anywhere beneath us, and it had nothing to do with the graveyard or the abbey. The sound was coming from the sky and whatever it was, it was growing louder. A rush of air, perhaps. Or a fast drum beat. Or ... wings. The beat of large, leathery wings hoisting aloft a huge body.

I turned my head up to the sky and the glowing white orb of the moon. A second later my heart stopped when I saw the outline silhouetted against it.

Cumbubbling bollocks. There was a dragon and it was coming right for us.

CHAPTER
EIGHTEEN

Although this was the group that had taken on a posse of vampires in hand-to-hand combat, the sight of a dragon made everyone scatter. Gordon, who didn't utter a sound, twisted in a lithe movement and threw himself over the graveyard wall and away from us.

Becky screamed, and so did Slim. Within a heartbeat, they were both sprinting for the abbey ruins as if hoping the old magic retained in the land and the crumbling stonework would hide them. Rizwan cowered behind the tree before making a run for the car park. Even Miriam darted away with Otis following her, his tiny arms flapping as furiously as his wings.

I gaped upwards, temporarily frozen. I might have stayed that way if Hugo hadn't thrown himself at me, grabbed my waist and hauled me towards one of the large stone monuments erected in memory of a long-dead dynasty. He shoved me and the silver chess box to the ground behind the stone, then used his body as a shield. Only Hester stayed where she was, hovering in the air as the dragon dived towards her.

'Hester!' I shrieked, trying to pull away from Hugo so I could return to help her.

'Stop it, Daisy!' Hugo barked. 'You have to stay down! Even you can't beat a damned dragon!'

The dragon's enormous shape filled the sky. It wheeled around Hester's tiny body before landing on four massive, clawed feet. The ground shook and the vibrations affected not only the yew tree but also the gravestones.

Then the dragon opened its mouth and roared, a chilling sound that echoed around us. The force of its bellow sent Hester tumbling through the air until she smacked into the tree trunk.

I struggled against Hugo. When he refused to let go, I gritted my teeth. 'If you don't move away now,' I hissed, 'I will not be responsible for my actions.'

'You can't attack it!'

'I'm not going to fucking attack it. I'm going to get Hester.'

Hugo muttered an expletive under his breath but his grip loosened. I dropped the box, behind the massive stone memorial and scrambled to my feet.

The dragon was advancing on the yew tree. I could no longer see Hester but I had to assume that she was still there. I eyed the beast, taking a moment to examine it from snout to tail and to work out how I could get close without being eaten.

I'd heard plenty about dragons and I'd seen tonnes of photos – there'd even been a viral video a few years earlier of a dragon swooping over the skies of Swansea. None of that could have prepared me for the sight of one up close.

It was huge, though not as massive as I'd expected. Its body was oddly compact, the size of a double-decker bus, and suggested phenomenal strength. Even under the cover of night, I could see the muscles rippling beneath its scales. It had folded its wings against its body, but I'd already seen them splayed out in all their glory as the dragon had flown in and I knew to be wary of their size and strength.

Most of the bobbing balls of magical flame that had helped

Gordon see what he was doing had been extinguished the second the dragon had appeared, but there was still some light from Hugo's. The fireballs were small but they helped me see enough of the dragon to be terrified.

Its tail was long, with barbed spikes along its length that glittered in the occasional flickers of light. I didn't need to touch the spikes to know they would be lethally sharp. The dragon's scales seemed equally sharp, although there was a terrible beauty to their green and purple shimmer. Its snout was vast but it didn't disguise its cavernous mouth filled with pearly-white teeth. There didn't appear to be any noticeable gaps, suggesting that this wasn't the creature that had lost its tooth here many years earlier.

It had two protruding fangs the size of my torso. This must be what it felt like to be a brownie faced with elves, humans, trolls and such-like. Even the dragon's eyes seemed impossibly massive and they gleamed a watchful golden yellow that was impossible to ignore. In fact, the sheen of its irises reminded me of Zashtum and her bizarre skin colour. There was cold intelligence reflected in those depths – together with a desperate hunger that made me shiver.

I'd faced a giant snake before but I'd never imagined I'd have to face something like this. I'd take a dozen snakes before I took on a dragon.

'Hester,' I whispered, urgency colouring my voice. 'Hester!'

There was no answer. It was possible she'd been knocked unconscious when she was blown against the tree. I sidestepped to the right to get closer so I could search for her but, as soon as I moved, the dragon blinked. Its translucent third eyelid slid across before its slitted pupil swivelled in my direction, and suddenly I was pinned to the spot. It wasn't Hugo's body holding me in place this time, it was the fixed gaze of a giant reptile.

I licked my lips. 'Hi there.' My voice shook.

The dragon blinked again. It seemed to be assessing me. Did it understand English? I knew dragons possessed language skills, but maybe it only communicated in Welsh. I didn't think it would be particularly impressed if I chanted the few words I'd recently learned; a dragon probably didn't need to hear a poem entitled 'Ode to the Penis'.

A thought occurred to me and I dropped my gaze to check beneath the dragon's girth. Ah. This one was female. I should avoid the poem.

I pointed at the tree. 'My friend is over there. She's very small and very helpless.'

A tiny, furious voice drifted upwards. 'I am *not* helpless!'

I breathed out, relieved that Hester was alright – at least for now. 'All I want to do is make sure she's okay, then we'll get out of your way.'

The dragon huffed, her breath clouding the air, then she pawed the ground. Hmm. Did that mean I could nip forward and grab Hester, or did it mean stay the fuck away? Before I could decide, Hester coughed and flew upwards, heading straight for the tip of the dragon's snout. My stomach dropped to my feet.

'You're amazing!' Hester squeaked. 'I've always wanted to meet a dragon!'

The creature turned her gaze away from me towards the brownie. She huffed again and blew out another breath. This time it was gentler and Hester managed to stay where she was, although her delicate wings had to flap double speed to manage it.

'You are beautiful.' Hester stroked the tip of the dragon's enormous nose and her nostril twitched. Hester stroked it again, and again it twitched.

My eyes widened. 'Hester,' I warned, 'I wouldn't—'

It was too late. Hester reached out for a third time and, as her fingers lightly touched her snout, the dragon sneezed. The combination of dragon snot and the rush of air sent Hester tumbling backwards and into the tree yet again.

Acting instinctively, I jumped forward. 'Hester!'

The dragon roared and swung towards me, her nostrils flaring in alarm and sending forth a lick of fire.

I sensed movement behind me and the dragon tensed further. 'No, Hugo!' I half-yelled. 'Not now!'

As he reached me, he raised his hands in submission. The dragon's eyes narrowed and it looked as if she were relaxing a little – but that was the moment that Gordon, concerned about the shouting, raised his head from behind the stone wall that encircled the graveyard.

The dragon reacted instantly and sent a jet of fire towards him. With one swift snapping motion, she unfurled her massive wings. If Hugo hadn't pulled me out of the way, I'd likely have been smacked in the face and lost several teeth. I could already smell the unmistakable aroma of my singed hair – and I'd not been the target of the dragon's fire.

The dragon swivelled around then spiralled upwards and away from us, her wings beating hard and fast as she rose into the moonlit sky.

I scrambled to my feet. Hugo did the same, the silver chess box still clutched under his arm. 'You bloody fool, Daisy!' he yelled at me. 'She could have killed you with a single breath!'

I glared at him. 'I'm not the fool! I had everything under control until you appeared!'

'It wasn't me that caused the problems. It was Gordon. In fact—'

I didn't get to hear the end of Hugo's sentence because his words were drowned out by the dragon's renewed roar. I craned my neck, watching as she executed a perfect mid-air tumble in the glinting moonlight. Then she turned her huge body until she was facing us again, her snout pointing downwards.

She opened her mouth and blasted a long stream of fire towards Hugo and me. Apparently she wasn't leaving, she was attacking.

There wasn't time to think. I leapt to my left and Hugo jumped to his right as the dragon nose-dived at us. I threw myself to the ground, conjuring up a wall of water to protect Hugo and me from the scorching flames. Steam hissed and spat.

I covered my head with my hands until I heard Hugo shout, then I pushed away my instinct to protect myself and leapt to my feet. I was already too late: the dragon was on him.

My arms flailed as I ran towards her. 'No!' I screamed. 'Leave him alone!' I darted towards her snapping jaws and razor-sharp teeth, and for a second she paused and glanced at me. Then she whirled her head towards Hugo and lunged again.

For a horrifying moment I was certain he was dead, bitten in half by the enraged dragon. When she reared, however, I realised that he was still in one piece. I blinked, confused, until I realised that there was something clenched tightly in her mouth – the silver box. She'd snatched it from him.

The dragon gave me one more warning look before she flapped her enormous wings and took off. This time she didn't come back.

I ran to Hugo. His clothes were singed and charred, and he was soaking wet from the water I'd magicked into existence. As he gazed at me there was no pain in his eyes, only furious irritation.

'She took it.' He shook himself, sending a shower of droplets into the air. 'The dragon took the chess set.' He glared at me. 'And you doused me in a gallon of water. Again.'

I pulled a face. 'Look on the bright side,' I said. 'At least this time it was deliberate.'

Hester was furious. At first I thought it was because she'd been covered in dragon snot, and so did Otis. 'It could be worse, Hes,' he said. 'After all, it's not from a troll. One quick wash and you'll be fine.'

'I don't care about the snot!' she screeched. 'I was making friends with her! I had a connection with that dragon and you lot ruined it! We could have moved up in the world, Otis! We could be working for a dragon now instead of a stupid elf. Now we're stuck with Daisy!'

I raised an eyebrow. 'She doesn't mean it,' Otis said quickly.

'I do!'

I folded my arms and regarded her calmly. 'I've said several times that you're not beholden to me. You can leave at any point.' I cared for the brownies a lot and I'd be desperately sorry if they left; I hadn't lied when I'd told Hugo that they were my people. But they weren't mine to command. They never had been and never would be.

Hester's cheeks were bright red as she gulped in air. Otis flew close to her and gently touched her shoulder. She flinched, then her body sagged and she looked at me again. 'Sorry, Daisy,' she mumbled. 'I don't really want to leave. I like you. I do.' She sniffed. 'But that was a *dragon*. You know?'

'Yeah, I know.' I smiled gently. 'I don't want you to leave, either. But you can, whenever you want to.'

Her bottom lip trembled. 'Thank you.'

The rest of the group circled the area warily, nervous that the dragon might return. I was certain that she wouldn't because she'd already got what she'd come here for. She wasn't interested in us; she never had been.

'I don't think,' Becky said in a trembling voice, 'I've ever been quite so scared in all my life.'

Miriam patted her arm reassuringly but she also looked pale. It didn't matter that she was an expert swordswoman; no sword in the world would defeat a dragon.

Rizwan rubbed the back of his neck and tried to look brave but it didn't last long. Eventually he gave up and shuffled closer to Hugo. 'You remember what happened to the MacAllens, right?'

The others nodded. I frowned and shook my head.

'They were a family of treasure hunters,' Hugo explained.

'Skilled treasure hunters,' Gordon threw in.

Hugo's eyes narrowed but he refrained from making any snide comments. 'Their feats are legendary,' he continued. 'They found extraordinary amounts of treasure. There's a whisper that they located King Arthur's sword and it's now locked away somewhere for safe-keeping. Nobody has ever confirmed or denied it.'

'I've never heard of them,' I said.

Hugo's mouth tightened. 'That's not surprising because they're long gone now. Eighteen years ago they were out on a hunt near Snowdonia when they uncovered a small cache of gold coins. They weren't particularly valuable but that didn't seem to matter – those coins were considered to be treasure by one of the three Welsh dragons.'

He looked at me grimly. 'Supposedly it was the female one with purple scales. She attacked the MacAllens in a bid to get the coins. Witnesses said they tried to leave the treasure and walk away but she didn't care. Every single member of the family was turned to ash. Not even a scrap of bone remained.'

Slim shook his head. 'We should have walked away as soon

as we found the dragon's tooth. That chess set was never supposed to be ours.'

'We weren't searching for it because we were greedy,' I argued. 'We had good reason to look for it.'

'Well then our venture was a success,' he said, folding his arms. 'The mythical magical chess set is safe – that dragon has it. No fiend can get it now.' He looked at the ground, which was becoming more visible with dawn's approach. 'And we're lucky that we've not been barbecued.'

Rizwan shuddered. 'Incredibly lucky.'

I switched my attention to the area around my feet. Patches of grass were still smouldering and a small bouquet of dried flowers on an old gravestone nearby remained alight. Everything smelled of bonfire. Even the old yew tree displayed signs of fire damage.

A shiver ran down my spine and my fingertips tingled. Hugo turned to me, alarm lighting his face. 'Daisy—'

Water magic exploded out of me, icy wet molecules coalescing every scrap of moisture in the air. Becky squeaked. A second later, it wasn't only Hugo who was soaking wet. We all were.

'For fuck's sake!' Rizwan yelled.

Oh no. I wrapped my arms around my body. 'I'm sorry,' I said. 'I'm so sorry. I didn't mean that to happen.' My limbs were shaking and there was a churning nausea in the pit of my belly.

Gordon wiped the water from his face and stared at me. Rizwan, Miriam, Slim and Becky looked horrified. Hugo's expression, however, had transformed into a blank mask. 'It wasn't deliberate that time,' he said.

CHAPTER
NINETEEN

It was a bedraggled, forlorn group that returned to Scotland. It didn't help that most of the others wouldn't look at me; I suspected they were now as wary of me as they had been of the damned dragon.

Fortunately, Hester and Otis had recovered from their hangovers and they chattered non-stop during the long journey home. I needed the distraction because Hugo checked on me hourly, as if I were in danger of suddenly bringing forth more water magic and submerging his Jeep from the inside. But I'd already upped my spider's silk dosage and I was fine. Absolutely, completely fine. Maybe if I kept telling myself that, it would come true.

'You shouldn't go home alone,' he said when we finally drew close to Edinburgh. 'Come back to Pemberville Castle. We can spend more time working on your meditation skills and controlling your magic so you don't have another outburst.'

'You've given me the basics,' I said. 'I'll keep practising and come to you when I've mastered those techniques. But I've got things to do.' I waved my hands around. 'People to see. I'm a busy person.'

He raised an eyebrow. 'Are you?' he asked sceptically.

'Yes.' On that count, I wasn't lying: there was some urgent research I needed to carry out, not to mention a visit to see a certain fiend-banishing witch.

Hugo glanced at my face. I knew he wasn't happy, but I wasn't his responsibility and I wouldn't be alone. 'There's no shame in admitting you need help, Daisy.'

The only help I needed was some tiny white pills. 'I'll be fine.' My voice was firm. 'I'd tell you otherwise.'

A muscle throbbed in Hugo's cheek. 'You don't have to take more drugs.'

I did.

'It's incredibly dangerous to keep increasing your dose.'

It was.

'It won't end well.'

It would not. I smiled. 'Don't worry about me, Hugo. I've got this.'

~

I made it to the hospital just before visiting hours ended. Naturally, despite my excellent sense of direction, I managed to get lost on my way to Mud McAlpine's ward. For some time now I'd suspected that hospitals deliberately made their layout as complicated as possible to distract people from the horrible reasons they had for visiting.

After asking several tired, harassed members of staff, I found the right room and reassured the nurse on duty at the front desk that I wouldn't be long.

There were four patients inside, each one strung up to IV tubes and beeping machines. Given the severity of their conditions, Mud probably wouldn't be in any state to hear what I had to say.

I located his bed in the far-right corner. To my surprise, although his eyes were closed he looked much healthier than he had the first time I'd met him and his chest was rising and falling regularly. Some of my anxiety eased; Mud was in the right place. He'd probably needed some proper medical intervention for a long time, regardless of any fiend attacks.

Unsure if he was asleep or merely resting, I slipped towards his bed and sat down on the plastic chair next to it. He immediately started to speak, although his eyes remained closed. 'Daisy Carter must be here with news,' he whispered. 'But is the news good? Or is it dreadful?'

I stared at him. How did he know it was me? I'd never heard of witches possessing telepathic visual power. And given the lack of herbal plants in the sterile hospital ward – and his medical issues – I couldn't imagine even a witch like Mud McAlpine using any magic.

'Mud knows only one user of spider's silk, and Mud knows what spider's silk smells like.' He opened one eye to look at me. From the glimmer of amusement I saw there, he was delighted that he'd effectively read my mind.

'What does it smell like?' I asked, fascinated. I'd never been able to scent anything beyond a very faint chemical smell.

'Rot,' he replied simply.

I grimaced, wishing I hadn't asked. 'How are you feeling?'

'Lord Hugo Pemberville is not here,' he said.

No, I hadn't told Hugo I was coming; this was something I wanted to do alone. 'Are you recovering?'

'Where is the mythical treasure?'

'Mr McAlpine—'

He wrinkled his nose. 'Mud is fine. Mud is feeling great. Mud will soon be doing the can-can.' He lifted his head an inch off the pillow then a flash of pain crossed his face and he fell back again. Mud would certainly not be doing the can-can any time soon.

I gave in to the inevitable and told him what he wanted to know. 'We found the treasure.'

Both his eyes were suddenly wide open. He scanned my face before reading enough in my expression to understand what was happening. 'But Daisy Carter does not have it now.'

'No.'

'Lord Hugo Pemberville does not have it now.'

'No. I'm sorry.'

He sagged against the white pillow. The healthy aura he'd possessed when I'd walked in seemed to be fading away by the second. 'Who has it? Who took it?'

'Not a fiend,' I said quickly. 'It was a dragon.'

His head jerked. 'Dragons only care for gold,' he whispered. 'It was the chess set. Daisy Carter found the chess set. None of the other mythical treasure is golden.'

I could say one thing for Mud: he certainly knew his stuff. 'Yes,' I said quietly. 'It was the chess set.'

A weary smile lit his face. 'Mud wishes he could have been there.'

'It was amazing.' Until it wasn't. I drew in a breath. 'But we don't have the chess set now. The dragon has it.' I leaned forward. 'Dragons are big and scary.' I touched the singed edges of my hair. 'And they have a lot of fire at their disposal. Special fire. Dragon fire. A fiend wouldn't attempt to go against a dragon.' I paused. 'Right? The chess set is safe?'

Mud's eyes met mine then looked away. 'Fiends are not afraid of fire, Daisy Carter. You already know that. Even dragon fire poses little challenge. The risk for a fiend is easily worth the reward, and they will risk a great deal for one of the thirteen mythical treasures. Dragons are strong but they are far from invincible.'

He sighed. 'Lord Hugo Pemberville promised he would look for the treasure. He did not break that promise. This is not his fault. Nor is it Daisy Carter's.'

I stared at him for a long moment. 'This isn't over yet, Mr McAlpine. No fiend will get their grubby mitts on that chess set – and no dragons will be harmed.' Not if I had anything to do with it.

∼

Otis and Hester were waiting outside, flitting anxiously around the main entrance and causing palpitations in the hospital visitors who noticed them.

'Well?' Hester demanded. 'What did he say?'

Otis jabbed her with his finger. 'More to the point, how is he doing? Is he recovering?'

Her face screwed up. 'Alright, let's go with that first. Is Mr McAlpine still breathing?'

I didn't smile. 'Yes. He's still very ill but he's doing a lot better. I think he'll be okay if he has a lot of rest.'

Otis nodded happily then he clocked my expression. 'The threat of a dragon won't make a fiend back off,' he said. 'Right?'

'Right.'

Hester looked delighted. 'So we're going after the dragon?'

'We have to,' Otis said. 'We have to secure the treasure and keep it safe.'

'And see the dragon again!' She beamed at me and bounced up and down. 'We can go now. My clothes are still packed.' She spun around, raised her hand to her mouth and whistled loudly for a taxi. Unsurprisingly, none appeared.

I stayed where I was. 'What did you two find out?'

'A few bits and pieces,' Hester said dismissively. 'Nothing of great importance.'

I looked at Otis. He fidgeted. 'The story about those old treasure hunters, the MacAllens, appears to be true. They were killed by a dragon.' He paused. 'The dragon that we met.'

'There's no proof it was our dragon!' Hester pouted. 'There were no witnesses, so nobody knows for sure what happened to them.'

'There were no witnesses because everyone died,' he told her. 'The coroner's report stated that the only thing that could have killed them and left nothing but piles of ash was dragon fire. And there were four purple-and-green dragon scales close by. Since the Second World War, there have only been three dragons left in Britain. Two are male and have red scales, and one is female.' He added grimly, 'And she has purple-and-green scales. The evidence is damning.'

'Poppycock,' Hester muttered, but her eyes slid away.

I wasn't surprised by the revelation, though I still felt a lurch in the pit of my stomach. 'What about the fiends?' I asked. 'Did you find out anything about them?'

This time Hester was more enthusiastic. 'Yes! They're highly dangerous and must be stopped at all costs.'

I looked at Otis; he was reluctant but he explained. 'We sneaked into the library at the Royal Elvish Institute and found a few bits and pieces. It's estimated that there are only nine fiends living in Britain, although that number will be eight now that Zashtum has gone.'

'That's eight too many!' Hester burst out.

I agreed with her whole-heartedly. 'Anything else?' I asked.

'While every fiend is cruel and sadistic, with Zashtum out of the way only two of them are considered to be real threats to the population at large. They're a lot older than the others and are hungry for power – they've stolen magical objects in the past and drained them. While no fiend has any regard for the sanctity of life, those two are believed to be particularly ... brutal. Their names are Vargas and Athair.'

Otis lifted his chin. 'The other six are still dangerous, but those two are the worst. The good news is that there's evidence to suggest none of the fiends like each other. They don't work together. Fiends are solitary creatures who guard their own power and position with violent jealousy.'

I supposed that was something; dispatching a lone fiend felt feasible, but taking care of eight of the bastards at once seemed impossible. 'Okay. That's good. What about *killing* fiends?'

This time both brownies scowled. 'Hugo was right,' Hester said. 'You don't kill a fiend – you can't. Given the right circumstances, a powerful witch can banish them from this realm but nobody has ever managed to kill one. If you don't have the skills to banish one, the best you can hope for is to injure them so that they need to crawl into a hole for several decades to recuperate.'

That sucked. Still, at least I was already accustomed to playing the role of underdog.

'Vargas hasn't been sighted for thirty years,' Otis said. 'Nobody knows where he's lurking, but he's clearly gone to ground. It's not unusual for fiends to stay out of sight for long periods of time – after all, until we had the misfortune to cross her path, Zashtum was last seen eight years ago when that train crashed near Bristol.'

My eyes widened. 'She was responsible for that?' Hundreds of people had died in that crash.

'The investigators discovered traces of fiend magic,' Otis replied. 'And several witnesses saw her at the time, laughing hysterically next to one of the derailed carriages.'

I shivered. Thank goodness she was out of the way now. 'And the other one? Athair?'

Hester answered. 'He's been seen numerous times in recent years. The sightings often coincide with the disappearance of magical items and the subsequent discovery of brutalised corpses. Athair is bolstering his magic – he's planning something and has been for a long time. There's nothing to suggest he'd worry about killing a dragon – he'd pull out all the stops to get his hands on an object as powerful as one of the thirteen mythical treasures.' Then she added, more quietly, 'And if he does, he'll be unstoppable. Even an army of witches would struggle to banish him.'

Only the British Museum had the means to keep that damned chess set safe. I massaged my neck. 'There's no choice. We have to retrieve the treasure from the dragon and get it to London where no fiend can touch it.'

Hester pumped her tiny fists in the air. 'And rescue the dragon in distress in the process!'

Somehow I doubted the dragon would see it that way. But sure. I shrugged. 'There's no choice.'

Otis's shoulders slumped. 'Back to Wales, then.'

'Yep. But not straight away. We're going to make a quick pitstop first.'

CHAPTER
TWENTY

Pemberville Castle looked even grander at night. Although it was cloudy, there was enough moonlight to illuminate the towers and turrets. There were only a few lights on the ground floor and everywhere else was dark. With luck, most of the Primes – and Hugo – were already asleep. I certainly hoped so.

Hester was buzzing, a broad grin on her face. Unsurprisingly, Otis was upset. 'It's not too late to change your mind about this, Daisy. All you have to do is explain everything to Hugo.'

I'd already made my decision; this was the best – and safest – course of action. It would keep Hugo and the rest of the Primes safe.

'We've been through this,' I whispered. 'The dragon will spook if a posse of people show up at her door. One person on their own has more chance of success than a large group. My days are already numbered so it makes sense that I'm the one who risks their life. Hugo will understand.' Eventually. Or so I hoped.

'He'll hate you.'

But he'd be safe. 'That's a risk I'm willing to take.'

Otis tutted sadly but I wasn't going to argue with him about it. I tiptoed forward and called out in a low voice, 'Duchess? It's me! Daisy!'

There was no immediate answer. She was probably fast asleep, but I knew she'd wake up the moment I tried to cross the bridge in front of the castle entrance. I shuffled another inch or two and tried again. The plan was to keep her quiet, not encourage a troll-based hullabaloo. 'Duchess!' I hissed.

'You're interrupting my beauty sleep!'

I exhaled. She was awake. 'Please,' I said. 'I need you to stay quiet. I need—'

It only took her a second to launch herself out from underneath the bridge. She planted both her feet on the stone and glared at me. 'What? What do you want?'

'Uh...' My mouth worked uselessly. The sight of Duchess in a nightcap and gown as if she were Wee Willie Winkie had caught me off guard. I shook myself and tried not to stare. 'I ... uh ... need to sneak into the castle without anyone knowing. Will you let me cross the bridge? Quietly?'

Her pale eyes glittered. 'Why do you want to sneak inside?'

The truth couldn't hurt. 'I want to steal something.'

In an instant Duchess's expression transformed from irritated to gleeful. 'Well, well, well! So little Daisy is nothing more than a grubby thief? How delightful! Be my guest.'

I didn't waste any time; Duchess could be mercurial. Before she changed her mind, I started to cross the bridge, swinging around her large body to get to the other side.

'It's about time that high-elf bastard got what's coming to him!' Duchess chortled. 'Smarmy high-elf wanker!'

I should have kept moving, it would have been the smart thing to do. Instead, I halted in my tracks. Yeah, sometimes I was my own worst enemy. 'That's not fair.' I turned to face the troll.

'Daisy!' Otis flicked my earlobe in alarm. 'What are you doing? Stop talking and keep moving!'

I ignored him and focused on Duchess. 'Hugo has been very good to you. He lets you into his home for afternoon tea. He's extending your quarters and making sure you're comfortable. You're constantly rude to him, yet he's polite to you.' I hesitated. 'Mostly polite to you.'

Confused, Duchess placed her clawed hands on her hips and tilted her head. Unfortunately for all of us, I was only getting warmed up. 'He is kind and loyal,' I continued. 'He's not perfect, but he's willing to admit when he's wrong, and he cares about his people. He's a good man.'

'And,' Hester contributed, 'he's incredibly sexy and the mere thought of him makes Daisy squirm with lust.'

'Exactly!' I said, then I coughed. 'Wait, no. I didn't mean that.' I pulled a face. 'All I'm saying is that you shouldn't be mean about him. He's ... nice,' I finished lamely.

Duchess was still staring at me. 'If he's so nice, why are you stealing from him?'

I shifted my weight. 'It's a long story.'

'If you say so, girlie.' She waggled her eyebrows and I suddenly recognised the glint in her eyes. Uh-oh. It was time to stop talking and start moving.

'Anyway,' I said quickly, 'I've got to go now!' I turned and darted for the castle door, half-expecting Duchess to attack me from behind for daring to admonish her. Instead, all I heard was her mocking laugh.

This time I didn't stop. With sweaty palms, I wrenched at the heavy door. To my relief it wasn't locked and I slipped inside.

Even with the door closed behind me, I could still hear

Duchess laughing. I grimaced and glanced around the grand hallway. At least it was empty and there was nobody around to hear her.

'So much for a surreptitious entrance,' Hester whispered.

'Yeah,' Otis said, agreeing with his sister for once. 'You almost blew it there.'

Aware that my cheeks were burning, I motioned for them to keep quiet. 'Let's find what we came here for and get out of here,' I muttered.

I sidled towards the corridor beyond the sweeping staircase, avoiding the suits of armour and listening hard for any sounds of life. Hester and Otis were snickering softly. Like the brave burglar I was, I pretended not to hear them.

It was dim beyond the entrance area, so I hoped that the rest of my sneaky heist could be carried out without interruption. I slipped down one corridor then another, back-tracking only once when I realised I'd taken a wrong turn. Eventually I found the right room and paused to listen at the door. When I was certain it was empty, I held my breath, inched it open and peeked inside. I'd made it this far; the hardest part was over.

I wasn't daft enough to turn on the lights. Instead, I felt my way around the Primes' vast office space, managing to avoid banging into any furniture. After a few moments my eyes adjusted to the darkness, making it easier to see what I was doing.

I tiptoed around one display cabinet after another before I finally spotted the one I wanted. I hastened towards it.

'It's not too late to turn back,' Otis said, eternally hopeful.

I forced a pained smile; it was far too late. I brushed away his concern and reached for the cabinet door. It squeaked faintly as I opened it and I winced, but I didn't stop.

I withdrew a folded piece of paper from my pocket and laid it carefully on the shelf. then I picked up the ancient dragon's egg. It was heavier than I'd expected but there was no time to marvel at it. I wrapped it carefully in the blanket I'd brought with me, opened my backpack and dropped it inside. Sorry, Hugo. I bit my lip. I really was sorry.

'Alright,' I whispered. 'We've got what we came for. Let's get out of here.'

As I spun around, preparing to head for the door to make a quick exit, Hester buzzed in alarm. 'Someone's coming! I can hear voices!'

My mouth went dry when I realised she was right. Panic filled me and I stumbled as anxiety got the better of me. There was only one place to hide and it was far from ideal, but I didn't have a choice.

I regained my balance, dived towards the huge conference table and scrambled underneath it in the nick of time. I curled my body into a ball and hugged my knees to my chest, while Otis and Hester pressed themselves against a chair leg.

Less than three seconds later, I heard the oak door open. Two people walked in, flicking on the lights and illuminating every corner of the room. Shit. Cumbubbling shit.

I heard Miriam's voice. 'I know I've said it before, but it's worth repeating. Daisy will despise you for doing this.'

'She'll be angry but she'll get over it.' Hugo's tone was gruff and I registered guilt beneath it. My eyes narrowed. What was he talking about?

'I wouldn't be so sure about that.'

'We've been through this. Her magic is causing serious problems. She's struggling to control it, even with the techniques we've been teaching her. It's far safer if she stays away.'

'Safer for whom?'

Hugo emitted a long sigh. 'You know how risky this will be, Miriam – and how necessary it is. We can't allow a fiend to take that chess set from the dragon because the consequences could be catastrophic, but entering a dragon's lair is asking to be roasted alive.'

I glanced at Hester and Otis and they stared back at me, wide-eyed.

'Just promise me that you'll look after her if I don't make it,' Hugo went on. 'If Daisy can learn to control her magic properly, she'll have a chance of getting free of her addiction to spider's silk.'

Miriam's response was soft. 'You know she's probably already too far gone to be saved.'

I pulled a face. Hugo growled, the dark rumble making me tense even more.

'But, yes,' Miriam said. 'I'll do whatever I can to help her. We all will.' She paused. 'Although if you don't come back, we'll still have to worry about the fiends getting hold of that treasure.'

'My plan will work.' Hugo paused. 'I'm almost certain of it.'

'We can go with you—'

'No.' His tone brooked no argument. 'It's too dangerous. I'm going alone.'

The floorboards creaked and I heard his footsteps. I could see his legs: he was walking towards the display cabinets. Suddenly I was sure I was about to throw up – and when I heard the faint squeak as the cabinet door opened, I tasted the bile in my mouth.

'Where the fuck is the egg?' Hugo spat.

I shrank further into myself.

'It's gone?' Miriam asked, genuinely astonished. 'Are you sure?'

'Yes, I'm fucking sure.' I heard a rustle of paper. 'There's a note in its place. *Dear Hugo,*' he read aloud. '*By the time you read this, I'll already be in Wales. I am so sorry for taking your dragon's egg. I will try and exchange it for the chess set so the set can be moved to the British Museum and kept safe. I hope that one day you will understand that this is the best course of action and safest for everyone and that you'll be able to forgive me. We can't risk more lives than is necessary.*' He ground his teeth. 'No prizes for guessing who wrote this.'

'Daisy?'

Hugo exploded. 'Of course it was bloody Daisy! Who else would be this fucking stupid? I'm going to kill her! Then I'm going to lock her up in the tower for the rest of her natural life! She needs saving from herself!'

I looked at the brownies. They looked at me.

'She can't have got that far unless she's sprouted a pair of wings and is flying to Wales,' he snarled. 'She doesn't have a car. Get everyone up and send them out to look for her! How the hell did she get past Duchess? Speak to that bloody troll and find out when she was here. Daisy can't do this! We have to find her!'

Hester raised her eyebrows meaningfully whilst Otis waved his hands. I sighed silently before nodding a reluctant agreement. So much for my great plan.

I cleared my throat and opened my mouth. 'Don't get your panties in a twist, Hugo. And don't wake everyone up. I'm right here.' I unfurled my limbs and crawled awkwardly out from underneath the table before dusting myself off and standing up.

Miriam's expression was mildly astonished; Hugo, on the other hand, looked furious.

'Hi there,' I said. I waved at them both before stuffing my hands in my pockets.

'Hello, dear,' Miriam said. Hugo glared at me. 'I think,' Miriam continued, already heading for the door, 'I'll put the kettle on and make a cup of tea. The two of you can talk this out on your own.'

Hester emerged in a flash. 'Did you say tea?'

Otis zipped out. 'Take us with you,' he begged. 'Don't leave us here with them.'

She nodded and within five seconds, the three of them had vanished through the door, abandoning me to my fate.

Hugo and I were alone. And this wasn't going to be pretty.

CHAPTER
TWENTY-ONE

We stared at each other as the silence lengthened, a few uncomfortable seconds growing into one long minute. Then two. Hugo barely blinked. I twitched and shuffled and finally gave up. 'At least I left a note,' I said.

His hands curled into fists and he stepped towards me. 'A note? A fucking *note*? You stole from me, Daisy! After everything we've been through together, this is how you repay me?'

'Technically I've not stolen anything. I've removed nothing of yours from this room.'

'Semantics!' he snapped. 'You'd have been across the border by now if you could have got away.'

True. 'It's for a good cause.'

'You bloody idiot, Daisy!'

I demurred. 'Actually, I think it's a very smart move. The dragon has the chess set and she won't give it up without a fight. I can't fight her – even if the law permitted it, I can't fight her. An exchange of goods is the most logical way forward.'

'You should have come to me first. We could have discussed it.'

I extracted my hands from my pockets and crossed my arms. 'Oh, really?' I asked coolly. 'Because it's clear that you were planning to do exactly the same thing and not tell me about it. This is *my* treasure hunt, Hugo. It started with me and it will damned well end with me. Why didn't *you* come to *me* to discuss what you were planning?'

A muscle throbbed in his jaw. 'Because your magic is becoming a liability. It's safer for you here.'

'I know there have been a few instances when I could have done better, but I can assure you, Hugo, that my magic is under control.'

'Only because you've upped your dosage of spider's silk.' His blue eyes flashed dangerously. 'Don't think I've not noticed that you're taking more pills.'

'I'm also meditating and practising the techniques you taught me.'

'It's not enough.'

'I know that!' I burst out. 'I know what's happening to me! And that's exactly why I should be the one to go to the dragon. I'm the one whose life is already limited. I've got less to lose than you.'

Hugo growled again. 'It's too dangerous.'

'I don't need your protection.'

'And I,' he returned icily, 'don't need yours.'

I glared at him. He glared back.

There was a loud creak from the floorboards outside the room, and a moment later Duchess's head appeared. She was too large to fit through the doorway so she peered at us from beyond it. 'I came to see what was taking you so long, girlie. Now I understand.'

Hugo hissed under his breath, 'What is the point of having a gnarly troll live outside your home if they're not going to stop intruders from breaking and entering?'

'I'm not a guard dog,' Duchess sniffed. 'And I'm not gnarly. Security is your problem, not mine.' She looked at me. 'Is this the nice, loyal, good man called Hugo Pemberville you were telling me about? Because he doesn't look particularly twinkly or kind to me.'

A line formed between Hugo's eyes, his anger melting away to be replaced by something else. 'Nice?'

Duchess shrugged. 'Apparently.'

'Loyal?'

'That's what she said.'

'Good?'

From somewhere down the corridor, Hester shouted, 'Don't forget sexy!'

Something else altered in Hugo's expression. 'So,' he said, his voice softer, 'now I know what you really think of me, Daisy.'

'I didn't say that last part,' I muttered.

He took another step towards me. 'But you were thinking it. And you said the rest. Out loud.'

There was no point denying it because Duchess was already nodding confirmation. I rolled my eyes. 'You can be kind, loyal, good, twinkly and nice and still be a stubborn bastard who doesn't know what's good for him.'

'I see.' He relaxed his stance. 'Much in the same way that you can be brave, strong, compassionate and kind-hearted *and* a total idiot all at the same time?' He paused then added, 'As well as incredibly sexy even when you're wearing bunny pyjamas?'

I lifted my chin. '*Especially* when I'm wearing bunny pyjamas.' I gave him a meaningful look. 'They beat the sex appeal of neck-to-toe thermals.'

'I like to keep warm,' Hugo said. 'But I'm prepared to strip off to my tighty-whities if you'll be my hot water bottle.' He winked. Unbidden, a delicious shiver ran through me.

Duchess blinked at us. 'Are you fighting or are you flirting?' she called. Good question. 'Because fighting is much more fun to watch. But if you want to get it on here and now, I'm okay with that, too.'

Hugo ran his tongue across his lips then turned and walked to the door. 'Bye, Duchess,' he said. He closed the door to afford us some privacy before facing me once more. Initially I felt a frisson of anxiety until I realised that his expression was now serious. 'You realise we both came up exactly the same plan.'

I pushed my hair out of my eyes. 'Great minds think alike.'

'We can't leave the treasure with the dragon.'

I nodded. 'One of the fiends might still make a grab for it and harm the dragon in the process.'

'And gain enough magical power to cause the rest of us real problems.'

'But the dragon won't give up the chess set easily to any of us.'

'So we have to give her something in return,' Hugo said. 'Something valuable.'

I gazed at him. 'Gold might work. But it would have to be a huge amount.'

'It would be a long shot,' he agreed. 'We have to offer her something she genuinely covets.'

'And what would a dragon covet more than a dragon's egg?'

'The egg is ancient and there's no way it's viable, but it's the best option we have.'

'Yes.' I frowned. 'It will still be incredibly dangerous.'

'Certainly. We'll have to enter her lair and she won't like that.'

'And she may well decide that we're villains for having the egg in the first place.'

'Indeed – but it's worth the attempt.'

'Definitely.'

'We can't risk the Primes' lives.'

'No.' I paused. 'Neither should we risk yours.'

Hugo's eyes narrowed. 'Let's not start this again. We go together – between us, we can persuade the dragon to give up the chess set. And we make a pact to stop trying to protect each other. We're both adults and we can both make decisions for ourselves, regardless of the dangers involved.'

I yielded because there was no longer any other way; I couldn't persuade Hugo to stay at home any more than he could persuade me. 'Okay.' I sighed. 'Okay.'

'I'll drive.'

'If you insist.' I met his eyes. 'But if the dragon eats you, I will kill you.'

He smiled crookedly, the familiar dimple forming in his cheek. 'Ditto,' he murmured. 'And I won't forget everything else you said about me. We'll come back to that later.'

He should forget it because I'd not forgotten Miriam's words from moments ago. I was probably already too far gone to be saved, so Hugo shouldn't get attached to me. 'Mmm.'

He leaned into my ear. 'I hope your bunny pyjamas are in that backpack as well as the egg.'

'I don't hear any shouting,' Duchess said from the other side of the closed door. 'Does that mean you're shagging?'

Hugo quirked an eyebrow. 'Not yet,' he whispered. And he grinned.

∼

TWELVE HOURS LATER, we presented ourselves at the Office for Dragon Affairs in Aberystwyth, Wales. I'd expected a grand establishment with elaborate stone masonry, several floors of offices and at least a handful of dragon-inspired statues. I'd obviously been spending too much time in castles, though, because the ODA was little more than a dusty room in the back of a cement-covered office block.

There was only one member of staff: a bespectacled man with a shiny, bald head and a cheap suit. He had the harassed air of an over-worked civil servant, and he was none too pleased at the interruption. 'You want what?' he asked, his eyes wide with astonishment.

Hugo offered his most disarming smile. It bowled me over but it did nothing for Arnold Enger. 'It's not a case of want,' he said. 'It's a case of need. We need to know the location of the female dragon's lair.'

'That information is privileged,' Enger said. 'There are only a handful of people allowed access to it, and they've all had to sign the Official Secrets Act.'

'I'm perfectly happy to sign whatever you need.'

Enger stared at him. 'Fine,' he said, when an appropriate number of uncomfortable seconds had ticked by. He opened a drawer and pulled out a wad of paper. 'You need to fill out this form – in triplicate. Then you should send it to the address written there.' He jabbed an ink-stained finger at the London address on the first page.

'If you're lucky, you might get an answer within six weeks. In the unlikely event that your application proceeds, you will then be invited to sign the Official Secrets Act. That usually takes a month to arrange. Once that is done, you may return here with the necessary documentation and I will show you on a map where her lair is located.'

Hugo was apparently used to British bureaucracy because his smile didn't flicker. 'We don't have that sort of time.'

'I wouldn't worry,' Enger said. 'The dragon's not going

anywhere. She's only eighty-nine years old, so she has many decades ahead of her yet. There is no rush.'

'There is every rush. I understand that you have to be careful, but time is of the essence. We need to get to her lair.'

Enger pushed his spectacles further up his nose and peered more closely at him. 'Wait. You are Hugo Pemberville?'

Hugo grinned widely. 'I am.'

'Lord Hugo Pemberville?'

'Yes.'

'The celebrated treasure hunter?'

'Yes.'

I rolled my eyes.

'The man who found the Loch Arkaig treasure.'

Actually that was me. I found it first.

'Yes,' Hugo said, without a single glance in my direction.

'The man who located Boudicca's crown?'

'Yes.'

'The man who tracked down the golden statuette of Merlin?'

'That's me.'

It was Arnold Enger's turn to smile. His lips curved upwards and twitched slightly, and within seconds he was beaming triumphantly. 'My lord, it's a real pleasure to meet you.'

I sighed heavily. Here we go again.

Enger continued, 'You, my Lord Pemberville, will *never* be granted knowledge about any dragon's lair.' With that, he snatched the forms and shoved them back in his drawer.

I folded my arms; I was genuinely amused even though discovering the dragon's location was paramount to the success of our quest. I bet this kind of thing didn't happen very often to Hugo.

'What?' Hugo asked, blinking in astonishment. 'Why not?'

'You are a treasure hunter and treasure hunters seek gold.

Dragons hoard gold. No treasure hunters are allowed anywhere near dragons. Don't you know what happened to the MacAllens?'

'I'm not planning to steal anything from the dragon!' Hugo objected.

'Then why on earth do you want to find her?'

'She has an important item that—' He didn't get to finish the sentence.

'There!' Enger snapped his fingers. 'There we go. You cannot take *anything* from any dragon.'

Obviously it was time I helped out. 'We will ask her to *give* us the item in question. We won't just take it. But the dragon is in very real danger. There are fiends who know about this item. It's magical, you see, and if a fiend gets their hands on it then—'

It was my turn to be interrupted. 'Fiend?' Enger asked. 'What the hell is a fiend?'

'Your worst nightmare,' Hugo said.

Enger shook his head. 'Nope. Never heard of any fiends. And my worst nightmare is the paperwork this visit of yours is going to generate.' He pointed to the door. 'You're not getting any more information out of me or anyone else. It's time for you to leave.'

'But—'

Enger stood up, narrowed his eyes into an officious glare and stood on tiptoe so he could match Hugo for height. 'The door is behind you. Goodbye.'

And that, I thought sardonically as we were escorted outside, is what happens when you kept secrets like fiends from the wider public.

CHAPTER
TWENTY-TWO

Otis wasn't happy. 'But what are we going to do now? We have to find the dragon!'

'I'll go inside and find what we need,' Hester said. 'We sneaked into the Royal Elvish Institute's library, so we can certainly sneak into that grey council hellhole before anyone notices us.'

I wasn't convinced that even the brownies could find the information we needed but before I could say that, a couple marched out of the front door of the building. Without a glance in our direction, they started scattering salt and muttering an incantation. Oh. They were setting up a ward; no doubt it was specifically designed for our group.

'We need a Plan B,' I said. 'There must be another way to locate the dragon's lair. We're not in vast plains or endless steppes – Wales isn't that big. If we scour the map, taking into consideration where Strata Florida Abbey is and where there have been other sightings of the purple dragon, we should be able to narrow down possible locations.' I glanced at Hugo. 'Can't you set the Primes at Pemberville Castle onto the search as well?'

'They're already looking.' His mouth was set into a thin line and I guessed he was still annoyed by what had happened with Arnold Enger. 'So far they've narrowed it down to about two thousand square metres. That's a huge area to cover and the lair will be shielded by magic. We won't simply stumble across it.'

I continued to look on the positive side. 'Surely if we can't find it, a fiend can't find it either.'

'Their powers have evolved – fiends are far more sensitive to magic than we are. That's probably how Zashtum latched onto Mud in the first place. If there's a fiend out there looking for that lair, sooner or later it will find it.'

Ah. I scratched my head. That was vexing.

'But I doubt any fiend has located it yet,' Hugo went on. 'So we've got time. I don't know exactly how good the fiends' magic-tracking skills are, but general wisdom seems to think they need to be close to powerful magic to sense it.' He shrugged. 'Five miles, maybe ten at a push. They have more chance of stumbling across the dragon's lair than we do – but this is far from over yet.'

'You must have some old-school network contacts who can help.'

He grimaced. 'I've tried that route already. If anyone knows, they're not talking. We have to do this ourselves, I'm afraid.'

'This would have been a lot easier in the nineteenth century.' Hester's bottom lip jutted out. 'Back then everyone knew where the dragons lived. People used to go to the lairs and sit outside them with picnics.'

'And occasionally hunt the dragons, kill them and sell the contents of their lairs and their corpses on the open market,' Otis added.

Hester's shoulders slumped. 'It's true,' she said sadly. 'People did do that.'

Hugo grinned suddenly. 'You're a genius, Hester.'

She blinked, genuinely startled. 'I am?'

Triumph glittered in his eyes. 'I know exactly where to go to find the information we need.' He turned and glanced along the pavement away from the centre of Aberystwyth. 'It's within walking distance. We can leave the car here.' He took off without another word, obviously expecting the brownies and me to trail after him.

I frowned. A little explanation would have been nice.

'He's so masterful,' Hester sighed. Otis and I glanced at her. She shrugged. 'What? He struts like a hero. You don't walk like that, Daisy. You walk as if you're a Labrador puppy that's scented a sausage.'

I pursed my lips. I rather liked that idea. 'So?'

'Hugo walks like a general commanding an army. He doesn't have to turn around to check anyone is following him because he knows that everyone will.'

I folded my arms. 'Will they?'

'Yep.' Hester gestured after Hugo's retreating back. 'In fact, you'd better hurry if you're going to catch up to him. He won't wait for you. I've watched him with the Primes. He leads, they follow, and he doesn't hang around while they get their shit together. Not ever. If he won't wait for them, he certainly won't wait for you.'

No sooner had the words left her mouth than Hugo stopped marching and looked over his shoulder. 'Daisy? Are you coming?'

Otis chuckled. 'He might not wait for the Primes, but he does wait for Daisy.'

'Because he knows what will happen to him if he doesn't wait,' I replied. 'This is *my* treasure hunt.' I raised a hand. 'On my way, Hugo,' I called.

'You're smiling very broadly, Daisy,' Otis said.

'That's not a smile,' Hester told him. 'That's an ear-to-ear beam of shining radiance.'

I flicked her a side eyed glance but, for some reason, I still couldn't stop myself from smiling, radiantly or otherwise.

~

Hugo was right on one count at least – we didn't have to go far. Within ten minutes, we were strolling into the National Library of Wales, a vast, grand building that gave Pemberville Castle a run for its money.

Otis and Hester zipped around in excitement. 'I love libraries!' Otis squealed. 'This is a great idea, Hugo!'

I wrinkled my nose. 'Useable information about the dragons is protected,' I said, unwilling to match their enthusiasm just yet. 'We're not likely to find it easily in a book.'

'I disagree.' Hugo grinned. 'All we need is the *right* book. We won't find any information about the current location of the dragons, but we can find old tomes that show where dragon lairs used to be.'

I started to frown then I stopped. Oh. 'You're right.'

'I usually am.' He winked at me. 'You said it yourself already, Daisy. Wales isn't that big. There's a limit to the places that are safe for a dragon to reside. And why would they go to the trouble of making a new lair when there are old ones that will be just as comfortable? They aren't stupid. Today's dragons will be making use of the same locations as their ancestors. All we need to do is find a history book that mentions a lair near to Strata Florida Abbey and we'll find our modern-day dragon.'

Hester nudged me. 'He's not just a pretty face.'

Yeah, yeah. I gave Hugo a grudging nod and he blew me a kiss in return. Before he grew too smug, I pointed to the door.

'Come on. Let's head in there and find a member of staff to help us.'

'What's the rush?' Hugo asked. 'You could spend another moment or two acknowledging my brilliance.'

I gave him a long look and he laughed good-naturedly. 'You're right. My superiority in all things is a foregone conclusion.'

I put my hands on my hips but removed them when I saw the teasing glint in his eye. He was hoping I'd disagree. 'We are not worthy of your magnificence, great Lord Pemberville. Shall I kiss your shoes?'

He smirked. 'That won't be necessary.' He paused. 'This time.' He held out his arm. 'Shall we?'

What the hell. I took his arm, aware of the familiar jolt as I touched him. He moved his hand and his fingers brushed against mine. Then, while I shivered despite the warmth of the building, the four of us headed deeper inside the library.

'Think of all the knowledge contained within these walls,' Hester breathed, her eyes wide.

'And all the words,' Otis agreed. 'It's amazing! How many books are here?' he asked Hugo.

A twinkly-eyed woman left her desk and approached us. 'Six million,' she said proudly. 'Give or take a few.'

'Wow,' Otis whispered.

She smiled at him. 'It's rather wonderful, isn't it? And it's wonderful to meet you. My grandparents used to have brownies but I've not seen any since I was a child. I'm Sandy.' Her delight at the brownies' presence made a pleasant change to the wary shock they normally inspired in the general public.

At first I thought that would help our cause, but I saw her expression grow more sombre when she looked at Hugo. 'Lord Pemberville,' she murmured.

Uh-oh.

'We've had a call from the Office for Dragon Affairs,' she said. 'We were told to you expect you.'

Cumbubbling bollocks. Hugo was smarter than he appeared – but so was Arnold Enger.

'We've been instructed not to give you any books relating to dragons.' She wrung her hands together, clearly unhappy. 'Their authority supersedes ours. I'm afraid there's nothing I can do.'

Sandy appeared to be on our side, and she obviously wasn't a fan of censorship. I reckoned I could persuade her to see sense and let us use the books we needed.

Hugo wasn't even slightly nonplussed. 'I completely understand. We're not here for books about dragons, so you have no need to be concerned and you can tell the ODA to relax.'

'In that case, how can I help you?' Sandy asked.

Hugo gestured towards our linked arms. 'We'd like some information about the best places in Wales for some romantic trysts.' He pulled me closer. 'Places that are secluded, atmospheric, contain a great deal of history and,' he deepened his voice to an extraordinary husk, 'are very, very swoon worthy.'

Swoon worthy? Seriously? I glared at him. He pretended not to notice.

Sandy looked delighted. She gave us a broad smile and pointed at a desk and chairs nearby. 'If you wait there, I'll see what I can rustle up.'

As soon as we sat down, my glare increased in intensity. 'Really, Hugo?'

'I had to tell her something. All I need are some old books.' He leaned forward. 'We don't want Sandy to get suspicious so you should hold my hand. And look deeply into my eyes to prove that you're besotted by my presence.'

'I should have stuck to my instincts and left you in Scotland. If that dragon doesn't kill you, then I might.'

Hester rolled her eyes. 'Get a room.'

'That's what I keep saying,' Hugo murmured.

My cheeks started to warm. Fortunately, Otis stepped in to save me. 'I don't understand. How will old books about romantic places help us find a dragon?'

Hugo grinned. 'It's amazing what information you can worm out of unusual places, Otis.' He tapped the side of his nose. 'You'll see.'

~

SANDY WAS good at her job. Before long we had a pile of books sitting on the table between us. Unfortunately, while she'd done as Hugo had asked I was unconvinced that a book such as *The Beating Hearts of Bright Welsh Lovers* would help us.

'I wasn't always the paragon of excellence that you see before you,' Hugo said.

I snorted. Loudly.

'In fact,' he continued as if I hadn't made a sound, 'when I was a teenager, I was somewhat lazy. I wasn't studious – I preferred spending time outdoors rather than inside libraries. The less time I spent poring over books, the better.'

I wasn't sure where he was going with this. 'Okay,' I said slowly. 'So?'

'So I used my unwillingness to spend hours looking for shortcuts.' He ran his finger down the spines of the books in front of us before selecting the oldest, shabbiest volume. 'And I reckon that shortcut will help us now.' He opened it, smiling slightly as its pages creaked, then lifted it to his nose and sniffed. 'In fact, I'm certain it will.'

While I fully understood the alluring smell of old books, I remained confused. 'Hugo,' I said, staring at the book in his hands. 'I don't see how—'

I didn't finish my sentence. Instead, I shoved my chair back to put as much distance between myself and the book as possible. 'That page moved,' I said. 'You didn't touch it. It moved by itself.' My hand went involuntarily to Gladys. I knew there were sentient swords – but could there also be sentient books?

'What's going on?' Otis sounded nervous.

'Shhh,' Hugo cautioned. 'You don't want to scare it away.'

'Scare the ... book?' I asked, feeling foolish.

'Don't be silly, Daisy,' Hester said. 'You can't scare a book.' She looked at Hugo with wide eyes. 'Can you?'

He chuckled. 'No. But you can scare away this little fellow.' He moved his little finger to edges of the paper and a tiny slithering creature appeared from between the pages. It was the colour of parchment and little more than the length of my thumbnail although far more slender in width. It had a forked tail and two quivering antenna. It was as ugly as sin.

Hester opened her mouth to shriek but I grabbed her before she could make a sound and glanced over my shoulder to check on Sandy. Luckily she was busy with her own book piles.

The creature opened its mouth, allowing its tongue to dart out and lick Hugo's finger. I watched it, my body stiff. I was none the wiser as to what was going on, but my sense of ick was growing by the second.

Otis flapped his wings in delight and executed a perfect mid-air tumble. 'A bookworm!' He clapped his hands. 'That's a bookworm!'

'That it is. Hello there, you,' Hugo cooed at the creature. He gave a series of tongue clicks and the creature licked him again.

'You, uh, speak bookworm?' I asked.

'I'm a bit rusty but I think I can manage well enough to get us what we need.' He clicked his tongue again.

'Amazing,' Otis breathed. He looked at me. 'Isn't Hugo amazing?'

I was certainly surprised by him. 'Um...'

'It's alright, Daisy,' Hugo murmured. 'You can express your wonder later.' He stroked the back of the bookworm's body. 'These glorious little beings helped me immensely when I was young, but with the advent of the internet they're rarely used nowadays. They're probably quite happy about that – they don't like new books or the chemicals used in modern paper. But they love old parchment and old books.'

He smiled. 'And sometimes they're more useful than Google. There are some corners that even the internet can't get to but as long as you know the right questions to ask, you can get almost any information from these little guys.'

He held the bookworm up to his face and clicked his tongue again. Bafflingly, it seemed to understand. It tilted his head, appeared to nod then leapt away and vanished.

'This won't take long,' Hugo said. 'It'll seek out the information we need and come back to tell us.'

'I thought bookworms carried nasty diseases,' Hester said. 'And were vicious.'

'Not true. They're sweet, helpful creatures – once you get to know them. They're usually quite reticent and prefer to stay hidden. It took me a lot of trial and error to learn how to talk to them, but it was worth it in the end.'

'Was it?' I asked. 'Would it not have been faster to study the normal way like everyone else?'

He grinned. 'Sure. But it would have been far less fun. And anyway, who wants to be normal?'

Just when you thought you knew a guy... 'You have hidden depths, Hugo.'

'Stick around, Daisy,' he told me. 'There's no telling what you might find out.'

CHAPTER
TWENTY-THREE

Hugo's confidence was merited: the bookworm came through and returned within twenty minutes. With the help of an old map spread out on the table, it pinpointed three separate locations all close to Strata Florida Abbey by tapping each spot carefully with its antenna. Alright, I admit it: I was impressed.

'I gotta get me some bookworms!' Hester crowed. 'Imagine a whole army of them, seeking out all the knowledge that I require. The world will be mine for the taking!'

Hugo, Otis and I gazed at her. 'What?' she asked, innocently.

'I didn't realise you had plans to take over the world, Hes,' Otis said mildly.

Hugo nudged me. 'If I'd known we had a super-villain in our midst, I might have stayed at Pemberville Castle.'

'What will you do once you're queen of the world?' I asked her.

She waved a tiny hand at us in irritation. 'Whatever I want.' She paused. 'But there will definitely be dragons. Lots of dragons.'

I'd heard of worse plans. 'Well, until that glorious day let's focus on the existing dragons and find the one who's got our magic chess set.' I pointed at the map. 'We can drive to this village here and hike to each of the three sites to check them out.'

Hester started to tap dance. 'Bring it on!'

I returned the books to Sandy and thanked her profusely while Hugo clicked his tongue some more at the tiny bookworm, presumably to express his gratitude.

The four of us headed out of the huge library with a noticeable bounce in our steps. This was good, very good. We were making excellent progress. There was still the tiny matter of persuading the dragon to hand over the chess set before she decided to turn us all into ash and cinders, but I'd worry about that later. It was important to celebrate every win, no matter how small.

Even Gladys seemed thrilled. The closer we got to Hugo's Jeep, the more she hummed. By the time the battered vehicle was in sight, her blade was thrumming and sending tiny vibrations down my leg.

Hugo unlocked the door and jumped in, immediately followed by Hester and Otis who shoved each other to try and get the prime spot on top of the dashboard. As I reached for the passenger door handle, I felt a faint prickle on the back of my neck. I glanced down the street towards the unimpressive building where the ODA office was situated. Gladys was still buzzing loudly by my side.

Hugo opened the window and leaned across. 'Come on, Daisy. If we leave now, we'll get to the first location before sunset.'

'Wait,' I said. 'Just wait a minute.'

His brow furrowed. 'What is it?'

I didn't answer; I was already striding towards the building.

Nobody was outside and there was no sign of the two witches who'd drawn the ward outside the building, though that was hardly surprising. I peered at the windows, unable to spot any movement inside. Then I looked down at the salt ward and my heart missed a beat.

'Is something wrong?' Hugo asked, appearing at my shoulder.

I pointed. His gaze tracked my finger until he also noticed the barely visible break in the line of salt. He sucked in a sharp breath. 'It doesn't mean anything bad has happened. The council witches might have broken their own ward after we left. People must come in and out of this building all the time. I imagine the ward became too obstructive for normal business.'

It was the most likely explanation, but the back of my neck was still prickling and Gladys was still humming. 'True,' I said. 'Plus, council witches don't tend to be particularly powerful so it wouldn't have taken a huge burst of magic to break that ward.'

'Lots of people could have done it,' Hugo agreed. 'Another witch. A sorcerer irritated by bureaucracy. An elf.'

I licked my lips. 'A fiend.'

We exchanged glances. Neither of us needed to say anything else.

I plucked two pristine white spider's silk pills from my pocket and swallowed them, then slid Gladys out of her sheath. Her hilt was shockingly warm to touch.

Hugo and I stepped across the now-useless salt ward and entered the building. At first nothing seemed wrong. Admittedly, no staff were visible but we hadn't seen many people when we'd been there earlier. Everyone was probably at their desks hard at work. Probably.

Hugo motioned towards a closed door on our right. I swallowed, nodded and edged over until I could touch the doorknob with my left hand. I gripped Gladys more tightly in my right hand and rotated the knob. The hinges creaked as the door swung open and I glanced inside.

Three faces looked up. One was in mid-chew, a sandwich raised to his mouth, and another was lying on a small sofa, feet in the air. The third, standing by a shiny tea urn, frowned. 'It's lunch time,' she said. 'If you want an appointment, you'll need to return in an hour.' Then her gaze dipped to my hand. I hastily thrust Gladys behind my back before she got the wrong idea.

'Okay!' I said quickly. 'Sorry!'

'Our apologies,' Hugo added, relief audible in his voice. 'We didn't mean to disturb you.'

I closed the door and turned to him. 'We're too twitchy,' I said. I smiled. 'That's all.'

He smiled back at me, his eyes meeting mine. 'There's nothing wrong with being cautious. We have good reason to be careful.'

Gladys hummed a higher-pitched note. I hushed her and returned her to her sheath.

Another door further down the corridor opened. 'Hey! How did you get past my ward?'

I turned and recognised one of the council witches from earlier. 'It was broken. We only came in to check that everything was alright and—'

'Bullshit! I double-checked it ten minutes ago and it was fine!' The witch curled his hands into fists and strode furiously towards us. 'The two of you need to leave. Immediately!'

We didn't move. 'It was intact ten minutes ago?' Hugo asked. 'You're sure?'

'Of course I'm bloody sure!' the witch yelled, his cheeks turning a mottled shade of purple.

'We need to check on Enger,' I whispered. 'Now.' I started to run.

The witch did his best, moving into the centre of the hallway to block our path. He raised his hand as if he were about to strike me. 'Touch her and you'll regret it,' Hugo snarled.

The witch did the smart thing and backed off.

'Evacuate the building,' I told him. 'Now.'

I sprinted down the narrow corridor towards Enger's office with Hugo matching me step for step. The door to the tiny ODA room was closed. Hugo sprang in front of me and kicked it open. In a stomach-churning flash, I registered Enger's splattered blood dripping down the walls. Across the floor, a vicious, golden-skinned fiend with long black hair was straddling his body. In an instant, all coherent thought fled my mind.

Hugo reacted first, roaring with fury and launching himself at the fiend. I ran into the room after him and drew out Gladys, but the space was so small that it was difficult to wield her.

The fiend was already up and spinning round to face Hugo. With a sickening lurch, I realised that his mouth and his teeth were stained red with Enger's blood. Hugo smacked him hard in the side of his head, following up an instant later with a powerful gust of wind magic that would have knocked any normal creature sideways. Not the fiend, however; he merely laughed and the cold sound echoed around the room.

'Pathetic elf,' he sneered. He swiped at Hugo, his clawed fingers raking across his cheek and drawing blood. Holding Gladys in front of me, I tried to push my way in but there was no space unless I shoved Hugo out of the way.

Hugo's attention was focused on the fiend. He blew out another thrust of air magic that the fiend countered with a jet of fire. Hugo ducked to miss it, narrowly avoiding becoming toast.

I gritted my teeth. Air magic wouldn't cut it against the fiend, and I knew that Hugo was wary of attempting anything else for fear of bringing more harm to Enger. I had to get the ODA officer out of the way.

I hunkered down onto all fours and dropped Gladys so I could reach for Enger's ankles and drag his body to safety. His chest was rising and falling so he was alive – for now, at least.

As my fingers curled around Enger's lower limbs, the fiend charged at Hugo and the loud screech of a fire alarm rent the air. At least that damned witch had finally done the smart thing; everyone in this building had to get out before they were all killed.

I yanked hard on Enger's legs and concentrated on pulling him out of the room. He moaned slightly but the sound was barely audible over the crashing noise of the battle between Hugo and the fiend. I jerked my head up when Hugo cried out in sudden pain and registered the blood streaming down his forehead. I couldn't tell what the fiend had done to him but it didn't matter. He'd hurt Hugo. I couldn't have that.

Red mist descended over my eyes. I shoved Enger to the side so that he was out of the way as much as possible, then I grabbed Gladys again. I stood up, swung her blade at the fiend and sliced into his fleshy upper arm.

He head-butted Hugo and knocked him against the wall before spinning around to face me. 'Another elf,' the fiend sang. 'Another victim for my—' He stopped mid-sentence and his scarlet eyes widened. 'You!'

I slammed the tip of Gladys's blade forward, aiming directly for his heart, but he was too fast. He leapt aside in a blur of motion and I didn't get close. I swung Gladys at him again; yet again, he moved easily out of my way.

'Not this time, bitch,' he snarled. 'Athair will hear of this.' He raised his hand and I saw my death written in his eyes. There was a wall behind me; the doorway was blocked by Enger's unmoving body, and Hugo was slumped in the corner.

The fiend knew his magic was strong enough to kill me and I knew it too. I could feel the enchanted power of the impending attack pulsating through the fiend's skin.

I threw out the best defence I could muster, pushing out water magic in a bid to form a barrier between us, but I was panicking and it was weak. Even under the best of circumstances, the air would have been too dry to magick up an effective water barrier. The fiend would destroy my pathetic creation in a second.

I braced and raised Gladys in front of me as some sort of shield, then waited for his magic to slam into my body. There was a flash of blurry movement from the fiend then I heard glass breaking.

Suddenly everything went quiet.

Unable to move, I stayed where I was for one long second then dropped the thin wall of water. A cascade of liquid crashed onto the floor into a mini-tsunami. I ignored it and dashed to Hugo. His face was coated in blood.

'Hugo! Where are you hurt?' I ran my fingers over his skull and located two small wounds, one near his forehead and another on the back of his scalp. He groaned but managed a small smile. 'It looks worse than it is,' he grunted.

'There's blood everywhere.'

'Head wounds always bleed a lot.' He raised his hand to his forehead and grimaced. 'The damned fiend head-butted me.'

I winced sympathetically.

'Is he gone?'

'He threw himself out of the window,' I said. I leaned across and peered out. There was some shattered glass and a few smears of blood, but no sign of the fiend. We were safe – at least for the time being. Why he'd run, though, was something I couldn't explain.

The witch who'd confronted us in the corridor gasped and

rushed to Enger, who lay half in and half out of the room. I looked into Hugo's eyes and he nodded. I left his side to check on the ODA officer's wounds.

'I've called an ambulance,' the witch said, the words spilling out of his mouth in chunks of anxiety and fear. 'And the police. And the fire brigade.'

'Good,' I told him. 'That's good.' I reached for Arnold Enger. Bite marks on his neck and shoulders were visible through the ripped fabric of his once-pristine white shirt. 'Mr Enger? Are you awake?'

His eyelids fluttered open. The witch leaned over him. 'Arnie?'

'Torture me all you want!' Enger hissed. 'I won't tell you where the lair is.'

'Arnie, it's me. It's Erwin.'

'I won't tell you!' Enger said. 'I won't say a word!'

Two green-suited paramedics jogged down the corridor towards us and I moved back to Hugo's side. I'd only get in their way. Before they reached Enger, Hester and Otis zoomed past them, terror etched on their faces. Their wings were beating furiously and both of them looked ready for a fight. Suddenly I was very glad that they'd stayed away until now.

'Daisy!' Hester shrieked. 'Daisy!'

'I'm fine,' I told them. 'I wasn't hurt.' But I should have been.

I shook the thought away and focused on Hugo. I yanked off my shirt and used it to wipe the worst of the blood from his face and examine the wound on his forehead. He was right – it wasn't as bad as it looked – but that didn't reassure me. 'This is exactly why you should have stayed at home,' I muttered.

'I'm heartened by your concern,' he said softly, his eyes on mine. 'It's good to know you care.'

I glared at him. 'Of course I bloody care.'

The left side of his mouth crooked up into a half-smile.

The paramedics were already hoisting Enger onto a stretcher. 'He's lost a lot of blood,' one of them said grimly. 'We need to get him to a hospital asap.' She nodded at Hugo. 'You should be seen to, as well. You might need stitches.'

Hugo shook his head. 'I'm okay.'

There was bravery in the face of mortal danger and then there was cumbubbling stupidity. 'I'll make sure he goes to the hospital,' I said. I glanced at Hugo, then I dipped my head and kissed him lightly on the lips. 'You have to,' I told him.

He blinked. 'If it means I get another kiss, I'm all for it. But we don't have a lot of time.' He gazed at me. 'You know what I'm talking about.'

I spared another glance at the smashed window. That blasted fiend.

The paramedics disappeared down the corridor with Enger but were immediately replaced by two grim-faced police officers. The fiend might be hot on the trail of the treasure but it appeared that our quest to retrieve it first would be delayed whether we liked it or not.

CHAPTER
TWENTY-FOUR

While Hugo was being stitched up at the hospital, I answered the police officers' questions as best as I could.

'If creatures such as fiends exist, then why haven't we heard of them before?' one of them asked.

'Presumably because they're above your pay grade.' I shrugged. 'I wouldn't feel bad about it. They were above my pay grade as well until recently.'

'We have CCTV footage of the attack.'

Good. 'Then you know I'm not lying about what happened.'

The officer pursed his lips. 'Perhaps. But I'd like to know what you think of this.' He turned his tablet screen towards me.

Hester and Otis perched on my shoulder and peered at it. If they were hoping for cat videos, they were disappointed; instead, the three of us watched silently as footage of my magicked water barrier appeared and my figure became nothing more than a blur.

The image of the fiend remained perfectly clear: his hands were raised and his face was a mask of fury. He looked for all the world as if he were about to strike me down but instead he rolled his eyes in what could only be described as irritation and spun around to jump out of the window.

'The – fiend,' the officer was still struggling with the concept, 'seemed to be about to attack you then changed his mind. Can you explain why?'

It certainly wasn't because I was big and scary and the fiend thought I'd smack his golden arse into hell. 'Maybe he'd run out of time on his parking meter.' I bit my lip, instantly regretting my nonchalant comment. I was feeling nothing remotely like nonchalant.

'I don't know. He's stronger than me in every possible way. The best I could do was slow him down but I could never have killed him – it's doubtful I could even have hurt him. He could have struck me down in an instant and I thought that's what was about to happen. I can't explain why he chose to run away instead.'

I leaned forward, intent on making them understand the gravity of the situation. 'You need to round up the witches you have on your staff and get them to guard Arnold Enger around the clock. The fiend wanted information from him. He didn't get what he needed, so he could well come back. A few powerful witches might be able to banish him out of this realm, but nobody else can stop him. No matter who they are.'

'Mr Enger is in surgery,' the officer said. 'He'll be in no position to talk to anyone for days.'

'He's lucky.'

The policeman sucked air in through his teeth. 'I might say the same about you, Miss Carter.' He wasn't wrong.

~

It was dark by the time we got into the Jeep and started driving. Hugo's skin was paler than normal and he was sporting a few bandages, but thankfully he was mostly unscathed. I drove while he drummed his fingers on the dashboard. Otis and Hester had taken up position by the back window, determined to look out for any fiends following us.

When I turned away from the motorway and onto a series of winding country roads, Hugo finally broke the heavy silence. 'We should talk about the elephant in the room,' he said.

I swallowed hard and nodded. 'I don't know why the fiend seemed to recognise me. If he was capable of taking another form, like Zashtum was, maybe our paths have crossed before without me realising it. And I don't know why he didn't kill me because he could have done. It would only have taken a moment. I saw it in his eyes – I should be dead now and I don't know why I'm not.'

Hugo's jaw tightened and his drumming increased in speed. 'That's not what I'm talking about.'

Oh.

'Who knows why a fiend does or says anything?' he continued. 'We should be grateful that you're fine and leave it at that.'

I adjusted my grip on the steering wheel. A different elephant, then. 'I only took a double dose of spider's silk before we went into that building because it helps me concentrate. It focuses my magic and controls it more effectively. I know it dampens my powers a little, but being able to control what I do is worth it. It's been useful in fights, too. It helps me not to feel pain.'

Now Hugo looked even more annoyed. 'I'm not talking about that either,' he said through gritted teeth.

I was confused. 'Then I don't know what you're talking about. What elephant?'

Hugo muttered something under his breath before turning to me. 'You kissed me. It wasn't a big kiss, and I'm confident you can do better, but you still kissed me of your own free will.

You weren't in withdrawal or hallucinating, you weren't underneath any mistletoe. You kissed me because you wanted to.'

I kept my eyes firmly on the dark road in front of us. I'd barely touched his mouth with mine. 'You were hurt.'

'Not badly.'

'I wanted to prove I cared.'

'Slim, Miriam, Becky and Rizwan care. None of them would have kissed me.'

'They might have.'

'They wouldn't.' Hugo suddenly sounded very smug.

'It was a peck. Nothing more.'

The dimple in his cheek appeared. 'Next time it'll be much, much more.'

'There won't be a next time.'

'Yes, there will.'

I spotted a layby up ahead, pulled the Jeep into it and turned off the engine. He wanted to address the elephant? Fine.

The amusement in Hugo's eyes faded and was replaced by something far more serious, far more intense. 'I know you're afraid to act upon your real feelings because of your addiction,' he said.

'Your best friend died because of spider's silk, Hugo. I'm already halfway there.'

'It won't kill you. I won't let it.'

'You won't have any choice.'

He watched me carefully. 'You owe me a favour.'

I recoiled slightly. 'And you want it to be a sexual favour?' I thought he was better than that – *far* better than that.

'No. Bloody hell! What kind of man do you think I am?'

I shrugged awkwardly.

'Once all this is over,' he said, 'once we have the chess set secure in the British Museum and the fiends have slunk back into whichever holes they usually lurk, you will repay that favour by coming to stay at Pemberville Castle.'

From the rear of the car, Hester piped up, 'Goody!' I turned and scowled at her.

'I'm with Hester,' Otis said. 'That sounds great to me.'

'I will continue to train you in meditation and magic control. Once you've mastered them, we'll work on your addiction. I know a lot about it after what happened with Philip. I can help you.' His eyes met mine. 'We're both stubborn as hell, Daisy. We're both determined.'

While both those things were true, he had to realise he was being far too optimistic. 'You can't cure me. I'm not a damsel in distress who needs a good man like you to save me.'

'I wouldn't dream of thinking that. I'm not going to cure you, I'm going to help you cure yourself. You can't say no, Daisy. You owe me a favour.'

'It'll end in tears.' I wasn't being pessimistic, just realistic.

'It's worth that risk.' For the first time, I spotted something desperate in his eyes. 'Give me three months. You can do that.'

I sighed. 'I don't have much choice, do I?'

'Nope.' His expression lightened. 'When your addiction is out of the way, if you still don't want to act on the attraction between us I'll stop mentioning it.' He leaned in and lowered his voice. 'But we both know that won't happen. You won't be able to stop yourself.'

'Because you're so desirable that I can't possibly say no?'

He smirked. 'Exactly.'

I gave him a long, cool look. 'You will regret this. *If* we make it back from this venture alive, and *if* I can learn to control my magic, and *if* I can wean myself off spider's silk, and *if* I decide that I will act upon whatever this is,' I waved a hand between us, 'then you'll be lost forever in *my* spider's web. Because you're right. I *can* kiss better than that. Once you've tasted me properly, Hugo, I'll ruin you for every woman who comes afterwards.'

Hester sucked in a delighted breath. 'Fighting talk!'

'Go Daisy!' Otis yelled.

Hugo only smiled. 'I can't wait, princess.' He ran his tongue across his lips. 'I can't wait.'

~

Part of me wondered if things would become awkward after our conversation in the car, but strangely I felt more at ease. Hugo seemed happier, too. He was humming to himself the following morning when we broke camp and he looked more relaxed than I'd seen him for a long time. It was as if a valve had been released on the pressure cooker that contained us. The steam had escaped, if only temporarily. That was a good thing.

Given how close the fiend was to our goal, we needed to be in the right frame of mind for success. If Hugo wasn't concerned about the way the fiend had acted towards me, I wouldn't worry about it either. Besides, I could have misunderstood both his words and actions – as Hugo had said, goodness only knew what went through the mind of a fiend.

However, there was one thing the fiend had said that concerned me greatly and I chewed it over as I tidied away my sleeping gear and we checked the map. When we started the trudge towards the first potential lair, I mentioned it to Hugo. 'Prevailing wisdom states that fiends are solitary beasts who dislike each other.'

'I've never heard anything to the contrary,' he agreed, shifting the weight of his backpack until he felt comfortable.

'The fiend yesterday mentioned Athair.' I glanced at him. 'He said *"Athair will hear of this"*.'

Hugo frowned. 'I missed that.'

'To be fair, you'd been knocked on the head a few times and blood was gushing down your face. You're forgiven for not hearing every word.'

Otis flapped over to Hugo and hugged his earlobe. Hester stayed where she was on my shoulder but I felt her stiffen. 'Athair is one of the stronger ones left in Britain,' she said. 'If the fucker we met yesterday wasn't Athair, does that mean that the fiends are working together now?'

'It sounds that way.'

'What if they band together and attack the dragon? What if they hurt her? What if they kill her?' I felt a barrage of tiny thumps on the side of my neck as she punched me. 'Stop meandering, Daisy! You have to run! We have to get to the dragon's lair *now*!'

'The first possible lair is seventeen miles away, Hester, and it's uphill all the way. We need to pace ourselves.'

'But ... but ... but...' she spluttered.

Hugo scratched the stubble on his jaw. 'It's a concern, but we don't have the ability to beat one fiend, let alone several, so nothing's actually changed. We move quickly, find the dragon, warn her about the fiends and save the day.'

He sounded very confident. 'You make it seem easy,' I said resentfully.

'It'll be a piece of cake.' His tone was breezy but when I looked at him, I saw that he was worried.

We had no real defence against the fiends and no real way of attacking them. Our only hope was to find the dragon before they did.

CHAPTER
TWENTY-FIVE

From outside, the lair didn't look much. I crouched behind a boulder and gazed at the dark, narrow opening surrounded by rocky crags, gorse bushes and sparse tufts of grass. Not far below us, a small flock of mountain sheep were grazing contentedly. Nothing suggested danger.

'It seems deserted,' Otis whispered.

I agreed; there was no sign of any dragon prints and there was no indication of any fresh dragon scat. There were charred marks on the rocks, suggesting that they had been damaged by dragon fire once upon a time, but I didn't get the sense that it had happened recently.

'What do you think?' I asked Hugo.

His expression was tight. 'It looks empty, but we need to check inside to be sure. There's an hour to go before the sun sets so we should search before nightfall. Dragons are clever creatures and our purple madame might simply be well-versed at hiding her habitat.'

I nodded. 'We've come this far.' I carefully lowered my backpack and withdrew the old dragon's egg. Then I took another spider's silk pill out of my pocket. When I felt Hugo watching me, I glanced up. 'I—'

'It's okay.'

It didn't look okay. I bit my lip but swallowed the pill anyway – and I followed it up with a second one as a chaser. I was still enjoying the bitter fizz when Hester's patience ran out and she took off from my shoulder, zipping towards the cave.

'Stop!' I hissed. If she heard me, she didn't react.

Otis, eyes wide with alarm, flew after her. Within seconds both of them had been swallowed up by the darkness of the lair. 'Honestly,' I said, 'if dragons, fiends and spider's silk aren't the death of me, those brownies will be.'

'They're small enough to escape notice if our dragon *is* in there,' Hugo said. 'You're not.' He stood up and walked past me. 'I'll go first. Wait here until I give the word.'

As if. 'You're the one who was hurt yesterday,' I said. '*You* wait here.'

'Remember our pact.' He raised his eyebrows meaningfully. 'We treat each other like adults and don't protect each other unnecessarily.'

Damn it.

'Besides, you're the one who gets claustrophobic in tight dark spaces, so, you—' He didn't get to finish his sentence. From beyond the wall of darkness, there was a muffled scream. I stiffened – that sounded like Hester. I spun and sprinted inside. Hugo was right with me.

It was darker than I'd expected. Without pausing, I conjured up a tiny ball of flame to light my path. I knew the entrance was right behind me so there was no rational need to feel the same crushing fear I'd experienced in the depths of Smoo Cave. Unfortunately, my nervous system disagreed: my chest already felt constricted. I swallowed hard, pushing away my terror as best as I could.

'Hester!' I called, my voice shaking. 'Otis!'

From deep within the lair there was another screeching yell. I swore under my breath and turned right towards the direction of the shout. Behind me, Hugo conjured up a fireball of his own. Between his magicked light and my own, the lair's interior was more visible although there wasn't much to see beyond a few old bones and more charred marks on the stone walls.

I doubted we would find our dragon; the air was too stale and we'd have heard her by now if this was her den. But something was in here with us.

The walls were closing in, pressing down upon me, while the shadows cast by the fireballs danced around my feet. I was finding it difficult to breathe normally. 'Hester?' I whispered as my feet came to a stuttering halt. I sucked panicked air into my lungs and hugged the dragon's egg close to my chest. 'Otis?'

My body was shaking, but then I felt Hugo's hand press firmly against my back. He didn't say anything – I didn't need him to. I wasn't alone. My trembling subsided and I nodded at him, grateful for his presence and that he wasn't urging me to leave the lair while he forged ahead.

'There's a tunnel down there.' Hugo pointed to a slope that led away from the entrance. 'The brownies must have gone that way.' I caught a glimpse of his tight expression in the flickering light. 'We can do this. *You* can do this. You're Daisy fucking Carter.'

He was right. I was. I gritted my teeth and plunged down, heading for the tunnel, my feet skidding on the sharp scree and shards of old bones that littered the floor. I slipped and slid several metres, barely registering the old claw marks on the walls. Then I turned a corner and suddenly there was enough natural light streaming down from a metre-wide gap in the roof of the cavern for us to see without the help of the magicked fire.

I caught a quick glimpse of passing clouds and felt the last of the claustrophobic tension leave my body, then I focused on the flitting figures of Otis and Hester. They were zipping from side to side, doing everything they could to stay out of the path of the enormous creature in front of them.

It wasn't a dragon; neither was it a fiend.

Hugo was already moving forward and I sensed the magic gathering in him as he prepared to attack. Now it was my turn to offer a reassuring hand. 'It's alright,' I said. 'I've got this.'

He must have heard something in my voice because he relaxed slightly and turned to me. I smiled, only slightly nervous now, and stepped forward.

'Alright,' Hester shouted. 'If you want a fight, you one-eyed bastard, you've got a fight! We can take you on. We'll pummel you to the ground! We'll make mincemeat out of your flesh! We'll carve out your eyeball and eat it for dessert!'

'Hester, enough of that,' I said mildly.

The brownies turned to me and so did the creature in front of them. He blinked his single eye and tilted his head. 'Hello again,' I said to the Fachan.

I wouldn't say he looked thrilled to see me but he didn't appear particularly upset either. 'Daisy Carter.' He bowed. 'You have returned to me as promised.'

'You know this ... person?' Hugo asked, totally baffled.

I realised I'd never told him the story. 'This is the Fachan – he's the one who gave me Gladys. I met him when I fell in Smoo Cave. He challenged me to a fight, then let me go when he realised that I wasn't a satisfying opponent.'

'You were pathetic,' the Fachan rumbled helpfully.

'Don't call Daisy pathetic!' Otis yelled.

'Yeah,' Hester said. 'We're still going to beat you. I'll take your liver and grind it into dust. Otis will spoon out your brains!'

'I like these two,' the Fachan said. 'They are brave warriors.'

Uh-oh. 'They're not warriors,' I said quickly before he challenged them to a real fight. 'And neither is he.' I nodded to Hugo, who was continuing to stare at the Fachan in genuine fascination.

'I will fight you before I fight them,' the Fachan declared gravely. 'Are you ready?'

Not a chance. 'Definitely not.'

His single bulbous eye narrowed. 'You have brought Gladius Acutissimus Gloriae Et Sanguinis with you. You must be ready to face me.'

I shook my head vigorously. 'No. I'm still a beginner.'

The Fachan sniffed. 'Show me.'

'Can't you take my word for it? I'm not here for you. I had no idea you'd be here.'

He didn't say anything else, only stared. I sighed and passed the dragon's egg to Hugo.

He leaned towards me and whispered. 'Are you sure about this?'

Nope. 'It's not a problem.' I pulled Gladys out of her sheath and began a series of practice swipes, using the techniques Miriam had taught me.

The Fachan watched. 'Pathetic,' he said eventually.

Hester started to open her mouth but I jabbed Gladys towards her. 'Enough from you,' I muttered.

'Even for a high elf your progress is dismal,' the Fachan said.

I noticed Hugo jerk out of the corner of my eye. 'I'm not a high elf.'

'That's what you said last time.'

'It's still true.' I managed a smile. 'We'll get out of your way. You're probably very busy.' I started backing up; it would be wise to get away from the Fachan while we still could. Then, because taking my own advice was something I was still working on, I hesitated. 'Why are you here?' I asked. 'We're a long way from Smoo Cave.'

'It is true. Home is far away.' He bared his teeth. 'But this hunt is worth the travel.'

This time Hester reacted before I could stop her. 'You're hunting dragons?' Her screech echoed around the cavern. 'I will rip your throat out!' She lunged towards him, but fortunately Otis managed to grab the tail of her blouse and hold her back.

The Fachan regarded her mildly. 'I do not hunt dragons.' His lip curled. 'I am not a monster.'

'What *are* you hunting then?' Hugo asked.

There was a faint scuffle in the tunnel behind us and two voices drifted in our direction.

'There's no treasure here.'

'There's no dragon, either – but I can definitely sense something magical. We should check it out to keep Athair sweet.'

A few bone shards skittered towards us. A moment later, two fiends appeared and gaped at us in the dim light.

The Fachan smacked his lips. 'Them,' he said with immense satisfaction. 'I'm hunting them.'

Hester and Otis might have been prepared to battle the Fachan, but the two fiends made them squeak in alarm and spin away. Fear juddered through me, but even so I raised Gladys.

Hugo also reacted immediately, blasting the shocked pair with a heavy burst of air magic that knocked them off their feet. So our magic *could* affect them, even if it was only because they'd been taken unawares.

The Fachan gave Hugo an irritated glare. 'This my hunt, elf. Stay out of it.' He glanced at me. 'You too. You're too pathetic for this sort of fight.'

My ego was more than capable of taking that hit. I relaxed my grip on Gladys's hilt and stepped back. 'Have at it.'

Hugo started to move towards the fiends but I grabbed his arm and shook my head. 'Let the Fachan do this. It's what he wants.'

The Fachan sniffed, dismissing us both. He turned to the fiends, who were struggling to their feet. 'We will do battle now,' he intoned. 'Unsheathe your weapons.'

The fiends exchanged glances. 'Who the fuck is this guy?' the first one asked.

'Not a bloody clue, Horst. But you know who she is, right?' He pointed at me.

'Yes.' Horst's red eyes flashed. 'Baltar was correct.'

'Enough talking!' the Fachan roared.

'Who's Baltar?' Hugo whispered.

I swallowed. 'Maybe he's the fiend we met yesterday.' I didn't understand why all these fiends knew me, but I couldn't exactly question them about it. They were completely occupied by the Fachan who had unsheathed his massive sword and was swinging it around his head in a lethal arc.

'You will regret this,' Horst snarled. He leapt forward, ducked underneath the swinging sword and threw himself at the Fachan. He didn't have a weapon – but I wasn't convinced he needed one with those pointed four-inch talons.

Horst opened his jaws to reveal his sharp yellow teeth and snapped at the Fachan's throat. I drew a sharp breath but the Fachan only laughed and spun his sword in the opposite direction before slicing into Horst's upper arm. Dark blood spurted out, spraying the cavern floor: the Fachan had nicked an artery.

I tightened my grip on Hugo's arm in grim anticipation but, as we watched, Horst's wound sealed itself in mere seconds. 'Shit,' Hugo whispered. Shit, indeed.

The other fiend, whose name we didn't know, was on the move. He paced around the cavern as the Fachan focused on

Horst then he smiled nastily and launched himself at the Fachan's back.

'Look out!' I shouted. 'Behind you!'

I shouldn't have worried; the Fachan was already ducking. He rolled aside and neatly returned to a standing position in the blink of an eye. The same couldn't be said of the fiend whose momentum meant that he couldn't stop his flying attack. He collided with Horst and both of them crashed to the ground in a tangle of patchy golden limbs.

I frowned and peered more closely. Huh. Unlike Zashtum, and presumably Baltar yesterday, these two looked different. Their skin wasn't perfectly smooth and golden and there were several spots on their bodies where a more natural colour was visible. Perhaps they were younger than the others so they were less powerful. The thought filled me with sudden hope.

Then I spotted that the fiend called Horst had pointed ears and I swallowed hard. Once upon a time he'd been an elf; he'd been just like me.

A quick sharp pain flashed through my ear; I yelled and jumped a foot in the air before realising it was Hester. 'This is our chance,' she said. 'We can flee now while they're busy.' She hit my ear again. 'Come on!'

Otis appeared in front of my face, his wings flapping furiously. 'Once we're outside, you can use earth magic to collapse the lair. Half the mountain will land on top of them. Even the fiends will struggle to survive that.'

'No,' I whispered.

Horst was already back on his feet, kicking out at his companion. He spat at the Fachan but this time didn't attempt to rush him. Instead, his lips started to move, his patchy skin bulged in several places and his red eyes glowed. Wary of the Fachan's sword, he was clearly planning to use magic instead.

'Daisy!' Otis hissed.

Hugo looked at me. 'You're worried about the Fachan.'

'I'd have died in Smoo Cave if it wasn't for him. He helped me.' I licked my lips. 'A lot.' He had also wanted to fight me to the death, but I wouldn't hold that against him.

'If there are two fiends here,' Hugo said, 'there might be more at the other locations. I know you don't want to abandon the Fachan, but if the fiends are working together the others might have already found the dragon. We can't waste time!'

Cumbubbling bollocks, he was right. But if the fiends killed the Fachan, they'd come straight for us and we'd never make it to the next lair. We'd also be in danger of leading them directly to the dragon.

The second fiend was on his feet again. The floor of the cavern was starting to rumble as Horst's magic coalesced.

'You have no honour,' the Fachan told him. He took three steps forward and swung his heavy sword at Horst's head. The fiend dodged it with frightening speed, then he spat again. This time there was a loud crackle and the air sparked and fizzed. Bloody hell. Somehow he was drawing on the static energy in the air. That was magic that no elf was capable of.

'Go,' I hissed at Hugo and the brownies. 'Go now! I'll catch up.'

'There is no fucking way I'm leaving you here, Daisy,' Hugo swore.

The air surrounding the Fachan and the fiends was filling with sparks of tiny lightning bolts. 'I swear to God, Hugo, I will catch you up. If the Fachan fails, I'll bring the cavern down. But the fiends are already too powerful and if they get hold of that damned chess set, their strength will be even greater. We cannot allow that to happen.'

'Daisy—' His voice was strained.

'Remember our pact,' I said.

'We're not leaving you!' Otis squeaked.

Several of the smaller sparks looped together and shot towards the Fachan. He raised his sword in the nick of time and the bolt bounced off the blade. But the second fiend was also muttering now, preparing to combine his magic with Horst's.

I gave Hugo a shove. 'You will go. All of you.'

'For fuck's sake.' He grabbed my waist and planted a brief, hard kiss on my lips. 'Don't you dare fucking die.'

I met his blue eyes. 'I won't.' I shoved him again. 'Go.'

Hester's eyes had filled with tears but she understood and she nodded. Otis gulped a farewell as Hugo reached for my fingers and squeezed them. Then the three of them dashed towards the tunnel and vanished, heading out of the lair while I sucked in a breath and turned back to the battle in time to see the Fachan block yet another bolt of lethal lightning.

As ideas went, this probably wasn't one of my better ones.

CHAPTER
TWENTY-SIX

T he dark space was illuminated thanks to the many tiny sparks of electricity as both fiends advanced upon the Fachan. His feelings were clear from his expression: although his single eye glittered with grim intent, his thin lips were curved at the corners. He was enjoying himself. Unfortunately, so were the fiends.

Horst took the right-hand side and the second fiend took the left. My hands slippery with sweat, I watched them exchange quick glances then attack, their faces frozen into identical grinning rictus masks.

Horst narrowly avoided the next swing of the Fachan's sword and bit down hard on the Fachan's upper arm, his sharp teeth latching on. The other fiend matched him on the other arm; now both fiends had their jaws embedded in his flesh.

The Fachan roared and started spinning, his feet moving with such speed that the nasty pair became a blur, with first their feet then their legs rising into the air until I was watching some sort of macabre, bloody spinning machine. The Fachan pirouetted on the spot for several long seconds, determined to shake off both the golden-skinned bastards.

Gladys buzzed with impatience in my slick hands, desperate to join the fray. 'He wants to do this alone,' I muttered to her.

She only buzzed louder and her blade jerked. I hushed her once more; I was prepared to step in at any moment, but the Fachan wouldn't thank me and I knew I wouldn't be much help. Not against two fiends.

Eventually, the Fachan's spinning reached such momentum that Horst was forced to release his toothy grip. He crashed down to the cavern floor. The other fiend had a stronger jaw and his teeth remained entrenched in the Fachan's bicep. I could see rivulets of blood dripping down the fiend's cheeks, although the pain didn't appear to bother the Fachan. He laughed coldly and then, with one heavy swoosh of his sword, slammed it into the fiend's back. I sucked in a breath. I was no expert but it looked to me as if he'd severed his spinal cord.

The fiend collapsed and thudded to the ground. His eyes rolled back into his head and for one optimistic moment I thought he was dead. However Horst, who was already back on his feet, toed his companion and laughed. 'Get up, you stupid bastard.' He looked at the Fachan. 'You must know you can't kill us.'

The Fachan gazed back implacably. 'Perhaps not. But I can make you hurt.' And he drove the tip of his sword into Horst's chest.

Horst screamed and a high-pitched sound of pure pain filled the cavern. He fell to his knees, the sword still embedded in his body. The Fachan allowed himself one small smile, then glanced at me.

'He was correct,' he rumbled. 'I cannot kill these two. But their injuries will take some time to heal. I will leave them here and return to my home, Daisy Carter. If you destroy this cavern, it will take them many weeks to escape from beneath the rubble.' He smacked his lips. 'It will be good.'

He touched Horst with the tip of his pointed leather boot. 'I thought they would be more of a challenge. Perhaps next time I meet them they will have learned more and will provide more entertainment.'

I blinked. He was remarkably matter-of-fact.

'Can't you chop off their heads?' I asked. Everything I'd learned suggested otherwise, but if anyone could ensure the fiends' demise it was the Fachan. Hope springs eternal. 'Burn their bodies? Make absolutely sure they'll never return?'

He shook his head. 'Fiends are not natural creatures. As long as even one scrap of their DNA remains, they will recover – but the more injured they are, the longer it takes.' He shrugged. 'Eventually they always come back.'

As if on cue, Horst moaned. The Fachan sighed, raised his sword and swung it down with incredible force. Alarmed, I took a step backwards and my back collided with the rough cavern wall just as Horst's head was severed from his body. Nausea rose in my throat.

That was when Horst's eyes swivelled upwards. 'You'll pay for this,' he whispered.

The shudder of horror that rippled down my spine was intense but the Fachan didn't appear bothered. He ambled over to the second fiend, who still wasn't moving. Methodically, he started to hack at his body parts, first removing a hand then a foot then an entire leg. I couldn't help myself: I turned to the side and started to heave.

'Have you eaten something that does not agree with you?' the Fachan enquired curiously.

Still retching, I waved weakly at him. Apparently disappointed at my fragile constitution, he pursed his lips and turned back to Horst's body. This time I closed my eyes; I'd already seen more than enough.

Suddenly, from behind me, I heard a whooping war cry

followed by the pounding of feet. I opened my eyes and raised my head to see a third damned fiend sprint out of the tunnel to my left and launch himself at the Fachan. It was Baltar, the one we'd encountered at the Office for Dragon Affairs – and he was blisteringly angry. 'I'm going to get you this time, you one-eyed freak!'

The Fachan straightened up and swung his sword in the nick of time towards his new opponent. As he blocked the attack he said, 'You again. Didn't you learn your lesson the first two times I took you down?'

'Third time lucky,' Baltar snarled and lunged. He was faster than the other two and avoided the sword's thrust. 'I have learnt a great deal since our last encounter.'

So these two had battled before. I hugged Gladys closer and pressed myself against the cavern wall.

'In that case, I look forward to our renewed fight,' the Fachan said.

He started to execute a series of masterful thrusts with his sword, catching Baltar's exposed skin several times, but each time the wound sealed over within seconds. From the watchful look on his face and the way that Baltar avoided the worst of the strokes, I knew he was a far stronger opponent than the other two fiends.

The Fachan stepped forward and swung his sword to the right. For a moment, his left flank was exposed. Baltar spotted it before I did and his face morphed into a delighted snarl. He launched himself towards it, his clawed hands outstretched and raking into the Fachan's flesh. Then, before the Fachan could adjust his aim, Baltar sprang backwards out of reach.

'You were right,' the Fachan told him. 'You have improved.'

Baltar continued to grin.

'But,' the Fachan said with a touch of sadness, 'not enough.'

He swung his sword once more, this time smacking it into the side of the fiend's head and almost decapitating him.

There was blood everywhere; most of it belonged to Baltar but I knew that some was from the Fachan. The wound on his side was seeping, though it didn't seem to slow him down.

Baltar wiped his eyes, presumably to clear his vision, then he roared and leapt around the Fachan towards his exposed back. The Fachan was ready. He propelled himself upwards, jumping off the ground with such lithe grace that my jaw dropped. He was tall and gangly, but in that instant he looked like a professional dancer. He performed a perfect mid-air somersault, landed in front of Baltar on his tiptoes and head-butted him before following up with a sword slash that cut through the fiend's upper torso.

Baltar stared in wide-eyed shock – and no small amount of hatred – then pitched forward onto the ground with a thud. Just like that, it was over.

I peeled away from the cavern wall and gazed down at the fiend's sprawled body. 'Well done,' I said shakily.

'It was an easy fight,' the Fachan responded dismissively. He didn't even appear winded. 'Fiends are strong but in the end I am always stronger.' He wiped his blade on his thighs and smiled at me. 'That was fun.'

He touched the deep cut on his side, pursed his lips and eyed me. 'Are you sure you do not wish to battle me at this time? I find I am in the mood for more sport and I am now handicapped. You will have a slight advantage.'

Emphasis on the word *slight*. I managed to stop myself snorting. 'Another time,' I said, praying that I would never, ever, have to face the Fachan in combat. Not only did I like him, I was certain that however hard skilled I became with a sword he'd skewer me in seconds every time.

He rolled his massive shoulders in a shrug. 'It is unusual for the fiends to work together like this, or to be near to each other. I have never seen it before. They are normally alone.'

'I can explain that,' I said. 'They've probably banded together because one of the thirteen mythical treasures has been located. They're trying to get hold of it to drain its magic for themselves.'

For the first time I saw a flicker of worry on his face. 'That would not be a good thing.'

'No,' I agreed. 'But with three of them out for the count, we can get it to safety before any more appear.'

'Make sure you do, Daisy Carter. You should not underestimate the fiends' capabilities.'

'I won't.' I licked my lips. 'Have you met the one called Athair?'

The Fachan stiffened. 'Athair is involved?'

'I heard the name mentioned by him.' I nodded at Baltar's unmoving body.

'If you encounter Athair, you should run,' the Fachan said. 'That one is unstoppable. It has been many decades since he and I fought. He is strong; if we met again, I do not know if I could beat him.'

Shit: that was quite the pronouncement given he'd just despatched three fiends in quick succession. 'Okay,' I said. I crossed my fingers for luck. Fortunately, running was something I could do.

The Fachan smiled suddenly. 'It was good to see you again, Daisy Carter. Until next time, I bid you adieu. I shall return to my home via the underground passages that run the length of the country. I suspect you will prefer the open air.'

He suspected right. I smiled at him – but as I did so, out of the corner of my eye I saw Baltar's hand twitch.

I reacted quickly – but not quite quickly enough. Baltar was not as wounded as he appeared. He withdrew a small dagger from beneath the folds of his trousers and at the same time rose upwards with such speed that I knew he'd simply been biding his time and waiting for the right moment.

He knew exactly which spot to aim for.

I shouted a warning at the exact moment that the dagger pierced the Fachan's skin in the same spot as his existing wound. Baltar followed it up with a walloping blow to the side of the Fachan's head and he staggered backwards, fell to one knee and dropped his sword.

Panic overtook rational thought as Baltar cackled and raised his other hand, which held another sharp dagger. As the Fachan lifted his hands to block the blow, I sucked in a sharp breath and launched myself at Baltar's back. As I screamed, I raised Gladys and drove her tip forward. It wasn't elegant and I didn't know what I was doing. The meagre training I'd had with Miriam had fled from my mind and I acted out of nothing more than instinct.

Baltar turned, his eyes widening. He clearly hadn't expected that I would get involved. He prepared to block me but my lack of training confused him. He probably thought I'd throw a series of carefully timed lunges but I didn't – I simply slammed Gladys forward and threw her at him with a howl of rage.

She was more aerodynamic than I'd realised. She left my hand and spiralled straight ahead until her tip slammed into Baltar's throat. He blinked once in astonishment then he keeled over backwards, landing first on top of the Fachan then slipping to the ground with a dull thud.

Horst's disembodied head scowled. 'Baltar?'

I ignored him and vaulted towards the Fachan. Baltar's dagger remained deep in his flesh, and bloody ripped skin surrounded the wound. The Fachan gasped and stared up at me. 'This is ... unexpected.' He raised his hand. 'Help me up.'

'I'm not sure that's a good idea.'

'Help me!' he ordered, steel in his voice.

Okay, okay. I swallowed and did as he asked. It was an effort to get him back on his feet and he staggered several times, almost knocking me over. Eventually, however, he was upright. He grimaced and touched the dagger embedded in his body. Before I could protest, he yanked it out. Cumbubbling bollocks. Another untimely surge of nausea attacked my weak body.

'Well done, fiend,' the Fachan muttered. 'You got me.' He glanced down at Baltar then his expression transformed from pain to shock.

Horst's head was still talking. 'Baltar? Are you alright?'

From somewhere in a dark corner where the other fiend's body parts lay, a second voice drifted across. 'What's wrong? What's happened?'

Horst was starting to sound panicky. 'Baltar? Baltar!'

I frowned and looked down at the fallen fiend's face. His eyes were open and his face was slack; frankly, he looked dead. I waited a beat, half expecting him to rise up and attack again. When he didn't move, I reached forward and yanked Gladys out of his throat. He didn't blink; he didn't even twitch.

The Fachan gave me a long look. Clutching the wound in his side, he knelt down by Baltar and his long pale fingers touched the fiend's golden skin. I kept Gladys at the ready; the fiend wouldn't surprise me again.

After several seconds, the Fachan rose slowly. He was clearly in a lot of pain but he was doing his best not to let his wound get the better of him. 'Tell me,' he said. 'Tell me what you did.'

I wrinkled my nose. 'What do you mean? I threw Gladys at him. That's all.'

'Did you use magic also?'

No, though I probably should have done. I hadn't really been thinking straight. 'No.'

The Fachan reached across and poked me. I jerked away. 'What are you doing?'

'What *are* you?'

I stared at him.

'The fiend is dead,' the Fachan said.

My lip curled. 'Yeah, yeah.'

'Check for yourself.'

I peered again at Baltar. Sure, he looked dead, but fiends didn't die.

Horst's voice rose. '*She* killed him? That bitch killed Baltar?' He sounded angry. But he didn't sound surprised.

I flicked a look at his decapitated head which still lay several metres away. His patchy golden skin was very pale – I supposed that was to be expected, given his condition. But the fear in his eyes surprised me. I raised Gladys and stared down the length of her blade. So fiends *could* be killed.

'Gladius Acutissimus Gloriae Et Sanguinis. Who would have thought it?' I looked at the Fachan. 'This was a powerful gift you gave me.'

He didn't say anything, just continued to look at me. Gladys hummed happily.

The ground beneath my feet started to tremble, then the tremble evolved into a shake. Several pieces of rock broke off from the cavern walls around us. 'Is this you?' I growled at the Fachan.

'No.' He pointed down at Horst. 'The fiend is doing this.'

He was right. Horst's eyes were closed and his mouth was moving as he whispered words that would invoke earth magic. I reached for him to try and stop him somehow, but before my fingers could so much as brush his hair there was a powerful jolt and I was thrown sideways.

This time it was the Fachan helping me up. 'You must leave,' he told me. 'Now. The cavern is going to collapse.'

More rocks were breaking away from the walls and tumbling down. There was a thunderous bang and a loud crack appeared above us, starting from the hole that displayed a glimmer of the outside world and leading right across the roof.

'I'm not abandoning you here,' I protested.

He scowled as if he were mortally offended by the suggestion that he needed my help. 'My wounds will heal. There are many underground passages leading from here that will allow me to return to my home in the north. It will take me many days but I will manage on my own. If we are to survive, we must both leave now.'

I gazed into his one massive eye to try and ascertain the truth. Eventually I nodded. 'Alright,' I said. 'Alright.'

'Go now, Daisy Carter. We shall do battle together another day.'

I frowned, but the Fachan had already turned towards the back of the cavern. I waited a beat before looking again at Horst. Gladys had killed Baltar; perhaps she could do the same to Horst. It would be better for us all if he and his fiendish companion joined Baltar in hell.

Fortunately for him, there was no time. The ground moved again and more rocks started to rumble. I had seconds to get out of there with my life intact.

I pulled a face. And then I ran.

CHAPTER
TWENTY-SEVEN

I sprinted out of the old dragon's lair as if the Wild Hunt itself were after me. The crescendo of collapsing rock spurred me on and I pumped my short legs for all they were worth. By the time I threw myself out into the fresh night air my lungs were burning and searing pain was jolting through every muscle, but I didn't stop and I didn't look back. I kept going until I was absolutely certain that I was a safe distance away.

I ended up halfway down the hill that led to the lair, flung myself behind a boulder covered in damp moss and only then did I raise my head to survey the damage.

Initially, it didn't look too bad. The lair wasn't at the summit of this hill – it was barely three-quarters of the way up, with an entrance that had been concealed from view until you were right beside it. When I looked for it now, there was nothing but a cloud of dust. The ground beneath me continued to shake but the scene above didn't appear to be disastrous.

Then the clouds shifted and the almost-full moon shone its glory down on the hillside as the dust cleared. Bloody hell: it looked like some sort of gigantic rock-eating monster had wandered by and taken a massive bite out of the hillside.

I thought of the damaged fiends trapped beneath the weight of all that stone and couldn't muster up even a trace of sympathy for them. Horst was the one who'd started the earth magic that had made the lair collapse on top of him and his buddy. He'd clearly decided that being buried by half a mountain was preferable to the lethal risk that Gladys presented.

If the Fachan was right – and I had no reason to think he wasn't – sooner or later the pair of them would find a way to reform their bodies and scrabble out, but I reckoned it would take weeks, if not months, for that to happen. That meant we were four fiends down out of nine, with both Zashtum and Baltar gone for good.

'Let that serve as a warning to the rest of you,' I said aloud. 'Mess with me and you'll suffer.' Not that I could take any real credit for anything that had happened, but still: I'd been a part of every takedown, even if only in a small way.

I touched Gladys's hilt. 'Thank you,' I murmured. 'You're the best sentient sword a girl could wish for.'

This time, Gladys didn't reply.

I gazed at the devastation for a long minute then straightened up. The noise of the cavern's collapse had probably echoed across these hills so there was no doubt that Hugo and the brownies would have heard it. It was time to catch up with them and show them I was safe.

I orientated myself and set off at a quick march in the direction of the second lair. If I moved quickly and didn't sleep, I could join them by morning.

There wasn't a clear path and I had to pause regularly to check my bearings. I also had to move more slowly than I'd have liked because the last thing I needed was to twist an ankle by placing my foot in the wrong spot.

FIENDISH DELIGHTS

At one point, as my eyelids grew heavy and my progress was painfully slow, I mistook the ghostly shapes of distant sheep for potential attackers. The surge of anxious adrenaline was more than enough to startle me awake and encourage my tired legs to keep going. All the same, by the time the first streaks of daylight started to appear, I was exhausted. A triple espresso would have been fabulous. It was fortunate that I had something better.

I delved into my pocket and located my stash of spider's silk. There was enough to last me at least ten more days. I swallowed one pill and, when my limbs still felt sluggish, I took another one. Then I shrugged. Needs must. I dropped a third pill into my mouth. That ought to do it.

I'd been taking spider's silk for long enough to know exactly what to expect, and I'd taken a higher dosage than this on a handful of occasions when the situation had merited it. Consequently I wasn't surprised when the bitter fizz made my tongue numb, or when I felt the swirl of magic inside me become more muted – but the sudden palpitations and the sweating were a shock.

I took three steps, thought better of it and sat down suddenly on a patch of wet grass. There was an odd high-pitched ringing in my ears, as if I'd spent most of the night in the mosh pit at a head-bangers' rock concert. But it wasn't all bad: the colours of the damp landscape sprang to life, sharpening in a bizarre fashion that reminded me of Dorothy stepping into Oz for the first time. It was extraordinary.

I blinked several times and rubbed my eyes but the effect didn't diminish.

'Well, that's weird,' I whispered to myself. I touched my chest; my heart rate was still too fast, but as long as it was still beating I couldn't complain too much. I shoved the tip of my index fingers into my ears and wiggled them around. The tinnitus became even more screechy before thankfully subsiding to a more comfortable level.

I stayed where I was for a good five minutes, nervous that hallucinations might start kicking in or that I'd keel over if I tried to stand up. When my strange symptoms neither increased nor decreased, I rose shakily to my feet. I was still alive and I was now wide awake, but I knew deep down that the edges of my mortality were starting to curl towards me like a piece of slowly smouldering parchment.

There was nothing I could do about it right now. Taking three doses of spider's silk had been necessary to keep me on my feet so I could catch up with Hugo, Hester and Otis. I had always known there would come a day when the balance of the positive effects of the drug and the damage to my health would tip out of my favour. I'd hoped I'd have longer. Hugo's plan to help me once all this was over might work, but I doubted it. I suspected that he doubted it would help, too.

In any case, I had more immediate goals. Now that it was daylight, I could move faster. I reckoned there were only another three miles or so to the next old dragon's lair, so I had to be gaining on my companions. They might even have already found a grumpy purple dragon and an ancient magical chess set. Fingers crossed.

I stopped worrying and let my feet quick march. Golden success, here we come. Before long I was nimbly traversing the landscape in a way that a Welsh mountain goat would have admired. I hadn't completely succumbed to the spider's silk, though, because I stopped myself from bleating in delight as I ran. I decided I'd save that for later.

My heart rate was normal by the time I reached the summit of the next hill and looked down upon a patchwork of pretty landscape. If I turned to my right, I could see the ruins of Strata Florida abbey nestled in the valley far below. To my left was the second dragon's lair and, although I couldn't see it, I knew it wasn't far. It was cold but the sky was clear and there was only a light wind; it was chilly but it proved incredibly helpful when two familiar voices drifted across on it.

'We should stay here until he comes back, Hes.'

'No, that's a stupid idea. We can't see anything, and I'm fed up with being left behind. Let's go this way. We don't have to go far. We can come back quickly.'

Something eased in my chest. I pushed myself onto my toes and called out, 'Hester? Otis?' When I squinted in the direction of their voices, I finally spotted the pair of them hovering about a hundred metres away. They saw me at the same time and gave identical screeches of joy before zooming straight for me.

'Daisy!' Otis threw himself at my face, colliding with my cheek and giving me a wet smacker before peeling away and kissing my nose. 'You're safe!'

'Of course she's safe,' Hester said. 'Daisy wouldn't let herself get killed without us.' She burrowed into the curve of my neck and sighed happily. 'There was a very loud bang,' she said. 'Did you collapse the cavern?'

'Not me. It was one of the fiends.'

Suddenly anxious, Otis jerked backwards. 'Where is he? Is he still after you?'

'He buried himself and his friend.'

His face went slack with astonishment. 'Why?'

'It's a long story. I'll tell you later.' I glanced around. 'Where's Hugo?'

'There was an odd noise and he went to investigate it,' Otis said. 'He told us to wait for him to come back.'

I stiffened; there might be more fiends out there. 'What sort of noise?'

'Humming,' Hester said.

Otis objected, 'It was more of a whistle than a hum. It was probably the wind.'

'It wasn't the wind, you nincompoop!'

I gritted my teeth. I needed them to focus. 'When?' I asked. 'When did he leave?'

Hester abandoned my neck and flew upwards to join her brother. She placed both her hands on her hips. 'Oh, I see. You're worried about Hugo but you weren't worried about us? So much for loyalty!'

'Hester,' I said, doing my best not to panic, 'you're here. You're both fine. Hugo is missing.' I looked around but I couldn't see any sign of him. 'Which way did he go?'

At least Otis understood. He pointed behind him. 'He disappeared around that corner. You see those trees?'

I nodded. That wasn't far – but my concern didn't dissipate.

'I'm sure he's okay, Daisy. He's very capable,' Otis tried to reassure me.

'Why didn't you go with him?'

The brownies exchanged awkward glances. 'He was getting a bit annoyed,' Otis admitted. I waited. 'At us,' he muttered.

Oh. Their incessant bickering could be vexing. I'd long since learned to block them out when they started sniping at each other, but I could understand why Hugo would have wanted a break from them.

'He was already in a bad mood because of leaving you behind,' Hester said. 'He got grumpier when we heard that huge bang last night. He wanted to go back and rescue you.'

'But mostly,' Otis said, 'he was irritated by Hester when she kept saying that the dragon liked her best.'

'No! He was irritated by *you* when you kept saying that the dragon wouldn't have sneezed all over me if she liked me.'

'It's true. She could have sneezed over Daisy. She chose to sneeze over you. Ergo—'

I interrupted him. 'Ergo, let's go find Hugo.'

Hester opened her mouth but I wagged my finger at her. Thankfully, she thought better of speaking.

With both brownies flapping beside me, I set off towards the small copse of fir trees that Otis had pointed out. I couldn't hear any whistling or humming, but I couldn't hear Hugo either and I certainly couldn't see him. My anxiety ratcheted up with every step, even though I kept telling myself that he was powerful enough to look after himself.

We'd almost reached the trees when there was a rustle. I slowed and my stomach clenched. A moment later Hugo emerged, striding lazily from beneath the branches. When he caught sight of me, his face lit up. 'Daisy! There you are!'

I probably should have concealed my concern, but I was so relieved to see him that I dashed forward and gave him a tight hug. Hugo's arms instantly went around me and he squeezed my body.

'That's quite some welcome,' he murmured in my ear. His arms tightened and, for a moment, I wasn't sure he'd ever let me go. 'Are you alright?'

'I'm fine,' I said, extricating myself from his embrace. I scratched the back of my neck and squinted at him. 'Where the hell have you been?'

'Call of nature.' He grinned awkwardly.

'And the humming?' Hester asked.

'It was whistling!' Otis said.

A tiny frown marred Hugo's forehead. 'That was nothing. Just the wind.'

Otis smiled smugly. 'Told you.' Hester rolled her eyes.

Hugo paid them no attention. Instead his gaze remained focused on me. 'What happened? Did you deal with the fiends?'

'The Fachan mostly took care of them. We won't see them again for a long time. The one from yesterday showed up as well.' I licked my lips. 'He's, uh, dead now.'

Hugo rocked back on his heels. 'Dead? Properly dead?'

'Uh-huh.'

'You're sure?'

'Uh-huh,' I repeated. I bit my lip. 'It's as much of a surprise to me as it was to him. I'll tell you all about it later.'

'I can't wait to hear the full story,' he murmured. He hooked his arm around mine and my skin twitched in response. 'It's really good to see you again.'

'Are you going to kiss now?' Otis asked.

Hugo's body stiffened.

'Because,' Hester said, 'we're very close to the second lair and we ought to go there first. We've delayed long enough.' She raised her tiny eyebrows. 'I want to see my dragon!'

I moved away from Hugo and nodded. 'Yes, let's deal with the dragon first and worry about everything else later.'

I glanced at the trees. They were planted close together and it was difficult to see anything beyond shifting dark shadows and densely packed, spindly branches. 'You've still got the dragon's egg?' I asked Hugo.

He patted his backpack. 'I have.'

I smiled brightly. 'Then let's go.'

CHAPTER
TWENTY-EIGHT

I held back so that Hugo could take the lead then I motioned towards both brownies. They could squeeze into my pockets for the last of the journey. Hester wrinkled her nose. 'We've been through this. It reeks in there, Daisy.'

I hardened my gaze. 'Just get in. I want to know where you are at all times until we've seen the next lair for ourselves.'

Otis was perturbed by my tone. 'Daisy—'

'Get in.'

He flinched then he did as he was told. Hester shook her head.

'I'm the one in charge here,' I told her. 'You're beholden to me. Do what I fucking say.'

She stared. 'How much spider's silk have you taken today?' she whispered.

Hugo's head whipped around and his blue eyes narrowed. I refused to look at him. 'Move it, Hester,' I growled.

She sniffed and flew down, holding herself stiffly. When she slid inside my pocket, she continued to indicate her unhappiness by jabbing me repeatedly through the fabric. I ignored her and waved at Hugo to keep going. He watched me for another moment before turning around to continue walking. I sucked in a breath and followed about a metre or so behind him.

We picked our way upwards, cresting first one hill then another. A few icy raindrops had started to fall and the wind had picked up, gusting in my face and making it difficult to move quickly. It didn't seem to bother Hugo and several times he extended the distance between us with his long-legged stride. Each time I doubled my pace, determined not to let him get too far ahead.

When I spotted the charred remains of a bush and the long scratches in the ground to my right, I forced myself to move faster. That became imperative when the faint reek of manure tickled my nostrils, because it wasn't a smell caused by sheep or goats. I couldn't suppress my shiver. We'd found the dragon lair. 'Hugo!' I hissed.

He didn't react; he simply kept ploughing ahead. I tried again. 'Hugo!' He still didn't stop. I ground my teeth. 'Hugo, you cumbubbling arse!'

He came to a stuttering halt and turned his head. I waved at him urgently. 'Slow down,' I said. 'This is the right place. We need to be careful now.'

He gave a sharp nod and I scurried forward until we were abreast. 'I think you're right,' he told me in a low voice. 'You see that spot ahead? That dark shape close to the clump of rocks?'

I peered ahead. To be honest, I couldn't see much of anything beyond grey scree and muddy ground but I nodded anyway.

'I think that's the entrance to the lair,' he whispered. 'It looks big enough and there are claw marks in front of it.'

I tried harder. Nope: I still couldn't see anything - but I still pretended that I knew exactly where he was referring to. 'Do you think she's inside there right now?' I asked.

'Possibly. Dragons are nocturnal so she's probably sleeping.

We'll have to tread very carefully. If she feels threatened, she's liable to roast us alive.'

I jerked slightly then nodded. 'Let's get a bit closer, call out and see if we can wake her up,' I suggested. 'Entering her lair unannounced while she's snoozing would be a very bad idea.'

Hugo nodded agreement and we crept forward. After about thirty metres, I finally saw the lair's entrance. Hugo was right: that had to be the spot. 'There's not much shelter here,' I said. 'It's open ground between this slope and the lair. We could do with a barrier if she decides to use her fire on us.'

'Good point.'

'Maybe we could use a few blasts of earth magic and build a barricade here. It won't shield us if she goes in for a full attack, but it might buy us a few precious seconds if we need them.'

Hugo toed the ground. 'There's a slight dip here. This would be a good spot.' He squared his shoulders as he gathered his powers then with perfect precision tossed out several low-key shots of magic to twist and manipulate the ground.

I watched his face for several seconds then I matched his efforts. It wasn't easy to control each magical burst, even with all the spider's silk coursing through my system, but I remembered everything Hugo had taught me about using a gentle touch.

Before too long our combined efforts had forced a metre-high barrier into existence. It wouldn't hold for long and I sincerely hoped it wouldn't be necessary, but it was a sensible precaution.

Hester's muffled voice drifted up from my pocket. 'What's going on? Is there a dragon out there? Can I come out?'

'No,' I snapped. Hugo looked at me. 'You know what they're like,' I muttered. 'They'll only annoy the dragon and cause more problems than we can handle.'

'Oy!' Hester yelled.

'I won't cause problems,' Otis added from the other pocket.

I ignored them and looked at Hugo. 'Let's do this.'

He nodded grimly. 'Let's hope it works.'

I chewed on the inside of my cheek. Yep. I started in a low voice. 'Hello?'

Hugo joined in. 'We won't come inside unless you invite us,' he called out. 'But we'd really like to talk to you.'

I spoke more loudly. 'We've met already. Down in the old graveyard? Before Christmas?'

Hugo leaned in to me. 'Do dragons know what Christmas is?'

I shrugged. There was a sudden deep rumble from beyond the dark hole that led to the lair. I froze. 'Of course I know what fucking Christmas is,' a distinctly Welsh voice snapped.

A belch of white smoke was ejected from the lair and I grabbed Hugo's arm without thinking. 'Don't worry,' he whispered. 'We've got this.' At least one of us was confident.

'Give me the egg,' I said to him. 'I was starting to establish a rapport with the dragon the first time we met. It makes sense for me to take the lead from here.'

Hugo turned his head away. 'No, I've got this. It'll be fine.' He stepped out from behind our makeshift magicked barrier. 'Stay there.'

Of course I ignored him. As the dragon's purple snout inched out of her lair, I joined him. His jaw tightened. 'I told you to stay over there.' Each word vibrated with anger.

'Since when have I ever done what you told me to?' I demanded. Hugo didn't answer. I hadn't really expected him to.

There was a second belch of smoke before the dragon's head emerged. She blinked at us lazily, as if she were completely unperturbed by our visit, but I sensed that she was a coiled spring more than ready to unleash her very worst if we made a single wrong move.

Despite the danger, I still felt awe. She'd been wondrous to behold in the graveyard but that had been night time; now, with daylight glinting off her shimmering purple and green scales, her beauty was extraordinary. 'Wow,' I whispered. I couldn't help myself.

The dragon inclined her head an inch in acknowledgment then padded out and revealed her whole body.

Hester, unable to contain her giddy excitement any longer, threw herself out of my pocket. 'Hi!' She zoomed straight for the dragon, ignoring my lurch as I tried to restrain her. 'I'm so pleased we could meet again! I'm Hester. It's a real honour to be here.' She curtsied several times in mid-air while the dragon regarded her curiously.

'You are a very strange little creature.'

Hester beamed. 'Thank you, Your Highness!'

The dragon rumbled, 'You may call me Aine.'

Hester hugged herself in delight. 'Hi, Aine!' She reached out to touch the dragon's nostril then, apparently remembering what had happened last time, thought better of it and withdrew her hand.

Aine's expression gave nothing away but she wasn't breathing liquid fire on us and I took that as a positive. All the same, it made sense to get to the point of our visit before we outstayed our welcome.

I stepped forward, ignoring Hugo's sharp intake of breath and hissed warning. 'Thanks for not killing us,' I said.

The dragon's slitted eyes turned to me. 'Yet.'

I acknowledged the warning with a nod. 'I apologise for intruding upon your home.'

'Then why are you here, elf?'

Hugo cleared his throat. 'You have something that belongs to us.'

I winced; I wouldn't have chosen those words.

Aine's massive nostrils flared. 'Something that belongs to *you?*' Her raspy Welsh voice dripped with disdain.

'What he means,' I said quickly, 'is that we'd really like to take back the chess set we found in the graveyard.'

Her eyes narrowed. 'It is not yours to take, no matter what you claim.'

'I'm sure you know there's great power contained within it.'

Aine huffed. 'I know more about it than you, elf.'

I swallowed hard. 'In that case, you know what will happen if a fiend gets their hands on it.' I lifted my chin. 'I'm assuming you know what fiends are.' I certainly hoped she did; I already had enough explaining to do.

She didn't blink. 'I am aware of fiends.'

That was good. 'They know about the chess set and they're coming for it. If you give it to us, we can keep it safe and stop them getting hold of it.'

'You think you can do better against a fiend than I can?' Aine enquired in undisguised disbelief.

'No. But the British Museum has—'

I didn't get the chance to finish my sentence. Aine lifted her head and let out a tremendous roar. The hairs on the back of my neck rose. Hester, who had continued to hover a metre or so in front of the dragon's snout, was sent tumbling backwards through the air.

'The British Museum?' Aine's body vibrated with fury. 'Thieving bastards.'

Uh-oh. I could already see licks of flame around her jaw. Before she decided that the mere mention of the museum was enough to incinerate us, I jumped in front of her. 'They're better than they used to be, I promise. I know they have a reputation for taking things—'

'Stealing! Not taking!' Aine roared.

I nodded quickly; to be fair, she had a good point. 'You're

right – but they don't do that sort of thing any more. They've learned.' At least I hoped they had; I didn't actually know how the British Museum was run these days. All I did know was that they were probably the only people in this country who could safeguard the magical chess set.

Aine wasn't even remotely mollified. 'Why would I trust you?' She lowered her head until her massive fangs were less than a metre from my head. Her breath clouded my face and I could feel the heat of her banked fire, but I held my ground. I had to.

'Daisy—'

I didn't turn to look at Hugo. 'Take it out,' I instructed. I met Aine's stare head-on. 'We have something for you. We suggest a fair exchange of items.'

Hugo joined me and rummaged in his backpack. I remained tense, only relaxing slightly when he finally extricated the ancient egg and unwrapped it. 'Here,' he said, with a distinct lack of ceremony. 'You give us the chess set. We give you this egg.'

It was impossible to read Aine's expression because dragons didn't give a lot away. She looked from the egg to me and back again before her jaws opened wide and I was confronted with her cavernous dark mouth. 'Or,' she said, 'I set you all alight and take the egg anyway. That's a far better idea.'

At least she was interested in the egg. That was a start. 'Sure,' I said, 'that would work for you. But it won't be any use when a fiend shows up.'

Hugo nodded as he gently stroked the smooth edge of the old egg with his long, tanned fingers. 'You're no match for a fiend, Aine. Their powers are far beyond yours.'

I didn't look at him. Out of the corner of my eye, I saw a small shape buzz past. Hester. I curled my hands into fists. That damned brownie.

She flew up and landed on the tip of Aine's snout. 'I understand that you don't want to negotiate,' Hester squeaked. 'Daisy here is only a stupid elf. She's not even a high elf. And she's lousy at life.'

For fuck's sake.

'But,' she continued, 'she's a good person and she's doing this for the right reasons. So's Hugo. You can trust them – and it's not like you can play chess anyway. The pieces are too small for you. Giving us the set will protect you from the fiends. You're the last remaining female dragon in Britain and all we want is to keep you safe and prevent any fiend from gaining more power.' She knelt down. 'If it will help sway your mind, I will remain here as your servant from now on.'

Otis popped his head out of my pocket. 'And me! I'll stay too!'

I understood that Hester was awed by Aine, but the last thing I wanted was for her to sacrifice herself. 'No! You can't do that!'

Everyone looked at me and I pulled a face. 'I mean, not unless you'd prefer to stay with Aine. But you can't give yourself up like that, Hester. Neither can you, Otis. You're my people.'

Hugo shrugged. 'They volunteered. And you said it yourself – they're pretty annoying.'

I still didn't look at him. 'No, the brownies are not part of the deal. If they want to stay once all this is over that's a different matter, but they're not part of this negotiation. We don't barter with lives.'

Aine blinked slowly before fixing on Hester, her slitted eyes crossing as she focused on her. 'You said she was lousy at life.'

Hester bobbed her head. 'Oh yes. But she's still a nice person.'

'Hmmph.' The dragon closed her jaws and shook her head

gently, making Hester slide off her snout. 'Wait here.' She turned and disappeared into her dark lair.

'I think it worked,' Hugo breathed. 'She's going to give us the chess set.' His hand reached for mine. As soon as our palms touched, my skin tingled.

'It looks that way.' A smile lit my face. 'Put the egg down there, by the mouth of the lair. Let's show her that we can be honourable and stick to our word.'

'Good idea.' He released my hand and crouched, placing the egg on a patch of bare ground.

'Perfect,' I called. 'You should come back here now. You don't want to spook her when she returns.' My smile widened. 'We've almost done it, Hugo. We've almost got the chess set.'

He started back to me, his blue eyes glittering. 'We make a great team, darling.'

'We're amazing,' I agreed. I opened my arms, indicating that I'd like a hug. He grinned and drew closer.

That was when I dropped my right arm, pulled out Gladys in one swift, terrified movement – and stabbed him.

CHAPTER
TWENTY-NINE

He reacted fast, registering my attack in enough time to half-spin so that Gladys's blade slid into the flesh of his left arm rather than his heart. Her hilt vibrated in my hand as Hester screamed in horror.

Otis threw himself out of my pocket. 'Daisy!' he shrieked. 'What the fuck have you done?'

Hugo's body turned to me and he bared his teeth in a snarl, his handsome face transforming into a vicious, ugly mask. Next he raised his right hand and walloped me on the side of my head. I was sent reeling backwards but I didn't let go of Gladys. I was still ready to fight.

'Stop it! Stop it!' Hester threw herself into the air between us.

I shook my head to clear my vision. 'Get out of the way, Hester.'

'Yeah, Hester,' he sneered. 'Get out of the fucking way.' He touched the wound on his arm and his fingers came away bloody. With slow, deliberate movements, he raised his hand to his mouth and sucked the blood away. 'Mmm,' he said. 'Tasty.' He grinned – and his body started to transform.

Hester and Otis gave simultaneous gasps of horror. I gripped Gladys's hilt with both hands and advanced as his limbs writhed, his skin bulged and his smooth skin transformed into a gleaming gold colour.

'Hugo's a fiend!' Hester yelled. 'Hugo's a fucking fiend!'

I waved her out of the way and advanced on him. 'That's not Hugo,' I bit out. I swiped the blade, aiming for his exposed throat.

He batted away my thrust easily, straightened up and splayed his arms out wide before executing a mock bow. 'It was a good performance though, right?' He smirked.

My words were strained, hissed out from between my teeth. 'Is he dead? Did you kill him?'

'What do you think?'

Agonising pain stabbed at the centre of my chest and my knees almost gave way, but somehow I stayed upright. 'I will destroy you,' I whispered.

'Really?' His smirk grew. 'Don't you know who I am, Daisy?'

I looked him up and down. He was tall, easily over six foot and his ears were pointed, indicating that he too had once been an elf. His skin wasn't patchy like Horst and the other fiend's had been; its sheen was akin to what I'd seen on Zashtum's body. But this fiend exuded more power than she had, and I could almost feel the magic rolling off him in waves. He was muscular, strong and entirely unrepentant.

'I'm going to take a wild guess,' I spat, 'and say that you must be Athair.'

Something odd flickered in his eyes and a dim part of me registered it as disappointment. He shrugged. 'You guess right,' he said. His head swayed from side to side. 'It's a real pleasure, Daisy. I mean that.'

I ignored his words and the shiver that ran through me. I pointed instead at his arm, 'You're still bleeding.' I swished

Gladys from side to side. 'Your wound hasn't healed. That's because of her.'

To my astonishment, Athair threw back his head and laughed. 'Is that what you think? That it's the sword that's did this?'

I inhaled shakily. 'She killed your mate. Baltar is dead. You're not immortal, Athair.'

'Baltar is dead?' He quirked an eyebrow. 'Bravo.'

I snarled, 'Soon you will be too.'

'Do it, Daisy!' Otis screamed. 'Give the bastard all you've got!'

I didn't need any encouragement. Blade swinging, I launched myself at him.

Athair danced out of the way, his feet nimble despite his large body. I tried to remember the moves that Miriam had taught me but eventually I gave up and simply threw everything I had at him. First, I flashed out a blast of earth magic to blow up a section of the ground and prevent him from darting to the side. Then I let out a battle yell and slashed at his torso. Gladys's tip scraped across his chest, drawing more blood and triumph spilled through my veins. I had this – I could do it. My heart wrenched. And I *would* do it for Hugo.

Athair didn't appear upset but simply smiled at me again. 'My turn now,' he said.

As soon as the words left his mouth, he threw out a scorching blast of fire magic. I dropped to my feet and rolled to avoid it, but I wasn't fast enough. Flames seared my arm and shoulder, and the strong smell of burnt hair filled the air around me. I growled and conjured up a bucketful of water, dousing myself with it. As I did, I registered another crackle and hiss as more fire streamed past.

It took me a moment to realise it wasn't directed at me. I wiped the water from my eyes and spotted Aine's head poking out from her lair before she breathed more fire in Athair's direction.

'Yes, Aine!' Hester yelled. 'Get him!'

His golden body was consumed in flames but I could see that he was still grinning. Powerful as it was, Aine's dragon fire had no effect on him whatsoever. I told myself that was a good thing because it meant I could kill him myself.

Aine pushed herself out fully out of her lair and snapped in Athair's direction. 'No!' I shouted at her. 'Stay back. Get yourself to safety!'

She swung towards me, her tail whipping as if she were as angry with me for trying to stop her as she was with him for attacking in the first place. But she didn't get it: if he killed me, people would mourn – alright, *some* people would mourn – but life would move on. If he killed Aine, that would be it: no more dragons, not in this country anyway. She was the last surviving female.

I muttered a curse under my breath then I played my remaining card left. I pointed at the old dragon's egg lying forlornly on the ground. Aine's head turned and she froze when she spotted it.

Otis yelled a sudden warning. 'Daisy!'

I spun around. Athair, who was still on fire, was striding towards me. I braced myself and tightened my grip on Gladys. Aine took a step towards me then stopped and veered towards the egg instead, scooping it up in her jaws before receding into her lair. Hester and Otis followed her.

I exhaled. Then Athair's fiery fist came flying towards my face. I tried to dodge the blow but I already knew in my heart that I wouldn't be fast enough. This was going to hurt. I grimaced in anticipation.

Nothing happened.

Athair stood directly in front of me, still grinning inanely as if all this were a hilarious joke. He'd pulled his punch at the last second, although for the life of me I couldn't work out why.

I didn't waste time asking questions. As the last of the flames around his body died down, I thrust Gladys towards him yet again. He dodged the blow. I thrust again. Again he dodged. He chuckled to himself – and that was when I knew I could beat him.

He was over-confident. Sooner or later he would make a stupid mistake because he believed that I didn't have it in me to bring him down. That was when I'd strike a lethal blow. All I had to do was get him to that point.

I pushed all my grief about Hugo into the pit of my belly, together with my worry about Aine, Hester and Otis. I'd have to maintain a pit of strength for the right moment without letting Athair realise what I was doing.

I forced myself to focus on the drills Miriam had taught me. I would run through them, jabbing at Athair; if he wanted to prolong this fight and play cat and mouse, I'd let him. All I needed was one brief moment when he screwed up and his guard slipped. It would happen; I was sure of it.

I stepped to my right before swinging a low blow to my left, then repeated the movement in the opposite direction. I jabbed Gladys's tip forward four times, executing each thrust with increasing speed. As I did, I kept a close eye on everything Athair did and every twitch of his body language. I only needed one opening. All I had to do was be patient.

'You're not much of a warrior,' Athair commented after another clumsy swipe.

I didn't bother answering, I was concentrating too hard for chat and I wouldn't let him distract me. *One, thrust left. Two, step back. Three, swipe right. Four, jab jab.*

Athair danced out of the way of each stroke with ease, but I'd spotted something: when he turned the left-hand side of his body, he was a fraction slower and his shoulder on that side was more rigid. Given that blood was still seeping from the wound on that arm, he was probably hurting far more than he was letting on. It wasn't a particularly deep cut but Athair probably wasn't used to his own blood.

One, thrust left. Two, step back. Three, swipe right. Four, jab jab.

'Your movements are very repetitive,' he said mockingly.

One, thrust left. Two, step back. Three, swipe right. Four, jab jab.

He sighed heavily, seemingly bored with my amateur drilling. I felt a prickle as he pulled on his magic before he slammed a violent burst of air in my direction that swept me off my feet.

I was thrown up and back, and my spine collided hard with the ground as I landed. I gasped for air as pain tore through my chest. For a few terrifying seconds my arms and legs refused to work, but then my fingers tightened around Gladys's hilt.

As Athair loomed over me, peering down from above with his maniacal grin, I swung the blade upwards and aimed for the left side of his body. A visceral surge of joy shuddered through me when I struck gold and Gladys sliced through his exposed forearm. There. His left side would be in even more pain now.

Athair yelled sharply and kicked at me in retaliation, but I was ready and rolled away. Now it was my turn to dodge. 'Bitch,' he hissed.

I smiled coldly: I'd provoked a genuine reaction other than mockery. But when I heard a voice behind me, my smile froze and I almost stopped breathing. 'Nobody calls my Daisy a bitch.'

Hugo. I scrambled to my feet and spun around. There he was. Dried blood coated half of his face, both his nose and right arm looked broken, but he was alive and there was a determined fury glittering in his familiar blue eyes.

He threw out his own blast of air magic towards Athair and

I spotted the dimple forming in his cheek. This time it was him; I was certain of it.

I ran to his side – I couldn't help myself. He was alright, and for this one moment nothing else mattered. As I joined him, Athair's expression soured further, even though Hugo's air magic had achieved little more than ruffling his hair. 'You shouldn't be here,' he spat at Hugo. 'This is between me and Daisy.'

I lifted my chin with delighted defiance. 'We're a team, Athair. You're on your own.'

'You still won't win,' he said matter-of-factly.

At that moment, Hester and Otis emerged from the lair holding the unmistakable shape of the chess set between them while their small wings flapped furiously. Aine must have handed it over. All we had to do was keep Athair occupied for long enough for them to escape with it. It was heavy and they were only tiny; it was clear that they were struggling, but they were giving it everything they had.

I reached for Hugo, my free hand quickly squeezing his. He responded. Then he crooked his finger towards Athair in an obvious taunt. 'Come on then,' he said.

I chipped in. 'Give it your best shot, you cumbubbling fiend.'

And with that, Athair charged.

I'd expected him to come for me, but his attack was aimed at Hugo. Athair thundered towards him, conjuring up a blistering fireball as he ran. Hugo ducked, dropped to his knees and narrowly avoided it.

I threw all my weight behind Gladys to attack Athair's left side again but I didn't get close. His right hand reached out across his body and wrapped around the tip of her blade so I couldn't thrust her any further forward. My jaw dropped as blood oozed around his fingers where Gladys had cut into his skin.

He yanked hard and pulled her from my grip before flinging her aside. A heartbeat later, he kicked upwards and his heel connected with Hugo's head. All I could do was watch as Hugo staggered and collapsed.

'You fucker!' I roared and threw out a blast of fire. Athair blocked it easily. He turned his back on me and marched towards Gladys, who had fallen to the ground several metres away.

I threw out air magic; the tail of Athair's shirt lifted, but he didn't break his stride. I threw out water magic; Athair clicked his fingers and conjured a blast of air to knock it away. I threw out earth magic, desperate to shake him off his feet; he simply jumped and sailed through the air with terrifying ease. Then he landed next to Gladys and scooped her up in his right hand.

'I'm done playing now,' he muttered. His arm tensed and he flung Gladys at the fleeing brownies. He'd known they were there all along. It didn't matter that they were already more than seventy metres away, or that I cried out a warning and sent as much air magic towards Gladys as I could in a desperate bid to stop her. I was impotent.

My sword cut an efficient, lethal beeline through the air then thudded into the side of the silver box that held the chess pieces.

Hester and Otis squealed as it was ripped from their tenuous grip. With a casual curl of his lips, Athair tossed out a wave of air that sent the brownies tumbling away. Then he sniffed and stalked over to the chess set and picked it up. 'Such magic,' he murmured, stroking the surface of the silver box. 'Such power.'

I knelt by Hugo's side. 'I'm okay,' he croaked. 'Go. You have to stop him.'

I paused long enough to brush his cheek lightly with a kiss. Then I straightened up and strode in Athair's direction.

The brownies were in a tangled heap on the ground, Hugo was behind me and Gladys was near Athair's feet: I was on my own and weaponless. My magic wasn't strong enough to beat Athair but I was still going to try. I couldn't let him walk away with all that power.

The ground shook slightly and there was a deep rumble to my left. As I neared the fiend, a jet of dragon fire spat past me and engulfed him in flame again. I didn't turn around. 'Aine,' I yelled. 'You need to get back. You can't be here.' From beyond the white-hot flames of her fire, the dragon's scarlet eyes danced.

Athair lifted his chin and suddenly I heard a roar of falling rock. I pivoted just as a section of the entrance to Aine's lair collapsed and landed on her tail, trapping her in place. I gasped in horror. No. Oh no.

Athair waved away the remaining flames with a nonchalant swipe of his arm, then he smiled at me, his expression strangely tender. I couldn't suppress my shudder of disgust.

'Watch this,' he whispered. He stretched out his arms and splayed his fingers. Little electric sparks danced at his fingertips. He was pulling on the same magic that Horst had produced in the disused dragon's lair. I had no doubt that Athair's version was stronger.

Heart pounding I sprinted, desperate to prevent him from shooting anyone with a magic bolt of lightning, but my feet were no match for his fingers. He crooked each one in quick succession and four sizzling bolts lit up the air.

The first one zapped towards Aine and shot past my head to reach her. I heard her roar of bitter frustration as the second bolt sped for Hugo. The third arched towards Hester and Otis and the fourth landed a foot in front of me, smacking into the ground and halting my progress.

Athair was grinning. 'Cool, huh?'

I turned to check on the others. Aine was struggling, trying desperately to free herself from the fallen rocks. There was a scorch mark on the ground in front of her long, purple snout where the lightning had struck. Hugo was trying to stand up, his body wavering, and there was an identical mark next to him. I knew before I looked that it would be same for the brownies. Athair was still toying with us.

He tilted his head and raised his eyebrows. 'You know I could have killed you all several times over by now.' His voice was soft, almost coaxing.

Hester pulled herself away from Otis. 'Then why haven't you, you wanker?' she yelled. 'Don't listen to him, Daisy! Don't let his words poison your ears! End that bastard, now!'

A flicker of irritation crossed Athair's gaunt face but his focus remained on me. 'You should ask yourself why you are still breathing, Daisy.'

My eyes travelled up and down his body. His clothes were charred rags from the dragon fire and his left arm continued to ooze blood. I had to keep believing that he wasn't invincible; I had to find a way to defeat him.

'I tell you what,' he continued, 'I'll throw you a bone. I'll let you keep one.' He smiled gently. 'You may have either the boy, the dragon, the sword, the treasure or one of the brownies. Choose one and I'll let you walk away. The rest die.' He nudged the silver box with his toe. 'Or they will be taken. Only one may leave this place safely with you. Which one is entirely up to you.'

Nausea rolled around my belly and I swallowed hard. I didn't get the sense that he was bluffing. I took one step towards him. 'Only one?' I asked. 'Why not two? Why not all of them?'

'You shouldn't protest too much. This is a boon that I've never granted to any soul before now. You should be grateful –

you should fall at my feet and kiss my shoes in gratitude for my generosity.'

Uh-huh. I took another step. 'How could I possibly choose?'

Athair pursed his thin lips. 'I'd suggest you choose the dragon – that would be my choice.' His voice hardened. 'Choose before I change my mind.'

My legs felt shaky. I was desperate for another hit of spider's silk but I didn't dare reach into my pocket for a pill for fear that Athair would mistake the move for something else. Instead, I gazed at him. 'You're asking the impossible.'

'No, Daisy,' he said. 'I'm not.'

Out of the corner of my eye, I saw Hugo pull back his shoulders and suck in a breath. Before he could move, the fiend zapped him with another lightning bolt. Hugo gave a sharp cry. 'Try anything, elf boy, and next time I'll stop your heart,' Athair growled.

'Hugo,' I whispered. He was on his knees, groaning with pain.

A fiery hiss ejected from Aine's nostrils. 'The chess set,' she said. 'Choose it. You cannot allow this creature to take it.'

Otis was having none of it. 'No! You have to pick Hugo. You need him, Daisy! You have to choose him. If there's any chance you can walk out of here alive, you'll need him with you to survive.'

'Screw that,' Hester muttered. 'Choose me! I don't want to die!'

I looked at her. She fixed me with a glare, her eyes narrowed, and suddenly I knew exactly what she was saying – I knew what they were *all* saying. I was backed into a corner and my options were limited but, as Miriam had said not long ago, there was always another way.

Everyone was ready.

'What's it to be, Daisy?' Athair asked silkily.

I turned to face him. His expression was expectant; I was surprised he wasn't rubbing his palms together in glee. I opened my mouth as if to answer him and the anticipation in his red eyes intensified.

In one swift, sudden movement, I dived to the ground and reached for Gladys. At the same time, Aine roared, heaved herself free and thundered towards Athair. Hugo blasted a wave of earth magic directly at Athair's feet that opened up the ground and made the fiend stagger. Otis and Hester zipped forward and threw themselves at his head, their tiny hands curled into fists so they could pummel him.

My hand found Gladys's hilt. From a kneeling position I raised her blade and swung it at Athair's neck, but I barely scraped his skin. He sprang away, howled in fury and flung out his own tremor of jolting earth magic. We all fell backwards, even Aine.

My head hurt, my back was bruised and bloody, and it was difficult to breathe. Tiny lights were dancing in front of my eyes and I was on the verge of passing out. A shadow fell across my face as I tried desperately to lift Gladys. My hand wouldn't obey the signals my brain was sending it. I was done for.

Athair crouched beside me. 'Interesting,' he murmured. 'I gave you a way out, offered you life, and yet you refused to take it. You continued to fight even though you knew you would lose.'

The best I could do was to hawk up a ball of phlegm and spit it at him, but I failed even at that. All it did was dribble down my chin.

'Daisy,' Hugo groaned from somewhere far to my left. 'Daisy.'

'Always with the interruptions,' Athair muttered. He reached for me and I flinched, expecting pain; instead, his fingers stroked my cheek. 'You should know that I never cared about the chess set – I already have all the power I could ever need. I only dangled it as a hook to see what you were truly capable of. You were never in any real danger because they were under orders not to harm you. I simply wanted to be sure that what I saw in you last time was not a lie. It was not. You have proved your worth, Daisy. It's you I want, not that old treasure.'

His features swam. I blinked, horror and confusion warring with a desperate need to slip into unconsciousness.

'You're more than I ever could have hoped for.' He brushed away a curl from my face and smiled. 'I will let you go. I will let you all go. You must remember that when we meet again. Remember that I could have killed them all and I chose not to.'

He paused. 'I am walking away because of you, Daisy. We do not have to be enemies. Don't forget that.' He lowered his head further until I could feel his cold breath against my skin. 'The old saying is correct.' He murmured eight chilling words into my ear.

A moment later, darkness descended. And then there was nothing.

CHAPTER
THIRTY

It was the smell I noticed first. Sour, faintly rancid but not altogether unpleasant. It was followed by a strange, wet, fuzzy thing slapping the side of my head. I raised my arm and tried to push it away, then I opened my eyes. When I glimpsed the row of massive sharp teeth looming over me, fear-induced adrenaline made me spring up and scoot away as fast as I could.

'She is awake,' Aine rumbled, unperturbed.

I stared at her then reached up to touch my cheek. It was still damp. 'Were you ... *licking* me?'

'The loud, angry one suggested it might help rouse you,' Aine said.

Hester and Otis were sitting on her stout purple shoulder. I narrowed my eyes at Hester. She pointed at her brother. 'It was him! It was Otis's idea. Not mine!' Otis merely snorted.

I wet my lips. Being tongued by a dragon was the least of my concerns. 'Hugo?' I asked fearfully. 'Is he—?'

'I'm here.' He placed his hand on my arm and I spun around. When I saw his bruised but still handsome face, I threw myself at his chest. His arms went around me. 'You're safe,' he murmured. 'We all are. The fiend has gone.'

I drew in a shuddering breath then pulled away and looked around. There was no sign of Athair. He really had gone. 'Your tail,' I said to Aine. 'Is it—?'

'It is sore but it will heal.' Her eyes gleamed. 'The fiend wounded me but he did not destroy me. Not even close.'

'He left the chess set,' Otis said. 'And it's still got all its magic. I can feel it. He didn't drain it.'

Hester smacked her lips. 'He was scared of Daisy. She hurt him too much and he decided to run.'

That was definitely not what had happened. I rubbed the back of my neck.

'Are you okay?' Hugo asked gruffly.

I nodded. 'A bit woozy, that's all.' My gaze dropped to one of the many scorch marks left by Athair's lightning. 'He said we'd met before but I have no memory of that. I didn't know fiends existed until you told me about them. But the other fiends said something similar.' Frustration beat at me. 'I don't get it.'

Athair's last words also echoed around my head – but I didn't dare confront them. Not yet. I wasn't ready.

'Given he stole my damned physical form and pretended to be me,' Hugo growled, 'you could have encountered him at any point. He could have been anyone. Same with the others. We've all been on the trail of the chess set – we could have crossed paths several times and not known it.'

I gave a jerky nod but my anxiety didn't ease. The power that Athair had displayed was extraordinary. Even with Gladys to help me, there didn't seem to be any earthly way in which he could be defeated.

'Daisy knew!' Hester called. 'Daisy knew that wasn't really you.'

Hugo's head tilted. 'How?'

'My skin prickles,' I admitted. 'When there's a fiend nearby, I feel itchy. And you – or rather Athair – said a few things that were out of character. Plus...' My voice trailed off.

'Plus?' he asked.

I sighed. 'There wasn't a dimple.'

Hugo blinked. 'Pardon?'

'When you conjure up magic your dimple appears,' I said. 'But when Athair was pretending to be you, there wasn't one.'

Something flared deep in his eyes. 'How very observant of you,' he murmured.

Yeah, yeah. I waved it off. 'He attacked you?' I asked. 'Before he took your form?'

Hugo nodded. 'I didn't hear him coming. He must have come up from behind and hit me on the back of my head. I went down like a ton of bricks,' he admitted. 'I'm sorry, Daisy. If I'd been paying more attention—'

I interrupted him. 'No. It wasn't your fault. I'm only glad he didn't kill you.'

'I might say the same about you,' he murmured. We gazed at each other, unspoken emotion building between us.

Aine coughed out a plume of white smoke. 'What is happening?' she asked, her eyes flicking between us.

'The longest session of foreplay the world has ever seen.' Otis rolled his eyes then clamped his hand over his mouth. 'I didn't mean to say that aloud.'

Hester snickered. 'He's not wrong.'

Aine stared for another moment or two. 'You are all strange creatures.' She raised one of her massive front legs and flexed her claws. 'And it is time for you all to leave. The danger is over. We shall find another new lair.'

We?

'May we take the chess set?' Hugo asked.

'I do not wish to see it again.' She belched out a plume of fire. 'Take it and go.'

'Aine,' I began, speaking slowly, 'why did you—?'

There was a scuffling sound from behind the pile of rocks at the entrance to the lair and I stopped. When I felt Hugo's body tense as he started to draw on his last magic reserves, I quickly stepped in front of him. 'No,' I said. 'It's alright.'

There was a little squeak followed by a faint flicker of fire that briefly illuminated the lair's interior. I caught a fleeting glimpse of a very small red creature with wide, blinking yellow eyes.

Aine rumbled and immediately moved, blocking the lair from our view. 'Leave,' she rumbled again. She gazed at us with sudden malevolence, as if the bonds between us that had formed during the battle with Athair had never existed.

'The egg,' I whispered, realisation dawning. 'But it was so old... How could that happen?'

The huge dragon watched me. 'Dragon fire may not be enough to kill a fiend but it is still full of magic. There are good reasons as to why we are not yet extinct, despite the attempts of your kind to kill us off. Call it a sort of prolonged hibernation, if you will.'

Hugo's jaw was slack. 'I had no idea.' I doubted anyone did.

Hester spun in mid-air, barely able to contain her delight. 'Do you need a nanny?' she asked.

Aine's chest rumbled again. I had the sense that we were severely outstaying our welcome. 'Let's go, Hes.'

'But—'

'We still have to get to the British Museum.' I was already retreating.

Her shoulders sagged. 'Fine,' she muttered. She looked at Aine. 'But if you're looking for a godmother, or you need suggestions about what to name her, then Hester is an excellent choice.'

Flames appeared around the edges of Aine's sharp, exposed fangs and her nostrils flared. I grabbed hold of Hester. It was definitely time to go.

∞

IT WAS A BEDRAGGLED crew that limped through the entrance to the British Museum. We'd taken considerable care during the journey from Wales to London, but there had been no sign of anyone following us. There was certainly nothing to suggest Athair or any other fiends were on our tail.

Our injuries and our anxiety about being attacked again had zapped our energy. Even a triple dose of spider's silk hadn't done much more than take the edge away from my pain and bone-deep fatigue. As we waited in a large vestibule away from the public area, I caught sight of myself in an ornate mirror. My hair was matted with dried blood, my eyes were sunken and my skin was as pale as parchment.

'Yeah,' Hester said. 'You look like death.'

Hugo, who was in a far worse state, placed an arm around my waist. 'We all do. This hunt has been like no other.' He could say that again.

It was galling to accept that we were only standing there with the magical chess set because Athair had allowed it, though none of us were willing to say that aloud. As long as the words remained unspoken, we could believe that we'd succeeded in our quest rather than been *permitted* to succeed.

'You haven't forgotten your promise, have you, Daisy?' Hugo asked. 'You owe me that favour. Your three months at Pemberville Castle awaits.'

Hester and Otis gazed at me hopefully and I sighed. My

reality had shifted in the last twenty-four hours and giving up three long months of my life to Hugo seemed even more pointless – and heart-breaking – than it had done before. But when I turned my head and looked into his eyes, I knew I couldn't go back on my word. 'I remember,' I whispered. 'Of course I remember.'

Hugo's arm tightened around my waist and for a moment I let myself enjoy our closeness. Then I pulled away.

A door opened and Sir Nigel strode in. As soon as he saw us, his eyes filled with concern. 'I can see I picked a terrible time to take a month's sabbatical.'

'We survived,' Hugo said quietly. His hand reached for mine. 'All of us. For now that has to be enough.'

'For now?' Sir Nigel asked.

I dropped my head. 'There are other fiends, and Athair is still out there. We couldn't defeat him. We couldn't come close.'

'You rescued Gwyddbwyll Gwenddoleu ap Ceido,' Sir Nigel said. 'That makes you heroes in my book.'

All four of us gazed at him with blank faces. 'The chess set,' Sir Nigel added helpfully. 'No fiend shall benefit from its power. It will be safe here, I promise you that. We have also dispatched our strongest witches to the old lair in Wales. The two fiends buried beneath the rubble there will be banished long before they recover. Your actions have made all of us far safer. You are to be highly commended.'

'Does that mean we get a reward?' Hester enquired.

Sir Nigel looked startled; it clearly hadn't been the first thing on his mind. I pulled a face. If this was when Hester started yapping on about diamond earrings again, I was going to get pissy.

'Because,' Otis said, jumping in, 'there's a witch in hospital in Edinburgh right now who laid all the ground work. Without him, we'd never have known about the chess set. He could do with some support with his recovery.'

Sir Nigel nodded gravely. 'Mr McAlpine shall have all that he needs. He deserves it.'

Hester flapped her wings in irritation and folded her arms. 'That's not all,' she said, pouting.

'Hester,' I began.

'Be quiet, Daisy,' she snapped. 'You need to learn when to shut up.'

Hugo stifled a chuckle and I glared at him.

'Go on,' Sir Nigel said.

'Do you have any old dragon eggs at this museum?' Hester asked.

I started.

'Several,' he answered. 'We stopped collecting them well over a century ago. The eggs we do have are incredibly old.'

Hugo's mouth lifted into a smile. So did mine. 'You need to give them back to the dragons,' Hester said. 'They don't belong to you.'

'Some of them are ancient,' Sir Nigel told her. 'While I agree that we should never have taken them in the first place, they are no longer—'

'Give them back!' Otis shouted. Sir Nigel jerked.

'Find a way,' Hugo said more quietly. 'They should be returned.'

'Alright.' He clasped his hands. 'I will see that it happens. Is there anything else?'

'Daisy would like diamond—' Hester started.

'No,' I said quickly. 'That's everything. Thank you.'

He smiled, then his gaze dropped to Gladys who was sheathed at my side. 'May I examine your sword?'

I felt an odd reluctance to part with her even for a moment, but I nodded anyway. I slid her free of her sheath and handed her over to Sir Nigel, hilt side facing him. She hummed faintly, but it was a soft sound that didn't appear to indicate displeasure.

'She is truly beautiful,' Sir Nigel said. He ran one finger down the flat side of her blade. Gladys hummed louder, clearly enjoying herself. 'There must be incredible magic forged into her steel. I had never heard of any weapon that could kill a fiend before now. There is nothing in any history books, not even a whisper that it could be possible. Until today, I would have sworn that the only way to defeat a fiend for good was for a powerful witch to banish them from this realm.' He hefted Gladys in his hands. 'That,' he said half to himself, 'or persuade another fiend to do the dirty work for us.'

Hugo's brow creased. 'What do you mean?'

'A fiend may kill another fiend,' Sir Nigel murmured. He held Gladys up to the light, still awed by her. 'If they are strong enough to do so. Unfortunately, they are rarely willing to try when there is a chance it will result in their own true death.' He shrugged and handed Gladys back to me. 'Your sword is an object of extreme rarity indeed.'

With slow, deliberate movements I re-sheathed her, hoping the trembling in my hands wasn't visible. The same refrain was echoing around my skull over and over again. Athair's last words weren't going to leave me alone now.

The apple doesn't fall far from the tree.

The apple doesn't fall far from the tree.

The apple doesn't fall far from the tree.

AUTHOR'S NOTE

Although most of this book is pure fiction (and the product of my vivid imagination!) there are a few elements that do exist both in real life and in mythology.

The Welsh poet Dafydd ap Gwyllim did indeed live from around 1315 until 1350. One of his poems is 'Cwydd y Gal' – 'Ode to the Penis'. He is believed to be buried beneath a yew tree by Strata Florida Abbey in Wales, although there are some theories that his remains are actually elsewhere.

Yew trees symbolise death and resurrection in Celtic culture. As I was writing about Dafydd ap Gwyllim's yew tree, the famous Sycamore Gap tree was vandalised then cut down, which certainly affected what I wrote about in this book.

Dragons have been the symbol of Wales since the seventh century.

The thirteen mythical treasures of Britain exist in legend. Although there is some debate as to what they are, they are typically common utensils with magical properties. According to https://www.sarahwoodbury.com/, they consist of '*a sword, a basket, a drinking-horn, a chariot, a halter, a knife, a cauldron, a whetstone, a garment, a pan, a platter, a chess board, and a mantle...'*

Acknowledgments

Thank you so much to everyone who helped bring Daisy's second book to life. Clarissa Yeo and JoY Cover Designs created the beautiful cover while Karen Holmes deserves a special thank you for her hard work editing the entire book.

Deep thanks must also go to Ruth Urquhart and the team at Tantor Audio for everything they've done to bring the audiobook to life.

It's hard work bringing my imagination to reality and every scrap of support from every corner makes a huge difference. I'm living my dreams and I'm grateful for it every single day.

Helen x

Also by Helen Harper

The *FireBrand* series

A werewolf killer. A paranormal murder. How many times can Emma Bellamy cheat death?

I'm one placement away from becoming a fully fledged London detective. It's bad enough that my last assignment before I qualify is with Supernatural Squad. But that's nothing compared to what happens next.

Brutally murdered by an unknown assailant, I wake up twelve hours later in the morgue – and I'm very much alive. I don't know how or why it happened. I don't know who killed me. All I know is that they might try again.

Werewolves are disappearing right, left and centre.

A mysterious vampire seems intent on following me everywhere I go.

And I have to solve my own vicious killing. Preferably before death comes for me again.

Book One – Brimstone Bound

Book Two – Infernal Enchantment

Book Three – Midnight Smoke

Book Four – Scorched Heart

Book Five - Dark Whispers

Book Six - A Killer's Kiss

Book Seven - Fortune's Ashes

The *WolfBrand* series

Devereau Webb is in uncharted territory. He thought he knew what he was doing when he chose to enter London's supernatural society but he's quickly discovering that his new status isn't welcome to everyone.

He's lived through hard times before and he's no stranger to the murky underworld of city life. But when he comes across a young werewolf girl who's not only been illegally turned but who has also committed two brutal murders, he will discover just how difficult life can be for supernaturals - and also how far his own predatory powers extend.

Book One – The Noose Of A New Moon

Book Two – Licence To Howl

The complete *Blood Destiny* series

"A spectacular and addictive series."

Mackenzie Smith has always known that she was different. Growing up as the only human in a pack of rural shapeshifters will do that to you, but then couple it with some mean fighting skills and a fiery temper and you end up with a woman that few will dare to cross. However, when the only father figure in her life is brutally murdered, and the dangerous Brethren with their predatory Lord Alpha come to investigate, Mack has to not only ensure the physical safety of her adopted family by hiding her apparent humanity, she also has to seek the blood-soaked vengeance that she craves.

Book One - Bloodfire

Book Two - Bloodmagic

Book Three - Bloodrage

Book Four - Blood Politics

Book Five - Bloodlust

Also

Corrigan Fire

Corrigan Magic

Corrigan Rage

Corrigan Politics

Corrigan Lust

The complete *Bo Blackman* series

A half-dead daemon, a massacre at her London based PI firm and evidence that suggests she's the main suspect for both ... Bo Blackman is having a very bad week.

She might be naive and inexperienced but she's determined to get to the bottom of the crimes, even if it means involving herself with one of London's most powerful vampire Families and their enigmatic leader.

It's pretty much going to be impossible for Bo to ever escape unscathed.

Book One - Dire Straits

Book Two - New Order

Book Three - High Stakes

Book Four - Red Angel

Book Five - Vigilante Vampire

Book Six - Dark Tomorrow

The complete *Highland Magic* series

Integrity Taylor walked away from the Sidhe when she was a child. Orphaned and bullied, she simply had no reason to stay, especially not when the sins of her father were going to remain on her shoulders. She found a new family - a group of thieves who proved that blood was less important than loyalty and love.

But the Sidhe aren't going to let Integrity stay away forever. They need her more than anyone realises - besides, there are prophecies to be fulfilled, people to be saved and hearts to be won over. If anyone can do it, Integrity can.

Book One - Gifted Thief

Book Two - Honour Bound

Book Three - Veiled Threat

Book Four - Last Wish

The complete *Dreamweaver* series

"I have special coping mechanisms for the times I need to open the front door. They're even often successful..."

Zoe Lydon knows there's often nothing logical or rational about fear. It doesn't change the fact that she's too terrified to step outside her own house, however.

What Zoe doesn't realise is that she's also a dreamweaver - able to access other people's subconscious minds. When she finds herself in the Dreamlands and up against its sinister Mayor, she'll need to use all of her wits - and overcome all of her fears - if she's ever going to come out alive.

Book One - Night Shade

Book Two - Night Terrors

Book Three - Night Lights

Stand alone novels

Eros

William Shakespeare once wrote that, "Cupid is a knavish lad, thus to make poor females mad." The trouble is that Cupid himself would probably agree...

As probably the last person in the world who'd appreciate hearts, flowers and romance, Coop is convinced that true love doesn't exist – which is rather unfortunate considering he's also known as Cupid, the God of Love. He'd rather spend his days drinking, womanising and generally having as much fun as he possible can. As far as he's concerned, shooting people with bolts of pure love is a waste of his time...but then his path crosses with that of shy and retiring Skye Sawyer and nothing will ever be quite the same again.

Wraith

Magic. Shadows. Adventure. Romance.

Saiya Buchanan is a wraith, able to detach her shadow from her body and send it off to do her bidding. But, unlike most of her kin, Saiya doesn't deal in death. Instead, she trades secrets - and in the goblin besieged city of Stirling in Scotland, they're a highly prized commodity. It might just be, however, that the goblins have been hiding the greatest secret of them all. When Gabriel de Florinville, a Dark Elf, is sent as royal envoy into Stirling and takes her prisoner, Saiya is not only going to uncover the sinister truth. She's also going to realise that sometimes the deepest secrets are the ones locked within your own heart.

The complete *Lazy Girl's Guide To Magic* series

Hard Work Will Pay Off Later. Laziness Pays Off Now.

Let's get one thing straight - Ivy Wilde is not a heroine. In fact, she's probably the last witch in the world who you'd call if you needed a magical helping hand. If it were down to Ivy, she'd spend all day every day on her sofa where she could watch TV, munch junk food and talk to her feline familiar to her heart's content.

However, when a bureaucratic disaster ends up with Ivy as the victim of a case of mistaken identity, she's yanked very unwillingly into Arcane Branch, the investigative department of the Hallowed Order of Magical Enlightenment. Her problems are quadrupled when a valuable object is stolen right from under the Order's noses.

It doesn't exactly help that she's been magically bound to Adeptus Exemptus Raphael Winter. He might have piercing sapphire eyes and a body which a cover model would be proud of but, as far as Ivy's concerned, he's a walking advertisement for the joyless perils of too much witch-work.

And if he makes her go to the gym again, she's definitely going to turn him into a frog.

Book One - Slouch Witch

Book Two - Star Witch

Book Three - Spirit Witch

Sparkle Witch (Christmas short story)

The complete *Fractured Faery* series

One corpse. Several bizarre looking attackers. Some very strange magical powers. And a severe bout of amnesia.

It's one thing to wake up outside in the middle of the night with a decapitated man for company. It's another to have no memory of how you got there - or who you are.

She might not know her own name but she knows that several people are out to get her. It could be because she has strange magical powers seemingly at her fingertips and is some kind of fabulous hero. But then why does she appear to inspire fear in so many? And who on earth is the sexy, green-eyed barman who apparently despises her? So many questions ... and so few answers.

At least one thing is for sure - the streets of Manchester have never met someone quite as mad as Madrona...

Book One - Box of Frogs

SHORTLISTED FOR THE KINDLE STORYTELLER AWARD 2018

Book Two - Quiver of Cobras

Book Three - Skulk of Foxes

The complete *City Of Magic* series

Charley is a cleaner by day and a professional gambler by night. She might be haunted by her tragic past but she's never thought of herself as anything or anyone special. Until, that is, things start to go terribly wrong all across the city of Manchester. Between plagues of rats, firestorms and the gleaming blue eyes of a sexy Scottish werewolf, she might just have landed herself in the middle of a magical apocalypse. She might also be the only person who has the ability to bring order to an utterly chaotic new world.

Book One - Shrill Dusk

Book Two - Brittle Midnight

Book Three - Furtive Dawn

Milton Keynes UK
Ingram Content Group UK Ltd.
UKHW040358111224
452348UK00004B/284

9 781913 116446